Where We Stand, Where We Fall

the politics of
Doctor Who

---

lizbeth myles

HERNE
BOOKS

First published in 2026 by

Herne Books
Unit 1, The Exchange
6 Scarbrook Road
Croydon CR0 1UH
info@hernebooks.com

This product conforms to the requirements of the
European Union's General Product Safety Regulations (GPSR).
EU Authorised Representative for GPSR:
Easy Access System Europe –
Mustamäe tee 50, 10621 Tallinn, Estonia
gpsr.requests@easproject.com

ISBN: 978-1-917665-05-6

Cover and endpaper artwork by Daryl Joyce.

A catalogue record for this book is available from the British Library.

Printed and bound in Great Britain by Bell & Bain, Glasgow.

CONTENTS

INTRODUCTION

'What would you die for? Who I am is where I stand.
Where I stand, is where I fall. Stand with me.'
The Doctor, *The Doctor Falls* (2017)

*D*octor *Who* has always been political.

It's always been shaped by the hopes, fears, and realities of the society around it. From the nuclear anxiety of *An Unearthly Child*, to fear that we longer agree on what reality even is in *The Reality War*. These ideas have been explored, directly and obliquely, through allegory, aliens and monsters, distant worlds and speculative futures.

Each of the six chapters here focuses on a different theme: nuclear warfare; environmentalism; transhumanism; feminism; and scientific responsibility. I chose these themes because they're ones I'm particularly interested in, and because they're ones that *Doctor Who* has enthusiastically engaged with across its history. None of these themes is confined to a story or two from a single decade, instead they are returned to again and again, evolving in new directions, with new angles, new nuances, to reflect changes in British society.

The show doesn't always get things right. It wears two hearts on its sleeve, but it can be clumsy, contradictory, and implicitly condone the very things it argues against. Its discussions of empire, tech, gender, and power are not a neat line sloping up towards ever more progressive, more just, positions. There's backsliding, there are horribly misjudged moments, and questionable conclusions. And those are important too, those struggles show the uneven nature of progress, and the shape of how cultural values can shift.

This isn't an academic book. That means there may be occasional bad jokes, digressions (I was very good and cut several paragraphs about black mould in Chernobyl's reactor number 4), and obvious bias (let me tell you about how much I adore the Moffat era …). Happily, this harmonises rather well with the show, which cheerfully uses wit, humour, and silliness to discuss serious themes. Solemnity doesn't necessarily deepen meaning. And, as the Doctor once said, he was serious about 'what [he does] … not necessarily the way [he does] it.'[1]

Hopefully, this book can show some of the brilliance of *Doctor Who*, illustrate the breadth and depth it's capable of, and why it's remained so compelling for over sixty years.

[1]   *The Time Warrior*

CHAPTER ONE

THE MUSHROOM CLOUD ON THE HORIZON

Nuclear Annihilation

The first detonation of a nuclear weapon took place near Socorro, New Mexico on 16 July 1945. The Manhattan Project had succeeded, the world entered the Atomic Era, and humanity reached a dizzying new height in its ability for self-destruction.

Ever since, the world has often come to an end. In computer games, film, and television, we've seen barren, radiation-soaked landscapes, peppered with the skeletal remains of civilisation. These depictions of nuclear devastation have been part of the cultural landscape since the genesis of nuclear weapons, as humanity grappled with the horror of how easily, and how quickly, we could destroy ourselves.

The term nuclear anxiety was first used in the 1960s, and is credited to anthropologist Margaret Mead.[2] It's defined as 'fear of nuclear war and its consequences', and is explored in a multitude of beloved television shows from that decade:

[2] A. Riad, A. Drobov, M. Alkasaby, A. Peřina, M. Koscik (2023). 'Nuclear Anxiety Amid the Russian-Ukrainian War 2022 (RUW-22): Descriptive Cross-Sectional Study', International Journal of Environmental Research and Public Health, 20:3551, 10.3390/ijerph20043551

The Twilight Zone, Star Trek, The Invisible Man, The Man from UNCLE, The Champions, The Avengers and, of course, *Doctor Who*. Indeed, the original series of *Doctor Who* was produced entirely during the Cold War period, and never lost its taste for exploring the possibility of nuclear holocaust.

But even after the dissolution of the Soviet Union, nuclear anxiety never entirely went away. Russia has continued to make nuclear threats to the West since the 1990s, and these threats have only intensified since the war in Ukraine began.[3] And so, twenty-first-century *Doctor Who* has also had its share of engagement with nuclear anxiety. What is perhaps surprising is that the theme is there from the show's very first story, *An Unearthly Child*.

> *'I tolerate this century, but I don't enjoy it.'*
> The Doctor, *An Unearthly Child* (1963)

An Unearthly Child is the four-part story that opened the show on 23 November 1963. The pilot episode introduces the original characters and concepts of the show: two schoolteachers, Barbara and Ian, follow an unusual student, Susan, home after school. (Which sounds pretty dodgy, even though they only have altruistic motives.) She disappears into a junkyard and her perplexed teachers follow. There they encounter a strange old man, the Doctor, who tries to get rid of them, but they insist on speaking with Susan, who's nowhere to be seen. When they hear her call out from an abandoned police box, they push their way inside, and discover it's bigger on the inside than it is on the outside. The Doctor reveals that he and his granddaughter Susan are travellers in time and space, that the police box is called the TARDIS, and it's where they live. The Doctor believes being discovered by

---

[3] https://commonslibrary.parliament.uk/research-briefings/cbp-9825/

the two teachers has put them in danger, and his solution to the problem is rather unconventional: he kidnaps them. The TARDIS takes off from London and materialises in a barren landscape.

That barren landscape is prehistoric Earth, and a nearby tribe is engaged in a political struggle over who should be their next leader. Za, the current leader, is losing his authority. He's unable to make fire, and the tribe's loyalty is turning towards a stranger, Kal, who's out there hunting and making sure people get fed, while Za sits in the cave staring at a pile of twigs.

When Za spots the Doctor lighting his pipe, he takes the whole time-travelling team back to the cave where they must either make more fire, or die. They hatch a cunning plan to escape: stick lit torches inside some skulls to scare the cave people, then run away. The plan works and off they go on their next adventure which is also very much concerned about nuclear war. (This was only a year after the Cuban Missile Crisis; nuclear anxieties were probably a bit higher than usual.)

What does a Stone Age tribe have to do with nuclear annihilation? It's the fire. Za and Kal fight for leadership of the tribe, and the key to winning is the ability to make fire. Fire allowed us to begin developing culture. At some point people discovered that meat was a lot tastier when we cooked it; more importantly, it also made it more nutritious. A nice mammoth steak is much easier to digest once it's been grilled over a fire. And that means less mammoth is needed to feed everyone, so less time spent hunting, and more time for sitting around having thoughts, and dreaming up civilisation. This ability to create fire was a watershed moment in the development of humanity, and so was the successful detonation of a nuclear weapon. In taking that first technological step, we began a very long journey to a time when the fire we are capable of creating could destroy the world.

Nuclear arsenals increased from nine bombs at the close of World War II to a height of some sixty thousand in the eighties. Today, across eight nations, there's a total stockpile of around thirteen thousand, with some ten thousand of those being held by the US and Russia. And yet, it could be worse: in the fifties, in the United States, physicist Edward Teller proposed developing a nuclear weapon that was capable, in a single explosion, of destroying the planet. He had already been dissatisfied with the destructive power of the atomic bomb, and so he'd developed the hydrogen bomb, a weapon a thousand times more destructive than the bombs dropped on Hiroshima and Nagasaki.

This still wasn't enough – Teller wanted to create what he believed to be the ultimate deterrent, Project Sundial. He envisioned a ten gigaton weapon, around 670,000 times more powerful than the bombs dropped on Japan. After all, why have enough power to destroy the world with thousands of bombs, when you can do it with one?

So, when doomsday weapons appear in *Doctor Who*, it's not pure fantastical speculation; at least one man tried really hard to make it a reality. And he'd already been successful in convincing the US Government to give him the money to develop the hydrogen bomb. Thankfully those who knew about Project Sundial were horrified, and it was never developed. Less thankfully, there are still enough nuclear warheads on the planet to destroy every major city[4] and plunge the world into a nuclear winter.

The Old Mother of Za's tribe believed 'it's better to live without fire' because 'fire will kill us all in the end'. When she speaks, she's not talking to anyone in the tribe, but to the audience, offering a dire warning about our future.

---

[4]   Kurzgesagt, 'What If We Detonated All Nuclear Bombs At Once?', www.youtube.com/watch?v=JyECrGp-Sw8)

'The Kaleds were at war with the Thals. They had a dirty nuclear war. The resulting mutations were then accelerated by their chief scientist, Davros. What he created he then placed them in a metal war machine, and that's how the Daleks came about ... And ever since the Daleks were created, they've tried to conquer and enslave as much as the universe as they can get their grubby protuberances on.'

The Doctor, *Remembrance of the Daleks* (1988)

Doctor Who's second story, *The Daleks*, takes place on the planet Skaro, a world that's suffered the fiery fate Old Mother predicted for Earth. The first episode of the story[5] is appropriately titled *The Dead Planet*. The TARDIS team arrive in a petrified jungle, where trees are made of brittle stone, and there's no living vegetation. Barbara suggests the 'white and ashen' look of the place is because of a forest fire, but the Doctor determines the heat must have been 'indescribable', rather than a part of the normal ecological process, and points out the damage to the soil. He judges it incapable of growing plant-life.

The stone trees – and the discovery of a dead animal made of metal – make it clear they're not on Earth, and it's soon revealed that this world has suffered a nuclear catastrophe. The audience is a step ahead of the time travellers, as we're shown the TARDIS radiation detector entering the danger zone, but when the travellers discover a Geiger counter, they quickly catch up. They realise the collapse of the biosphere is due to a nuclear war, and as the Dalek city still stands, full of 'magnificent buildings', the Doctor determines the radioactive fallout is a result of a neutron bomb.

The neutron bomb was first tested only the year before *Doctor Who* began, and was designed so the blast was minimised,

---

[5]   In the first few years of *Doctor Who*, each individual episode had its own title.

but the radiation emitted was far greater than in a standard nuclear weapon. The idea was to destroy living tissue with neutron radiation, while buildings were left standing. The US wanted to be able to bomb a Soviet army invading Western Europe without destroying infrastructure, and neutron bombs would supposedly allow more precise, efficient, tactical strikes. It was, horrifyingly, considered a 'cleaner' nuclear weapon. These warheads, however, were never deployed in Europe, and the US ended their production in the eighties, their final neutron bomb decommissioned in 2011.

The neutron bomb explains why the Dalek city still stands, and it also means timely commentary on this brand-new weapon. One of the criticisms of the neutron bomb, compared to a regular nuke, was that it actually made it easier to start a nuclear war. Having that seemingly intermediate option makes it feel less dangerous to escalate from conventional weapons to nuclear weapons. I mean, they wouldn't be firing a proper nuke; it'd be a nice, clean one that caused less property damage. No-one could get really terribly upset about that, surely? It couldn't possibly bring about the end of the world. The civilisations of Skaro would disagree.

The Daleks are not the only survivors on Skaro: their mortal enemies, the Thals, live an agrarian existence on a distant plateau, but their harvest has failed due to lack of rainfall, and they're forced to come to the Dalek city to look for food. They hope to make peaceful contact, but, naturally, the Daleks are much keener on exterminating them.

In a Sparta and Athens vibe, the Thals were once a warrior culture, and the Daleks were best known as philosophers. But Dalek philosophy has now been reduced to violent xenophobia. They have no intention of aiding the Thals, and when the Daleks discover they need the radiation to survive, they plan to detonate another bomb to increase the planet's radiation levels, which would kill the remaining Thals. Another solution is never considered; asking for aid from the Thals or the Doctor doesn't even occur to them. Fuelled by nationalism and belief in their racial supremacy, they justify the horrors they commit through the lens of their own survival. They have physically mutated into another species, a species created by violence, driven by hate, and literally unable to live unless the war continues. In future stories, they'll no longer need the radiation for survival, but will hold on to their hate, and their desire to exterminate the unlike will be their defining feature through the decades.

The Thals are decent people. Friendly, helpful, a little bit pacifist, but they soon get over that. They're more than willing to make peace, though given they're facing starvation and their only hope is that the Daleks have spare food in their city, it's not as noble a gesture as it could be. But they are sincere. And while radiation poisoning and mutations aren't any fun for the Daleks, it's the Thals who are faced with the most lethal danger of nuclear war: starvation.

After the blasts, the shockwaves, and the radiation of a nuclear blast, there are the firestorms. These occur 'when coalescent fires cause sufficient updraft to form their own wind, blowing inwards from all sides and thereby increasing the intensity of the fire',[6] or lots of smaller fires join together to make one giant super-fire that's powerful enough to generate its own storm-force winds. In nature, they can be seen in major wildfires. They've broken out in cities during earthquakes, during firebombing raids in World War II, and after the nuclear bombing of Hiroshima. As well as the destruction at ground level, if they are powerful enough, the theory is that they could throw sufficient soot and dust into the atmosphere, to block the sunlight, and create a nuclear winter.

[6] A. F. Phillips, 'The Effects of a Nuclear Bomb Explosion on a City', Peace Res. 36, 93 (2004)

The concept of nuclear winter was first proposed in 1983, two decades after *The Daleks* was broadcast, in a paper titled *Nuclear Winter: Global Consequences of Multiple Nuclear Explosions*. Its authors included Carl Sagan, though he most likely lent his name to give it some added publicity. It posits that the most fatalities of an all-out nuclear war would come not with the blasts or the radiation, but when the absence of sunlight caused crops to fail, and billions would starve.

The Thals are not exactly in that position – their war took place hundreds of years ago – but their situation draws a line between nuclear war, biosphere devastation, and the failure of crops. Despite their anti-radiation drugs, they're portrayed as a small, primitive society, living at subsistence level. And in small, primitive societies, famine is a constant threat. Even the Romans, with their vast resources and one of the greatest empires of the ancient worlds, struggled with unpredictable weather, to such an extent that it's often considered one of the reasons for the fall of the Western Empire. *The Daleks* is interested not just in the immediate horror of nuclear war, but in the long-term effects it has on society.

One of those effects is adaptation to the high radiation levels of their world. The Thals have their anti-radiation drugs, and the Daleks need the radiation to live, but our intrepid time travellers arrive with no defences. Only a few hours after they leave the TARDIS, they begin to feel the effects of radiation sickness: headaches, fatigue, nausea, and cognitive impairment (no, Ian, you can argue as much as you like, but if your legs are paralysed, you can't walk). Based on these symptoms, and how long it's taken for them to manifest, they've received a dose of at least five hundred millisieverts (mSv). For comparison, the average person in the UK receives an annual dose of 2.7 mSv (though it'd be lower if we took out Cornwall – thanks to high levels of radon gas, Cornwall residents get an average of 6.9 mSv). A dose of 5000 mSv will kill about half the people who receive it within a month. For certain death, you need closer to 30,000 mSv.

Given the TARDIS team weren't all throwing up minutes after leaving the TARDIS, they didn't immediately get that fatal dose. It's unknown exactly how long they spend exploring, and walking to the Dalek city, but without treatment it seems they have a few days at best. It would be extremely difficult for them to have received a radiation dose from anything but gamma radiation – it would take lead lining or a few feet of concrete to block it – and the half-life of gamma sources are very short, generally a matter of seconds. Longer lived radiation sources that emit more dangerous forms of radiation – alpha and beta – have much longer half-lives (plutonium-239, used in nukes, has a half-life of 14,110 years). But they can be easily blocked – their clothing would be enough to protect them from alpha particles. Maybe they shouldn't have poked that stone animal. Most likely though, they're dying from a fantastical form of radiation, as radiation often is in science fiction. A silent, invisible threat that can do all sorts of strange things, so a threat from nuclear fallout that should last no more than five years lasts for five hundred. But realism isn't the point. *The Daleks* is interested in showing the full breadth of nuclear horror, and having our heroes dying slow, agonising deaths on their second adventure certainly fits the bill.

The Thals provide them with the anti-radiation drug the time travellers need to survive, one that they too are dependent on. But they also talk about their mutations, which have somehow come full circle to make them terribly pretty. (The attractive aliens are the good people, while the scary looking ones are evil. Of course they are. But swiftly moving on…) *The Daleks* offers two very different paths that could be taken for how humanoids would genetically mutate over the centuries, paths that are quite fantastical. But the question asked is a good one: how would life adapt to high radiation?

And it's only recently that we've discovered some answers, and discovered that in the aftermath of nuclear disaster, life can rebound with remarkable speed.

In 1986, the worst nuclear accident in history occurred in the Soviet Union, at the Chernobyl nuclear power plant. Due to flaws in the design, and safety procedures not being properly followed, a simulation of a power outage resulted in two explosions in reactor number four, releasing highly radioactive material into the atmosphere. Around 116,000 people were evacuated from the area that became known as the Chernobyl Exclusion Zone (the CEZ). Today, this zone – an area of approximately 2600 square kilometres in Ukraine, and 2100 square kilometres in Belarus – is still contaminated by high levels of radiation. But the CEZ is not a radioactive wasteland. While no longer home to humanity, in the decades since the accident, the land has been thoroughly reclaimed by nature.

There's an impressive array of wildlife – including wild boars, red deer, beavers, and European bison – that can be found throughout the zone, and their numbers have incresed over the years since the accident. The endangered Przewalski's horse had a small population brought to the zone in the hopes it could live there safely. Their numbers grew from the initial thirty animals in 1998, to one hundred and fifty by 2021. Perhaps the most successful inhabitants of the zone are the wolves, and the grey wolves in the Belarus CEZ have been particularly intriguing. As apex predators, they feed on irradiated prey that's fed on irradiated plants that grew in irradiated soil. And yet the wolf population in the CEZ is some seven times denser than in other protected area of Belarus.[7] And it's unclear as to why. Ongoing research

[7] The Biologist, Royal Society of Biology, Mike Wood and Nick Beresford (https://thebiologist.rsb.org.uk/biologist-features/out-of-the-ashes)

suggests that these wolves are not proving more resistant to cancers caused by the radiation, but they're proving more resistant to the *effects* of those cancers; their genes have become more resilient. Tree frogs within the CEZ have also experienced a possibly beneficial genetic mutation. When they've been found in higher radiation areas of the zone, instead of being a lush green, they're a peculiar black. The colour change comes from increased melanin in their skin, and means they've got better protection against ultraviolent radiation as well as protection from ionising radiation. The generations of frogs since the explosion seems to have rapidly evolved to their environment, although, as with the wolf population, understanding of these mutations is an ongoing process.

The flora's recovery is just as impressive. Within three years the plant life was regrowing in irradiated areas that would have killed any mammals. Plants are more resilient than mammals, since most of their cells are able to create whatever new cells the plant needs. They're not dependant on a whole bunch of different organs working correctly and in synch to live. Plants will respond to their environment based on chemical signals[8] and in the CZE there's evidence that they're adapting to better protect themselves from radiation exposure.[9] Damage is still done to their DNA, but in the highest radiation areas of the Red Forest (an area of pine forest that, after the disaster, turned red and died), they protect themselves against more serious damage by creating stress-protective antioxidants.

[8] A. Trewavas (2009), 'What is plant behaviour?*'. Plant, Cell and Environment, 32: 606-616, https://doi.org/10.1111/j.1365-3040.2009.01929.x
[9] G. T. Duarte, P. Y. Volkova, S. A. Geras'kin, 'The response profile to chronic radiation exposure based on the transcriptome analysis of Scots pine from Chernobyl affected zone', Environmental Pollution, Volume 250, July 2019, https://doi.org/10.1016/j.envpol.2019.04.064

But while the CEZ has turned into an unlikely nature reserve, it's not a paradise where animals can live free and safe from human interference. In the immediate aftermath of the Chernobyl explosion, vast tracts of forest died, and animals within high radiation zones were killed, or developed radiation sickness. Numbers have recovered, dramatic mutations are rare, we have evidence for some beneficial mutations, but the radiation still causes genetic damage. And, of course, a significant part of why they're seen to thrive is the absence of any pressure from humans hunting or repurposing the land. But even with the no-humans advantage, their survival is impressive. Both flora and fauna have proven resilient, and demonstrated that recovery from massive nuclear fallout is, to some extent, possible.

These ideas are touched on in *The Daleks* with the reveal that there actually is life on Skaro beyond the Thals and the Kaleds. Contrary to the dead planet we're first presented with, Skaro is not quite a barren wasteland after all. In terms of fauna, Skaro doesn't have anything so uplifting as wild horses grazing in young pine forests that have regrown after radiation exposure 'equivalent to 20 Hiroshima bombs'.[10] But animal life does continue to exist. We encounter only one example onscreen, but the Thals reveal that this creature isn't the only one of its kind. And the mere existence of this creature reveals the recovery of an ecosystem.

This inspiring example of resilience appears in episode five, *The Expedition*, and it is a giant tentacled monster lurking in a lake. It's easy to dismiss as a moment of crisis in an episode that desperately needed something interesting to happen, but it also adds to the texture of Skaro, and to the fallout, no pun intended, of the neutronic war. This lone creature has attacked and killed Thals before, and another unfortunate, a

[10]   'Back To The Wild', IAEA Bulletin, 47/2, February 2006

18

Thal named Elyon, gets grabbed on this trip. Why? Despite Alydon's assertion that there's 'horror in the lake' the creature's not attacking because it's evil, it's attacking because it senses a threat, or it needs sustenance. If you're going to go take a drink from a lake filled with alligators, knowing full well the alligators are in there, don't blame the alligators.

Our mutated squid friend is a predator, and since predators need prey to survive, and the Thals are not regularly offering themselves up as snacks, most of the time, they're eating something else. There must be other forms of life in that lake, prey for our tentacled friend. And, in turn, the prey needs to feed on something. The tentacled monster allows us to infer a food chain, an ecosystem, that shows Skaro is not truly dead.

This foreshadows the final scenes from the story, where the Doctor discovers that he was wrong about the soil. His tests have concluded that 'this soil is not quite so barren as [the Thals] think' and that this generation of Thals 'might live to see and hear the birds amongst the trees'. And near Chernobyl, that's exactly what's happening: the soil is recovering. It's now reached the point where agricultural lands just outside the CEZ that were abandoned could, potentially, return to farming.[11]

But my personal favourite of the comparisons one could draw between life in the CEZ and life on Skaro, I've saved for last: the fungus. To be specific, *cladosporium sphaerospermum*. This is the fungus I'll be referring to throughout, and I hope I'll be forgiven for not typing out its complete name every time.

What makes *cladosporium sphaerospermum* special is that

---

[11] J. T. Smith, S. E. Levchuk, D. A. Bugai, N. A. Beresford, M. D. Wood, Khomutinin Yu, G. V. Laptev, V. A. Kashparov, 'A protocol for the radiological assessment for agricultural use of land in Ukraine abandoned after the Chornobyl accident', Journal of Environmental Radioactivity, Volume 286, 2025

it's a radiotrophic fungus. It ionises radiation and metabolises it to grow, in a similar way plants photosynthesise sunlight, but instead of chlorophyll, the fungus uses melanin to absorb radiation.[12] Essentially, this fungus 'eats' the radiation. And it can do it in environments that would kill almost any other living thing. It can survive the most radiative part of the CEZ: the walls of reactor number four, where the explosions originated. And it doesn't just survive in this environment, it thrives. A natural way to clean up radiation raises many exciting possibilities, not least of all the idea that it could be used in space to shield astronauts on long voyages.

The Daleks also has a lifeform that thrives in irradiated conditions: the Daleks themselves. The Daleks are initially at work to lower the radiation levels on Skaro as 'after the neutronic war, our Dalek forefathers retired into the city, protected by our machines' having 'built this underground city as a kind of huge shelter'. And so, naturally, they assume that if they leave their city in the current atmosphere they'll die of radiation poisoning. They successfully manage to start lowering the planet's radiation levels, and if they weren't quite so paranoid and murderous, it could have been the start of the beautiful friendship between themselves and the Thals. But these shared ends last only a few episodes as the Daleks quickly discover that they are now dependent upon the high radiation levels; they 'need it as ... the Thals need air'. Despite their advanced technology, they leap instantly to the easiest, and most disturbing, option to protect themselves: detonate another nuke, and replenish the radiation in the atmosphere. Their logic is that they 'do not have to adapt to the environment' when they can 'change the environment to

[12]   E. Dadachova E, A. Casadevall, 'Ionizing radiation: how fungi cope, adapt, and exploit with the help of melanin', Curr Opin Microbiol. 2008 Dec, ;11(6):525-31. doi: 10.1016/j.mib.2008.09.013. Epub 2008 Oct 24,. PMID: 18848901; PMCID: PMC2677413

suit us.' The fact that they'll kill every other remaining lifeform on the planet isn't relevant.

Horribly, it's not that the Daleks don't understand empathy or kindness. They do and they use them to manipulate the Thals, telling them that they've 'no malice towards [the Thals], and they hope that they can work with [them] to build a new and safe world, free from the fear of war'. And then try to kill them as soon as they enter the Dalek city. While the Thals are confused by the betrayal, Ian, who would have lived through the Second World War, understands at once: the Daleks 'dislike the unlike' and are 'afraid of you because you're different from them. So whatever you do, it doesn't matter.' He takes a stance undoubtedly influenced by World War I: one cannot compromise with fascism, one can only stand against it.

But the Daleks' proposed solution of a neutron bomb isn't good enough for our fascist little tin pots. Twenty-three days to make a neutron bomb? Too slow. They need a faster solution, and decide to use their nuclear reactors to bombard the atmosphere with radiation. After five hundred years, their urgency might seem strange, but it's only now they are certain the Thals survived, and so they're driven not merely by their need to survive, but their need to destroy.

It's a deeply disturbing terraforming operation. They blasted their world with radiation, and have discovered a means to help it recover faster. Instead, they plan to ensure nothing can survive but them. They are consumed not merely by their own survival, but for them to be the only ones to survive. Why adapt, why compromise, why think of anything outside your pepper pot encasement when you can solve all your problems with destruction? It's a depressing contrast to our hardy fungus, which offers fascinating possibilities in scientific exploration, protection from radiation, and healing the planet from the most terrible accidents.

The Daleks was broadcast in the winter of 1963-64; the Chernobyl disaster occurred in 1986. And we still don't fully understand the long-term consequences of the radiation on the ecosystem. *The Daleks* is not prophetic, but it throws out a wide net of ideas, and it's delightful to see, seventy years later, how many of those ideas had legs, some very wobbly, but legs nonetheless. It's a fine testament to the effectiveness of *The Daleks* in exploring the aftermath effects of a nuclear war, to unravelling the horrors and the possibilities of survival.

Producer Sydney Newman famously, at least among the more committed *Doctor Who* fans, objected to the Daleks initially, believing them to be nothing more than 'bug-eyed monsters', and exactly the sort of thing he didn't want in his educational show. But despite the incredible success of the Daleks, who quickly became an icon of *Doctor Who*, *The Daleks* (the story) is educational viewing. It's just less interested in facts, and more into encouraging critical thinking. It explores the horrific consequences of a nuclear war, while asking ethical questions about our survival and offering two extremes. The Thals are peaceful, co-operative, and maintain their cohesion even when faces with starvation. The Daleks are cruel, paranoid, and react with violence to peaceful overtures. The first episode offers the simple message that nuclear weapons are bad and could kill us all, but then we follow the TARDIS team somewhere far more complicated. Instead of a tomb world, where all life is extinguished, the story asks for engagement with the trials survivors must face. It humanises the horror, allowing us to imagine ourselves in that situation, to see all that could be lost, and invites us to ask how we can prevent suffering such a future ourselves.

The Daleks offers hope. Yes, this is scary stuff, horrific things happen, and nuclear war is definitely not healthy for you, your loved ones, culture, civilisation, or the planet, but those anxieties are not meant to overwhelm or paralyse the

22

viewer. Exploring ideas about what would happen afterwards allows a more emotional connection with that possibility. These are the things we would lose, and aren't those things worth fighting for? It asks ethical questions about how, in extreme circumstances, communities can adapt and survive.

While *The Daleks* is mostly remembered for, well, the Daleks, it's really a remarkably sober tale for children's tea-time viewing that flows from exploring one horror of nuclear war into another. The time travellers almost die from radiation poisoning, the Thals are threatened with starvation, and cannot survive without regular medication. The Daleks have suffered massive genetic mutation that allow them to thrive, at the expense of all other life. Skaro is a desperate, broken world, trying to recover from the terrible mistakes of its past, yet still suffering five centuries later. While today the details of what would happen in the event of nuclear war are far better understood, the spirit, if not the precise letters, of those horrors are all present in *The Daleks*. It fully understands that nobody wins a nuclear war.

An Unearthly Child and *The Daleks* form an alpha and omega of technological development. Civilisation beginning and ending in fire, just as the Old Mother predicted. It touches on one of the most chilling responses to the Fermi Paradox, which questions why there is no firm evidence of alien intelligences: when a certain level of technology is reached, self-destruction becomes inevitable. It's obviously an explanation *Doctor Who* very much does not embrace, even in its first season – in five stories' time we'll see technologically advanced humans meeting the alien Sensorites – but there's still something disquieting about pairing the discovery of fire with the aftermath of a nuclear war. Neither discovery is condemned, indeed *Doctor Who* is a show that celebrates scientific advancement, and our main character is a scientist himself, but it always remembers that each step forward comes with a moral obligation: do no harm. Or, at the very least, try not to blow up your planet.

> *'Hasn't it got, like, defence codes and things? Couldn't we just launch a nuclear bomb at them?'*
> *'You're a very violent young woman.'*
>
> Rose Tyler and Harriet Jones MP,
> *World War Three* (2005)

Doctor Who never explores nuclear war in the same breadth again. If you were an optimist, you might say it's because the fear of nuclear war was never as intense as it was just after the Cuban Missile Crisis. It doesn't seem an outlandish idea, but nuclear anxiety wasn't gone; it still isn't. And with the classic series over before the Cold War was, it's a topic that's often returned to in those decades. Stories show the explicit threat of nuclear warfare, allegories of post-apocalyptic landscapes, or fighting for control of super weapons that can destroy planets, or galaxies, or the universe itself.

The next substantial engagement with nuclear issues comes some years later, during the second Doctor's era. William Hartnell has regenerated into Patrick Troughton, an incarnation with a much more whimsical personality. In *The Dominators* (1968), he and his companions, Jamie and Zoe, arrive on the planet Dulkis. This is a world that developed nuclear weapons, but never suffered a nuclear war. Cheeringly, after testing the nuclear weapon on an isolated island, the Dulcians decided nuclear blasts were a very bad plan and to never do it again. In fact, they successfully 'outlawed war' and created an exceptionally dull,[13] but very peaceful society with, arguably, the worst fashion sense in the history of *Doctor Who*. Curtains are not a good look on anyone.

[13] Dulcians, Dulkis, dull ... get it? I've always assumed it was deliberate. Maybe not.

The Dulcians' one flirtation with apocalyptic self-destruction was setting off a nuke on an isolated island that, post-explosion, was renamed the Island of Death. And instead of brushing it under the carpet in shame or horror, they used it for education. There were 'weekly visit[s] by parties of students to show them the horror of atomic radiation'. The soil was poisoned and the island remained uninhabited due to the radiation level being lethal without 'protective suits'. (At least until the titular Dominators invade and suck up all the radiation as fuel, leaving the island liveable ... sort of like the humanoid version of our friendly radiation eating fungus.)

The Daleks shows a world five hundred years after a nuclear war. *The Dominators* shows a world that launched a single nuke one hundred and seventy years ago, and 'for centuries ... have lived in peace'. The Daleks wanted to irradiate their world a second time, the Dulcians immediately saw the danger of annihilation from one test of their shiny new weapon, and said no, not for us. It can seem a naïve idea, and the story looks and sounds rather silly much of the time, but the core beneath feels fresh: this is a society that actually backed off from an avenue of advancing their technology, because they weren't prepared to put their civilisation at risk. And they succeeded. They don't even have anyone advocating for getting those nukes back. And there's certainly an opportunity for that angle in the story. The invading force, the Dominators, are aggressive, cruel, and murderous. And no one on the planet's ruling council considers anything but pacifism as a suitable response.

Their pacifist ways don't stop at no nukes or outlawing war. They've banned any sort of weapon.[14] Could we ever

[14]   Alas, this isn't interrogated further, but my curiosity was piqued as to how far this went. What did they define as a weapon when so many things could be used as one? Was it merely objects that were primarily used to kill? Did they have issues with very sharp knives? We shall never know.

have a world free of war, of violence? Weapons and war have been constants throughout human history, so it's a smidge unlikely we'll be giving those up any time soon. But what about nuclear weapons? They're new, relatively, and they could destroy the planet. There have been numerous treaties to reduce their numbers over the years, but was there ever a time when we looked upon what we'd created and thought 'terrible idea, let's stop it at once', as the Dulcians did? Yes. Yes, there was. For a brief time, it was a real possibility.

The year was 1946. And the newly formed United Nations' first resolution called for 'the elimination from national armaments of atomic weapons and of all other major weapons adaptable to mass destruction'.[15] Several months later the United States proposed a plan to make it happen. The architect was Bernard Baruch, and so it was known as the Baruch Plan. It was a serious, workable proposal that recognised a world without nukes was a safer, happier place than a world with them. There was a system of policies included on how to monitor and police this ban, and to keep control of the uranium and thorium needed to create nuclear weapons. And the United States, the one country with nukes, were the ones who wanted this to happen. And the one other country they absolutely needed to agree was the Soviet Union.

Bernard Baruch fully understood what was at stake. His words to the United Nations when he presented the plan remain deeply moving, perhaps even more so now we can look back on decades of nuclear anxiety. 'If we fail,' he said 'then we have damned every man to be the slave of fear. Let us not deceive ourselves; we must elect world peace or ... world destruction.' But the Soviets did not trust the Americans, and the plan was rejected.

[15]   United Nations: www.un.org/en/ga/68/meetings/nucleardisarmament/
disarmamentfora.shtml

The Soviet Union went on to test its first nuclear bomb in 1949, the British followed in 1952, France in 1960, China in 1964, India in 1974. In 1986 it was heavily suspected that Israel was in possession of some 200 nuclear weapons. Pakistan tested its first nuke in 1998, and North Korea in 2006. Earth is clearly not keen on getting rid of her capacity to destroy herself any time soon.

But many other nations had no interest in joining the apocalypse club. Agreements between states created nuclear-weapon-free zones (NWFZs) with the aim of halting nuclear proliferation. The first country to step forward was Poland, who called for a NWFZ in central Europe, afraid of the Soviet Union deploying nukes within its borders. Sadly, the political climate of the Cold War in the fifties rendered such a proposal impossible. But that effort was not forgotten and in the years that followed more and more states joined the non-proliferation effort, and banned nukes within their borders. There are now five NWFZs[16] that include 115 of the world's 205 countries.

When you watch *The Dominators*, it's very easy to argue the Dulcians are, in fact, very foolish indeed, and that it was sheer luck that saved them from being conquered. But we shouldn't ignore the hundreds of years of peace they've had. The story makes pacifism look pretty silly when faced with a merciless aggressor, while also declaring that it can work wonderfully. Just not indefinitely. And a world that successfully ended war for centuries is nothing to sniff about.

After seeing the two extremes of what can happen after a society develops nuclear weapons, *Doctor Who* returns to the theme in the fourth Doctor era, where Tom Baker – the most iconic of the Doctors, with his mass of curly hair and absurdly long scarf – now stars. After exploring aftermaths

[16]   United Nations, 'Overview of Nuclear-Weapon Free Zones': www.un.org/nwfz/fr/content/overview-nuclear-weapon-free-zones

we're now thrown into a hot war in *The Armageddon Factor* (1979). Two planets, Atrios and Zeos, have been lobbing nuclear missiles at one another for some time. On Atrios, an individual known only as the Marshal leads the war effort. He knows they're losing and is determined to create a 'final weapon' to destroy Zeos. Princess Astra is the planet's de jure leader, but she has little power since the Marshall has full control over the military. Astra advocates for peace, but the Marshall is consumed by winning, even if it will obliterate his own world.

The story opens with an over-the-top recruitment effort, in the form of a soap opera. This production tries to convince the men of Atrios to leave their families and join the war. We zoom out to see it's a video screen and discover it's the entertainment of choice in a hospital ward. What better way to keep up the morale of the patients than cheesy propaganda?

To make things even more fun for the injured, the hospital is also under attack by Zeos. Even though they're deep underground, the concrete roof collapses as nuclear strikes hit the planet. On the surface, the radiation levels are, as the Doctor delicately puts it, enough to 'fry eggs in the street'. In the bunker levels hundreds of metres below, the effects are mitigated with concrete and lead. But even parts of this underground structure have been lost to contamination, and citizens must wear radiation detectors to monitor their exposure.

The story quickly moves to the military command centre where a slew of reports come in detailing the damage: 'Area six obliterated', 'District ten, no contact', 'Heavy causalities through all upper levels'. The show may not have the budget to show a massive bombardment of nukes on this crumbling civilisation, but there's still something chilling about this stream of reports. There's no surprise, no horror, no fear, only dead-eyed acceptance. And the Marshall, with his need for victory, only cares about his counter-attack. He's lost all sight of what he's fighting for. His people don't matter, his world's future doesn't matter, only victory at any cost. The Daleks would approve.

When the Marshall demands the Doctor create his 'ultimate weapon', the Doctor counters with an offer to create a planetary shield to protect Atrios from attack; the Marshall refuses. He wants his giant explosion so he can 'crush ... the hated Zeon beneath the heel of Atrios'. When flat-out offered the choice between saving his people and destroying the enemy, he chooses to be a monster. He may not have started the war, but he refuses to finish it. Hatred of the other has consumed him. And he's more than a little paranoid: as soon as the TARDIS is spotted, he aims a nuke at it. All this paranoia and hate hit harder because the stakes are so high. This isn't Custer at Little Bighorn; it's a general who'd be chill with his soldiers shooting every civilian on the planet and then themselves, just so long as the enemy goes boom. Nobody wins a nuclear war, but the Marshall is determined to lose it in the most horrifying way possible.

Rather appropriately, given that *Doctor Who* is a time travel show, now that we've seen the aftermath of a nuclear war, and seen one in progress, we finally reach a cold war in 1984's *Warriors of the Deep*.[17] The year is 2084, and Earth is once more attempting self-annihilation with two superpowers poised on the brink of war in a wholly unapologetic allegory of NATO and the Warsaw Pact. The story takes place on Sea Base 4, an underwater military installation armed with nuclear weapons. The crew refer to these weapons as 'proton missiles', but from the way the Doctor describes them – 'the

---

[17] This is not the most well-regarded of stories. The fandom's nickname for it is Warriors on the Cheap. But I try not to judge a story by special effects alone.

sort of missiles that kill life, but leave everything else intact' – it sounds like it's future jargon for neutron bombs, like those used in *The Daleks*.

Unfortunately, or fortunately, the nukes can only be launched by a human operator synced to the base's computer, and the operator they have is a psychological wreck, unable to complete the launch due to intense anxiety. When one mistake means a world-wide nuclear war, that's not the guy you want on your team. Meanwhile, the reptilian Silurians, the first sentient beings to inhabit the Earth, who've been sleeping beneath its surface for millennia, are waking up. They don't like the talking apes who've taken over their planet, and they'd quite like it back.

It's a setup designed for paranoia. The crew of Sea Base 4 are already on edge with their cold war, their nukes, and an operator incapable of actually firing the things. The Doctor, and his companions Tegan and Turlough, arrive inexplicably at their top-secret military asset. And then ancient reptiles rise from the ocean and want to start a war so they can inherit the Earth. It's Cold War paranoia ramped up three-fold from its already intensely paranoid baseline. The superpowers are terrified of being destroyed, warped into a permanent state of mistrust, and unable to see a way forward that isn't deepening that divide, further entrenching them in a trap of constant vigilance and fear.

The fundamental tension between the blocs of humanity isn't resolved. But the stand-off between the humans in the base and the sentient reptiles results in a single surviving human and all of the reptiles dead. Humanity wins by one. The horror is that the Doctor tries to stop the slaughter, multiple times, and in the end he's the one who uses a chemical weapon to kill the last Silurians. The final moment of the episode is quiet and painful. The Doctor stands over their corpses, believing 'there should have been another way'. There should have. He tried a lot of them. But the fear and distrust was so deeply ingrained in all parties that it could only be resolved in the death of one side, or both. At least the planet survived, for now.

While no one actually launches a nuke in *Warriors of the Deep*, they're very keen on the ability to do so at a moment's notice. In *Doctor Who*, humanity does like its nuclear weapons. The idea of one single strike effectively ending a conflict echoes the justification behind the nuclear bombs dropped on Hiroshima and Nagasaki, and when faced with an alien threat, even sensible, ordinary people, such as companion Rose Tyler[18] can suggest something along the lines of, 'hey, maybe we should kill them all with the most destructive weapon we've ever created? I see no flaws in this plan.' This is how the Brigadier, to the Doctor's horror, ends the threat in *The Silurians* (1970); a single bomb to blow up their base[19]. Prime Minister Harriet Jones's attack on the departing Sycorax ship in *The Christmas Invasion* (2005) has often been compared to Thatcher's sinking of the Belgrano, but Jones's order isn't some jingoistic gesture, it's the same monstrous logic that's used to justify the nukes dropped on Japan: she's taking those lives because she believes it will secure the safety of her own people. Our future Welsh Prime Minster, Roger ap Gwilliam, doesn't even need a reason to fire a nuclear missile; he just wants to do it because he can.[20] And hey, if it's a really, really big threat like, say, the moon hatching into a dragon,[21] we can just fill the giant orbiting egg with a hundred nukes and call it a day.

The real-world Cold War finally appears in the

---

[18]   *World War Three*
[19]   Ironically, the Doctor commits a similar act to end the threat in *Warriors of the Deep*.
[20]   *73 Yards*
[21]   *Kill The Moon*. Please watch if you don't believe that the moon hatches into a dragon. Because it does. And then lays a Moon-sized egg.

imaginatively titled *Cold War* (2013), when the Doctor arrives on a Soviet nuclear submarine. At least this time the humans – most of them, anyway – aren't keen on firing nukes at anyone. Instead, it's the awakened Ice Warrior who sees the state of the planet, understands that a single shot can destroy it, and decides that's a great idea.

A fearful reaction response to a potentially planet-killing threat is understandable, but the ease of the jump to a nuclear blast for the supposed greater good is chilling. We're even willing to do it by blowing up ourselves and lots of other innocent people who've no say in the matter, whether it's Kate Stewart threatening to blow-up the Black Archive, a secret vault beneath the Tower of London,[22] and take London with her, or Martha Jones doing a Sundial with the Osterhagen Project, which gives her the ability to blow up enough nuclear bombs to shatter the Earth's crust.[23] Characters in *Doctor Who* find a plethora of ways to justify horrific acts of death and violence: it's necessary to win, there's no other choice, we have to be certain, we've no other way to win, so we'd rather die and take everyone with us than surrender. These responses are rooted in fear. And when we're trapped by terror, the monstrous can quickly become more soothing than repellent.

> *'Today the Kaled race is ended, consumed in a fire of war. But from its ashes will rise a new race: the supreme creature, the ultimate conqueror of the universe, the Dalek!'*
>
> Davros, *Genesis of the Daleks* (1975)

It would be remiss not to talk about *Genesis of the Daleks* (1975), one of the truly great stories of *Doctor Who*.[24] It

[22] *The Day of the Doctor* and *The Zygon Inversion*
[23] *The Stolen Earth*
[24] It was also the first *Doctor Who* story I had on VHS, so I'm a little biased.

presents an alternate origin story for the Daleks to the one in *The Daleks*. Or maybe Skaro has a cycle of apocalyptic wars and keeps forgetting about the last time Daleks evolved. But let's not get bogged down in one little continuity hiccup. This is *Doctor Who*, time is very flexible.

In *Genesis*, the fourth Doctor (Tom Baker, giant scarf, jelly babies, all teeth and curls) is sent to Skaro by the Time Lords. He and his companions, Sarah Jane Smith and Harry Sullivan, are tasked with either destroying the Daleks or finding some way to make them less destructive. And Davros, a brilliant scientist consumed by the desire to perpetuate his Kaled race by any means possible, is about to create the very first Dalek.

For the Doctor and his companions, it quickly becomes less about completing their mission, and more about surviving the horrors of the Thousand Year War between the Kaleds and the Thals. A war that finally ends when Davros betrays his own people, resulting in the destruction of Kaled civilisation, to protect the creation of his Daleks. And then he sends those Daleks to eliminate the surviving Thals.

This alternate story about the Daleks' origins sees Skaro on the brink of total devastation. All that remains of the Thal and the Kaled civilisations are underground bunkers and a domed city each. Everything else is wasteland, poisoned by centuries of weapons. Nuclear, biological, chemical, they've used them all, and their resources are near exhausted. By the time the Doctor arrives, the young Kaled general orders him to 'be hanged. Not taken out and shot as in the past' to conserve ammunition. On the battlefield, soldiers are equipped with combinations of advanced hand-blasters, and ancient projectile rifles; a gas mask that wouldn't be out of place in the First World War is worn alongside a radiation detector; uniforms are made of animal skin and synthetic fibres. Skaro has been sucked dry to feed the war, every resource on the planet turned to that singular purpose, and for a thousand years, it has not been enough.

The Daleks are born once again from apocalyptic horror. In *The Daleks* it's framed as five hundred years of radiation-induced mutation; in *Genesis* the mutations that create Daleks are a deliberate choice, made by Davros, to ensure the survival of the Kaled race. The chemical weapons used in the war have already started mutations in the species. Davros 'believed that there was no way to reverse this trend and so he started experiments to establish [the Kaleds'] final mutational form. He took living cells, treated them with chemicals and produced the ultimate creature.' This ultimate creature, of course, is the Dalek: cabbage-sized, tentacled beings that will be sealed inside a metal casing, and have no purpose beyond survival. In this nuclear war then, we do find a winner, one that considers all other life unworthy of living. This nuclear war is not simply obliteration, but a source of evil. Those steeped within it have become so twisted that even the end of the war means only the beginning of another cycle of death and destruction.

In one of *Doctor Who*'s most compelling scenes, the Doctor has the chance to destroy the Daleks in their infancy. He's not planning to use a nuclear bomb, but a couple of relatively modest explosives. Still, the parallel is there: that single overwhelming strike to eliminate a threat. 'Do I have the right?' the Doctor asks, one small step away from committing genocide. He knows full well the countless lives that will be lost to the Daleks. He's seen them invade Earth and bring down humanity, twice. But he hesitates to destroy them. He recognises that there will be unforeseen consequences to his actions, that new wars will ignite where there were once allies and friends. And yet, would that still not be better than the relentless horror of the Daleks exterminating life in all its other forms? In keeping with humanity's predisposition towards blowing stuff up, Sarah is very much for him just getting on with it, and finishing off the Daleks for good.

But the Doctor never makes a firm decision, never decides on the right thing to do. It's a choice that one could argue is a flaw in the writing, an unsatisfying beat because it remains unresolved, but I love it. When asked if he would kill Hitler as a child, he doesn't weigh the morality of killing an innocent child against saving millions of future victims, because nothing is ever that simple, that clean. If you could stop the order to drop those nukes on Japan, would you? Are you making space for a different Hitler? Are you condemning millions more to die in a war? There's no easy or comfortable answer. People generally don't enjoy ambiguity, they prefer certainty, being told this is right, and this is wrong. And the Doctor refuses to answer. Will you save lives, or will you cost more? He doesn't know, and it renders his two choices morally indistinguishable. The only correct answer, even if it's impossible, is the one the Doctor failed at in *Warriors of the Deep*: find another way.

This idea, this search for a choice beyond kill or be killed (or, in some cases, kill everything) is echoed in the fiftieth anniversary special *The Day of the Doctor*. In the timeline of the 2005 series of *Doctor Who*, sometime before it begins, the Doctor ended a Time War between his people and the Daleks by wiping out both species. He believed himself to be the sole survivor, and the guilt of that has haunted him. In *The Day of the Doctor*, the weapon of mass destruction is revealed, and the Doctor wrestles with the morality of pushing a button we know he's already pushed. But this time around, he makes another choice. He saves his people. In *Warriors of the Deep*, the Doctor wished there was another way; in *The Day of the Doctor*, he finally found one.

WHERE WE STAND, WHERE WE FALL

'Why do human beings kill human beings?'
A philosophical Dalek, *The Power of the Daleks* (1966)

From the very start, *Doctor Who* has enthusiastically engaged with what nuclear warfare means. It's explored the fear, the horror, the paranoia behind it, and its devastating consequences should it ever be unleashed. At its best it's used it as a way to test characters, to show how moral lines can bend, and fold in extreme conditions. How far would we go to survive, and would the ultimate cost be worth it?

The single most powerful moment in *Doctor Who*'s engagement with nuclear war, at least for me, is in the seventh Doctor story *Battlefield* (1989). Morgaine, the villain of the piece, is an immortal warlord and sorceress from another dimension. Throughout the story she and her knights kill with sword and sorcery; she's willing to sacrifice her own son for victory. Near defeat, her final act is to arm a nuclear missile. It's a weapon foreign to her universe, but it's the only choice she has left to destroy her enemies. She is stopped because the Doctor talks her down. In their confrontation, he describes nuclear war:

'Death falling from the sky, blind, random, anywhere, anytime. No one is safe, no one is innocent. Machines of death, Morgaine, are screaming from above, of light brighter than the sun. Not a war between armies nor a war between nations, but just death, death gone mad. The child looks up in the sky, his eyes turn to cinders. No more tears, only ashes. Is this honour? Is this war? Are these the weapons you would use?'

Morgaine is horrified. She kills without compunction, is unmoved at death, and yet this ... this obscene world-ending horror is not acceptable to her. She sees no honour in it, no meaning, only abomination, and she makes the choice to stand down. Nuclear weapons are beyond even her cruelty

36

and desire for power, and she will not use them.

It's a moment that distils how *Doctor Who* sees nuclear war: it's not just another weapon, but a moral event horizon. The show treats nuclear annihilation as mirror and metaphor, a terrifying creation of humanity's ingenuity combining with humanity's fear, and our desire to destroy what we can't understand. At its best the Doctor's power lies in his restraint, his persuasion, and his ability to imagine that there can be alternatives, no matter how difficult they are to find. Morgaine's reaction solidifies that idea. She's steeped in blood, kills without pity, but can still see that embracing nukes is embracing obliteration, not victory.

Doctor Who has used the idea of nuclear destruction to test the moral fibre of its characters, from the Brigadier's ruthless pragmatism in *The Silurians* to the Doctor's genocidal solution to the Time War. When survival demands atrocity, should we ever choose mercy? Yes, the show insists, because survival alone is not enough. We need compassion to live. And even at the edge of extinction, there must always be another way.

CHAPTER TWO
WOMEN VS TIME AND SPACE
Feminism

Doctor Who has always been about power. The Doctor's power allows them to travel anywhere in space and time, to have the intelligence, authority, and knowledge to save worlds, and defeat terrifying foes. But they don't do it alone: almost always, the Doctor has a companion at their side. And almost always, that companion is a woman.

Companions are the backbone of *Doctor Who*. They're the identification figures, humanity's representatives in time and space. Male companions are there at times, but rarely without a woman beside them[25]. And it's nice, for once, to have a woman be the default human[26]. She's the identification figure, through her we see the wonder and terror of the universe. The unknowable, alien Doctor has almost always been a man, and there's incredible power when he finally becomes a she, but to have the human default be female through six decades of adventures shouldn't be dismissed. The Doctor's the eccentric genius but we, humanity, are Barbara or Sarah or Ace.

---

[25] Notably, *The Massacre* and *The Deadly Assassin* have no female companions (barring two minutes of Dodo Chaplet at the end of the final episode of *The Massacre*).
[26] Even when she's not human. She's still the human viewer's identification figure. It counts metaphorically.

When it comes to women's roles in *Doctor Who*, it's painfully easy to tumble into cliché. Ten years' worth of characters are too often dismissed as 'sixties screamers'; the words 'plucky' or 'feisty' or 'strong female character' might be used to wince-inducing effect in any decade. But the truth is messier, and much more interesting, because women's roles in *Doctor Who* have always been more complicated. There's no jump from companions screaming in terror to fearlessly facing down destroyers of worlds; it's not damsels-in-distress to courageous heroines. It's a glorious mess of them all, in every decade. *Doctor Who* can manage tedious objectification as adroitly as inspired leadership for its female characters, sometimes in the same story.

And the companions have always been about more than Polly making coffee, or Mel's impressive lung capacity. From Barbara Wright's moral authority, to Belinda Chandra's willingness to sacrifice herself to save a world, the role of the companion has shaped the show every bit as much as the Doctor. The show's always been engaged with women's power, often trying to celebrate it, sometimes confused or afraid.

It isn't linear progress; these things never are. Barbara had some very sensible footwear to explore alien worlds in the sixties, while in 1984 Tegan ran around humanity's last colony in high heels[27]. Britain's first female Prime Minster was mentioned years before Thatcher's premiership, but the tenth Doctor brought down democratically elected Prime Minster Harriet Jones because he didn't like the way she dealt with alien threats to her planet.[28]

But the women of *Doctor Who* are never footnotes. They can be side-lined or passive in one story, only to return in the next with the wit and determination to save the universe.

[27] *Frontios*
[28] *The Christmas Invasion*

Like so much of *Doctor Who*, the way women are presented is a contradiction. They've been diminished and celebrated, but never forgotten. Ever since Barbara first insisted on investigating her very strange student, Susan Foreman, the Doctor's granddaughter, the women of *Doctor Who* have navigated, resisted, and remade their roles, defined their own place.

Women's roles in society have evolved significantly over the past sixty years, and *Doctor Who* reflects that. It embraced women in science in the 1960s, engaged with how they navigated patriarchy in the seventies, and spent a bit too much time objectifying them in the eighties. The revival brought normalisation of diverse women in diverse roles, yet sometimes stumbled by diminishing their agency. And in their thirteenth incarnation a woman finally embodied the authority of the Doctor.

Doctor Who reflects the culture of its time, sometimes the best of it, sometimes rather less so. And in doing so it's forced to make decisions on women's authority, whether that's in the TARDIS, in Parliament, on Gallifrey; in a lab or library or revolution.

> *'I thought you said you took General Science at A level?'*
> *'I didn't say I passed.'*
> The Doctor and Jo Grant, *Terror of the Autons* (1971)

Of all of *Doctor Who*'s engagements with women's power over the decades, there's none more nuanced than in the Pertwee era. At first glance, that may seem an odd thing to say. The third Doctor is one of the more chauvinist incarnations, and he can be appallingly patronising to his longest running companion, poor Jo Grant (though Brigadier Lethbridge-Stewart is also a frequent target of his snarky comments). But those moments are exceptions, not the norm, and this era's five seasons are the only time in the show's history that it explicitly and consistently engages with contemporary feminist ideas.

The timing wasn't a coincidence: second-wave feminism had just entered mainstream politics. In the first-wave, women fought primarily for the right to vote, and universal suffrage was achieved in the UK when the Representation of the People (Equal Franchise) Act 1928 was passed. Second-wave feminism began in the late sixties and flourished in the seventies. The origins date back to Simone de Beauvoir's groundbreaking work, *The Second Sex*, published in 1949. It challenged the idea of gender differences making women inherently inferior, and argued that gender is a social construct used to oppress women. Then in 1963, Betty Friedan's *The Feminine Mystique* was published, which attacked the idea that women could be fulfilled as human beings with nothing more than staying at home and raising children. These works were both heavily influential in a movement that focussed on expanding women's freedom in society: they challenged the stereotype of so-called traditional gender roles, fought for women's financial freedom, equal pay, and reproductive rights. Legal rights in the UK moved forward with the Abortion Act (1967), the Equal Pay Act (1970), the Matrimonial Clauses Act (1973), the Sex Discrimination Act (1975), and the Pregnancy Discrimination Act (1975). Of course this didn't mean the fight for gender equality was over, but these were great victories, huge leaps forward in women's freedom within society.

Doctor Who didn't just notice this political atmosphere, it embraced it. It wasn't the main theme of any story, but it was always there in the background, ready to bubble up at regular intervals. There are a few nods to feminist values in the late sixties as *The Invasion*'s Isobel Watkins objects to Brigadier Lethbridge-Stewart's 'bigoted, anti-feminist, cretinous remarks'[29], and the show decides every other story needs a brilliant female scientist, but it's from Jon Pertwee's debut story, *Spearhead in Space* (1970), that it really steps up its game. The three companions of the era – Liz Shaw, Jo Grant, and Sarah Jane Smith – show three distinct sides for how women in the seventies could successfully traverse and thrive in a patriarchal environment.

At the heart of the era is Jo Grant, a companion often dismissed as a ditzy idiot who asks the Doctor an awful lot of silly questions. It's a painfully inaccurate assessment of one of the most well-developed companion arcs in classic *Who*. Jo possesses quiet strength, an indefatigable moral centre, and the ability to have everyone else underestimate her as she navigates patriarchy and paternalism.

Jo arrives in *Terror of the Autons* (1971), and she's set up in her opening scenes to be a stark contrast to the third Doctor's previous companion, the brilliant scientist Liz Shaw. Liz has departed as she feels what the Doctor really needs is 'someone to pass [him his] test tubes and to tell [him] how brilliant [he is]',[30] which she might be a smidge overqualified for. The Brigadier believes that Jo's the person for the job; the Doctor quickly disagrees, as what he believes he needs is another scientist to work with. The Doctor insults Jo's intelligence in their first scene together, and she occasionally puts herself down – she refers to herself as 'exceedingly dim'[31] – having managed to fail General Science at A-level.

But after establishing Jo does not have the intellectual

---

[29] Isabel intends to go down to a sewer full of Cybermen. The Brigadier *is* right to object, but instead of justifying himself on the very reasonable grounds that she's a civilian, he says she can't go because she's 'a young woman'.

[30] *Terror of the Autons*

[31] *The Time Monster*

genius of her predecessor, the rest of *Terror of the Autons* is spent showing off her strengths. She single-handedly rescues the Doctor, she gets herself out of handcuffs, and she escapes the Autons by jumping off a speeding bus. Jo is a 'fully qualified agent'. She may not know her way around a science lab, but she's not afraid of a bit of physical violence, knows how to crack open safes, set explosives, and decrypt coded messages. Her unfettered compassion saves the world being destroyed by the last Daemon,[32] her refusal to be patronised results in a serendipitous discovery that ends the radioactive green maggot threat[33] and, most impressively of all, she saves the universe when the Doctor can't, because he's not prepared to kill her to save everything else, but she's prepared to kill him, and herself.[34] Her moral courage eclipsing the Doctor's is a truly magnificent moment.

Jo's method of dealing with sexism is the most subtle of the three third Doctor companions. She doesn't confront directly, doesn't bother to argue; when faced with a man telling her she can't do something, she will look at him with her big eyes, agree sweetly, then go off and do what she wanted anyway. In *Terror of the Autons* this allows her to rescue the Doctor, in *The Claws of Axos* she discovers the Axons have captured an ally, and in *The Curse of Peladon* she ignores the Doctor to go and search for murder evidence where the Ice Warriors are hanging out. And she's not punished for her choices. Each time the story says she was right to act. This era isn't about minimising the sexism of the time; it's about engaging with that sexism. It doesn't just show different ways that women navigate, but that it's a reality they have to deal with even from friends and allies.

The third Doctor has a tendency to patronise, and while

32 *The Daemons*
33 *The Green Death*
34 *The Time Monster*

he'll do it to everyone, it feels a bit harsher when it's aimed at the woman who's standing at his side facing monsters and villains. The Brigadier is a product of his time, chauvinistic, refusing to allow women to be put in danger if he can help it, even if they're eminently qualified. But these men aren't demonised for their behaviour, or their attitudes: the Doctor and the Brigadier are not participating in these patriarchal structures because they're bad people, they're inhabiting the norms of the time. It's not condemnatory, it's reflective. And it's contrasted with respect and admiration for the companions' abilities. We're presented with a paradox of them knowing these women can defend the Earth, and yet they still participate in patriarchal norms. None of the companions reject these men, indeed they'd all consider them close friends by the end of their tenure (perhaps something a little spikier between the Brig and Liz, or more flirtatious if their interaction in *Spearhead from Space* is anything to go by). It's this nuance that makes the Pertwee era so admirable in how it approaches gender politics. There's no pretending it doesn't exist, and there's no black and white. Even the Master apologises for a sexist comment after immediately being challenged by Dr Ruth Ingram in *The Time Monster*.

While Jo Grant ducked under sexism, Liz Shaw glares at it icily. She is utterly brilliant, and everyone knows it; she never tried to dim her genius, and no one ever expected her to. When the Brigadier needs a scientific advisor to assist in defending the Earth from unexplained or alien threats, she's the person he thinks best suited for the job. His respect for her intelligence is absolute, while not softening his chauvinism, much to her annoyance.

When it comes to the Doctor, Liz is not just unintimidated by the Doctor's intelligence but she's able to keep up with it. Unlike Jo, Liz never suffers a word of patronisation from the Doctor, but she too is stopped from putting herself at what the Doctor considers too much risk. Unlike Jo, she doesn't ignore the Doctor's instructions. It's a nice distinction that suggests Liz may recognise that she'd be putting herself in unnecessary danger, while Jo, with her specific training, knows she's being underestimated.

Her crowning moment is saving the world from the Nestene Intelligence. While the Doctor gurns, a tentacle wrapped around his throat, Liz has to repair a MacGuffin needed to defeat the Nestene. A couple of days ago she didn't even know aliens existed, now she's doing an on-the-fly fix on technology far more advanced that anything humanity's invented. After a plethora of brilliant female scientists playing support roles in the sixties, finally it's the brilliant female scientist who saves the day.

Sarah Jane Smith is easily the most hot-tempered of the third Doctor's companions, and nowhere is this more evident than how she responds to sexism. She's forthright, ambitious, and clashes head on with paternalistic attitudes. She's won't smile sweetly, or raise an eyebrow; she'll just tell you exactly what she thinks.

Her introductory story, *The Time Warrior* (1974), is a tour de force of who Sarah Jane Smith is. She's a journalist who uses her Aunt Lavinia's credentials[35] to sneak into a secret research base as she thinks she might get a good story out of it. When she's caught, she unapologetically admits it. And when the Doctor suggests the price of his silence is that she can make the coffee, she explodes magnificently in anger[36].

Her curiosity leads her into the TARDIS, and when she steps out again, a thousand or so years in the past, she attempts to reason out what's happened to her. And despite struggling to come to terms with being in the Middle Ages, she quickly gains allies, and leads an assault on a castle. The

---

[35]   Aunt Lavinia is another brilliant female scientist; a virologist this time.
[36]   *The Time Warrior*

really brilliant bit here isn't showing off Sarah's competence, though that is a lot of fun, it's the inspired choice to send her to the Middle Ages for her first adventure. Not only does the story have the chance to show her attitude to sexism, but it also contrasts it with historical realities.

There are two other women Sarah encounters in *The Time Warrior*: Lady Eleanor, wife to a nearby lord, and Meg, a serving woman in the warlord Irongron's castle. Eleanor is sharp and brave, ordering an assassination attempt on Irongron without her husband's knowledge. She instantly takes to Sarah, her strength and determination, and enthusiastically contributes to the Doctor's plan to defend her castle against Irongron's attack. Her social status gives her power, and she is more than willing and able to use it. Meg is at the opposite end of the ladder, and dependent on Irongron's protection to survive. When faced with Sarah's forthrightness she instantly shuts it down. Just like Eleanor, she understands her position, and it's a very different one. When Sarah starts to talk about freedom for women, Meg dismisses her as 'young and foolish'. If you want to live, you shut up and do as your told. She's not being cruel – she gives Sarah a job in the kitchens when she thinks she's starving – but practical. Her world is a harsh, capricious place, and her words are an attempt to protect Sarah.

In *The Monster of Peladon*, Sarah encounters another angle of oppression. The planet Peladon is a stridently patriarchal world, but the new monarch is a woman. Unlike Elizabeth Tudor or Mary Stuart, Queen Thalira has very little confidence in herself as a ruler, and believes she's 'looked upon as little more than a child'. The Doctor notices her thinking and rather than trying to change her outlook himself, he asks Sarah to 'have a few words with the Queen ... I have an idea you could give her some good advice.' A lovely moment for the Doctor, and for Sarah as she instantly takes up the task of explaining women's liberation to Thalira. When Thalira protests that 'she's only a girl' – appalled that poor Thalira has been socialised to think that way – Sarah responds with her particular style of uplifting fury: with a firm 'there's nothing only about being a girl ... the fact is you are the Queen, so just you jolly well let them know it.' And for added value, Sarah's not thrilled about classism either; in the closing scenes, there's a callback to her earlier words when Sarah responds to Thalira's dismissal of an admired citizen who happens to be a miner with 'there's nothing only about being a miner'.

There's a beautiful subversion of Sarah's feminism in *Robot* (1974). When she meets Doctor Hilda Winters and her assistant Arnold Jellicoe, she assumes that the leader of their Scientific Reform Society is Jellicoe, and addresses him as doctor. Winters dryly responds that she 'hadn't expected male chauvinist attitudes from [Sarah].' Her mistake is a nod to internalised sexism, that she is subject to the same social pressures as the Brigadier, and that her beliefs do not grant her immunity.

One of the most satisfying aspects of the Pertwee era is the care taken to contrast the character and aptitudes of its three companions. To show that although they share the same feminist values, they are very different people. One beautiful illustration of their particular approaches is in how each respond when threatened by a gun. In *The Ambassadors of Death*, Liz is kidnapped. She's calm, collected, and responds to her nervous gun-wielding captor with an icy 'It's all right, I won't hurt you.' Sarah has no time for dry wit. When a sawn off shot gun is pointed at her by a looter in *Invasion of the Dinosaurs*, she ignores the looter's order to turn around, and only does so when the Doctor pulls her away from him. As the looter runs, Sarah attempts to chase after him, but the Doctor holds her back. She refuses to be cowed, to the point of putting herself in unnecessary danger. Jo has the most delightful reaction: when hardened criminal Harry Mailer takes over Stangmoor prison in *The Mind of Evil*, Jo overturns the threat by biding her moment, and then grabbing the gun straight out of Mailer's hand and ending a hostage situation. Once again, she has a chance to show off her training as a UNIT agent, and that she's never squandered an opportunity to take advantage of being underestimated.

> 'What's a girl like you doing in a job like this?'
> 'Well, when I was a little girl I thought I'd like to be a scientist, so I became a scientist.'
>
> Captain Knight and Anne Travers,
> *The Web of Fear* (1968)

In the sixties, women were entering the workforce in ever larger numbers. As a teacher and a secretary, respectively, Barbara and Polly had two of the most acceptable jobs for a woman of the time, but in the Pertwee era, all three companions had occupations that were overwhelmingly dominated by men: a physicist, an agent of a paramilitary organisation, and an investigative journalist. It's a dynamic trio of occupations, and while they may not always be utilised to their best, their careers are never forgotten and they generally inform how each of them approaches challenges. It's a stark contrast to most other companions, in any era, where their occupations are mostly a side-note, with the notable exception of those medically trained – Grace Holloway, Martha Jones, and Belinda Chandra[37].

Simone de Beauvoir's most famous words, 'one is not born, but rather becomes, a woman',[38] are particularly relevant to this era. Each Pertwee era companion refuses to be side-lined or protected, and instead insists that she will choose

[37] And a quick nod to Harry Sullivan, also a doctor, also relevant to his time as a companion.
[38] Simone de Beauvoir, *The Second Sex* (1949)

her own position in society. They defied the norm of societal expectations, and embraced the way feminism encouraged women to not see themselves defined by any biological destiny or society's gaze, but as a person able to self-define. And *Doctor Who* not only gives them that space, but supports it: their male friends and colleagues almost always respond positively to the actions or the words they use to expand or defend that self-creation.

The patriarchy isn't framed as a villain, but as a flaw in society, reflected back at the companions from our other heroes, from male colleagues, friends, and villains. Women's challenges are not white-washed because the Pertwee era is more interested in dramatising those patriarchal attitudes, and showing how women can navigate them. It refuses to give neat answers to gender politics. And it's powerful because 'many women do not recognise themselves as discriminated against; no better proof could be found of the totality of their conditioning'[39] and here is a show that both practises patriarchy and fights against it. Liz, Jo, and Sarah navigate through intellect, charm, and confrontation. They use their individual strengths to deal with being patronised, underestimated, or pushed aside. And while their methods differ; their values converge: Jo thinks 'it's about time that women's lib was brought to Draconia',[40] Liz acerbically asks the Brigadier, 'Have you never heard of female emancipation?',[41] Sarah snaps out a furious 'subservient poppycock!' when told 'women ... have our place' before she remembers she's in the Middle Ages.[42]

Each of these companions finds agency and authority in her own way, and while most companions are challenged by

[39] Kate Millet, *Sexual Politics* (1970)
[40] *Frontier in Space*
[41] *The Silurians*
[42] *The Time Warrior*

alien worlds and unearthly monsters, the Pertwee era never forgets about the challenges women face in their own society.

> *'Polly ... put the kettle on.'*
>
> Ben Jackson, *The Smugglers* (1966)

While the 1960s laid the foundation of the Pertwee era's engagement with feminism, it wasn't particularly interested in its own present day. Instead, it offered breadth: a plethora of companions from the past, present, and future. The 1960s engaged with modern ideas, and the roots of second-wave feminism, eschewing nuance and depth, to instead show an extraordinary variety of women's roles across time and space. This decade brought new freedom for women, more choices and control over their own bodies than ever before with the contraceptive pill being made available in 1961, and the Abortion Act and NHS (Family Planning) Act passed in 1967. The Swinging Sixties had arrived, bringing with it a hefty dose of optimism, cultural change, and creativity.

The Troughton era also has three of contrasting companions, but while the Pertwee era has three contemporary women, the second Doctor's female companions are from the present, past, and future. Polly is the contemporary companion; she's a secretary with a sixties dolly girl aesthetic, epic eyelashes, and a penchant for imaginative solutions. She closely resembles the characterisation of the twenty-first companions: a young woman with a sense of adventure excited to travel in time and space, and leave a normal life behind. She is one of the sixties companions who suffers most from the unfortunate reputation for being a screamer, and has often been dismissed because she made some coffee in *The Moonbase*. How very backwards having women making the coffee. But Ben was asked to clear away some coffee cups first (which he couldn't be bothered with), and Polly's coffee-making led to the Doctor discovering the source of a deadly infection. She also offers to make coffee in *The Tenth Planet*, because she wants to help and she's in a space tracking station, not exactly her area of expertise. It may not be glamorous help, but it's practical.

But the brilliance of Polly lies not in her exceptional eyeliner or helpful coffee-making skills, but in how she solves problems. No matter the time or place, she offers plans that might sound odd at first, but usually end up working. In *The Smugglers* she comes up with the idea to pretend she and Ben are witches and scare poor Tom, a seventeenth-century stable boy, into releasing them from imprisonment. In *The Moonbase* she finds out the Cybermen have plastic on their chest, and decides to 'try an experiment'. She likes to keep her nails looking good, so has some nail varnish remover handy, and 'nail varnish remover dissolves nail varnish. Nail varnish is a plastic. So ... we sprinkle [the Cybermen]' she explains to a perplexed Ben. She saves the Doctor by pretending to be a god in *The Underwater Menace*, and in *The Highlanders* she traps an English officer in a pit by pretending to be an owl.

While Polly shows enthusiasm and quick, unconventional thinking during her travels, poor Victoria Waterfield spends a lot of her time terrified. Of all the companions in *Doctor Who*, she's the one most unsuited to life onboard the TARDIS, the one who does not in any way want to be there. In her first story, *The Evil of the Daleks*, she's orphaned when her father is killed and the Doctor offers to take her with him; in *Fury from the Deep* she sees a chance for a new family, and stays behind. In between she spends a lot of her time terrified, genuinely needing Jamie's protection in a way Polly and Zoe never do. At times it can be heart-breaking, but when she does summon her courage, it makes it all the more admirable. When she was told to stay behind in *The Tomb of the Cybermen*, she loses her temper; when captured by an Ice Warrior, she pummels him with questions, and figures out how to use technology centuries ahead of her. When the Ice Warrior points a gun at her to convince the Doctor to co-operate, she insists he tells them nothing. She's also a very well-educated Victorian woman. She understands how sympathetic vibrations work, and realises that the Doctor's making ammonium sulphide – stink bombs – to use against the Ice Warriors, and cheerfully throws one herself.

While Victoria is well-educated for her time, the genius of the Troughton era is late twenty-first-century astrophysicist, Zoe Heriot. She majored in pure mathematics, calculates when stars will go nova, and can figure out how to take out a Cyberman invasion fleet with a handful of missiles. In her spare time, she enjoys convincing computers to blow themselves up.

Her intellect is underscored in *The Krotons* when the teaching machines determine she's scored twice as much as the best of the native Gond students. And she's unapologetically aware of her own intelligence, believing that the Doctor is 'almost as clever as [she] is'. Zoe's tragedy is that she struggles to express her emotions. Her 'head's been pumped full of facts and figures which [she] reel[s] out automatically when needed,' but she 'want[s] to feel things as well.' Gemma Corwyn, the psychiatrist on the space station where they work, known as the Wheel, chillingly observes that Zoe 'seem[s] to have survived [the parapsychology unit's] brain-washing techniques remarkably well'.[43] When she stows away on the TARDIS, it's not just a choice to escape her life on the Wheel, but to discover who she really is.

Alas, the first Doctor's companions have no neat trios to compare, but they do have two duos that show a determination not to give up on an archetype just because the first one isn't terribly exciting. When the Doctor is first

---

[43] *The Wheel in Space*

encountered in *An Unearthly Child*, he's living in the TARDIS, parked in a junkyard, with his granddaughter Susan. In her first episode, Susan is a delicate shade of eerie, and it's that strangeness that leads Barbara and Ian to the Doctor's TARDIS, where he kidnaps them and the whole epic of the Time Lord's adventures in time and space begins. Susan is set up as a fascinating character. Unfortunately, that doesn't last much beyond that first episode. There's an intriguing moment of telepathy in *The Sensorites*, a charming friendship with Ping Cho as they travel together along the Silk Road in *Marco Polo*, but mostly, she's just not that interesting and is given very little of interest to do.

But as soon as she departs to get married on a post-apocalyptic Earth recovering from a Dalek invasion, the Doctor's granddaughter version two arrives. Not his literal granddaughter this time, but a young orphan from the twenty-fifth century named Vicki. And Vicki is fun, vivacious, mischievous, and happy to mock Barbara and Ian for their primitive twentieth-century ways. She gets bored easily, and is disappointed when her first TARDIS trip involves relaxing in a Roman villa for four weeks. She gets scared, but she always wants to run towards adventure.[44]

There's a similar vibe with Dodo Chaplet and Polly (who arrives at the very end of the first Doctor's era). Once Vicki's left the TARDIS, the Doctor picks up a second substitute granddaughter, who struggles to form any character at all. It's desperately disappointing, but the extent of the behind-the-scenes chaos makes it understandable. Poor Dodo. The first young woman from the modern day not really doing all that much with her life, and happy to go off on adventures, but imbued with an aura that provokes annoyance and frustration. It's a relief that fellow companion Steven Tyler seems to feel

[44] *The Romans*

those emotions just as much as the audience. Fortunately, her tenure was short, and Polly, like Vicki, immediately eclipsed her predecessor.

In between these two pairs is a third duo who contrast in a different way: Sara Kingdom is from the far future, and Katarina is from the distant past. Their characters are opposites. Sarah is cold, ruthlessly competent, and comfortable with violence; Katarina is gentle, uncertain, and unable to grasp what it means to travel in the TARDIS. Katarina seems to exist just for a tragic death, but Sara Kingdom, though also doomed, is a fascinating character. Prior to her first scene, Mavic Chen, Guardian of the Solar System – Dalek ally, and traitor to humanity – calls her 'ruthless, hard, efficient' and refers to her only as Kingdom. Her pronouns are not used. It's a deliberate setup so expectations are subverted when she turns out to be a woman. And she lives up to her reputation, shooting her own brother dead by the end of her first episode because she believes him a traitor. Sara discovers she's been deceived, and changes loyalties, but she never softens. She's a better fighter than Steven, but in true twenty-fourth-century style, he doesn't feel his masculinity is threatened by her competence. When the Doctor sends them both back to the TARDIS while he goes after the Daleks' superweapon, the Time Destructor, Sara refuses while Steven obeys. She pays for it with her life, but her duty demanded she help the Doctor if she could.[45]

But the greatest of the Hartnell companions is the sublime Barbara Wright. Her curiosity is catalyst for all of these adventures in time and space, when she convinces Ian Chesterton to help her discover why their pupil Susan is so strange. She's the first human to enter the TARDIS, the first to believe the Doctor's claim it can travel in time and space, and the compassionate, moral heart of the first TARDIS team.

[45] *The Daleks' Masterplan*

She's also the only female *Doctor Who* companion to have lived through the fifties as an adult, the only one who grew up during World War II. While later companions tended to be young, vivacious women, she has a much more settled, sensible energy. She's one of the very few companions older than thirty, and while she appreciates the wonders of the universe, she'd also very much like to get home. She looks to Ian for emotional support, and shows both fear and a determined bravery. She challenges the Doctor, tells him off for poor behaviour, and he apologises.[46] And when forced into a situation where violence becomes necessary, she'll hold a knife to the throat of an Aztec priest,[47] or fight off a mind-controlled Ian so she can smash up the life support containers of some evil tentacled brains.[48]

Barbara is also a character who has only grown more complex with the passing of time. Her actions in *The Aztecs*, aimed at altering Aztec society to save them from Cortez, may have looked noble in the sixties, but in the twenty-first century she's a white saviour, arrogant and naïve, come to save the poor primitives from themselves. Like Brigadier Lethbridge-Stewart, she's not a villain, but the product of her society. This lens makes *The Aztecs* an even more layered, fascinating story, and Barbara's character again added complexity. Barbara embodies moral authority, and it's an authority that's shown to have many positive effects, but one she can also misuse.

The companions of the sixties answer a question posed by Betty Friedan, whose landmark work, *The Feminine Mystique* was published the same year *Doctor Who* began: 'Each suburban wife struggled with it alone. As she made the beds, shopped for groceries ... she was afraid to ask even of

---

[46]   *The Edge of Destruction*
[47]   *The Aztecs*
[48]   *The Keys of Marinus*

herself the silent question – is this all?'[49] *Doctor Who*'s answer is, and always has been, no. If one goes adventuring in time and space, it is every bit as much an adventure for women as it is for men. And it's in the sixties companions, pushing back against society's expectations of women in the fifties, that that answer holds the most power.

> *'What a fine, fleshy beast!'*
> Shockeye describing Peri, *The Two Doctors* (1985)

Progress is never a nice, straight line, heading upwards towards a better world for all. Sometimes it's eighties *Doctor Who*. This isn't an irredeemable decade when it comes to women's representation, it can just get painful. At times, very, very painful. In the seventies, Leela's exceptionally revealing skin-tight outfit was clearly not there just because she was a member of a primitive tribe who wore animal skins, but she was still a solid character. With her, the difference between intelligence and knowledge was adroitly explored, and she was one of the few companions eager for violence, and unconvinced by the Doctor's restraint, no matter how many times he objected. The term male gaze was created by film critic Laura Mulvey in 1975, and while *Doctor Who* was certainly guilty of it with Leela, it really double-downed in the eighties. To sum it up in three words: Peri deserved better.

The prime example of eighties *Doctor Who*'s lack of forward momentum in its attitudes towards women is Peri Brown. Peri was a biology student rescued from drowning by the fifth Doctor's companion, Turlough, and dumped in the TARDIS to recover, where she's left alone in her bikini to splutter and fall unconscious.[50] Take a moment to think back to Liz Shaw's snarky first scene with the Brigadier, or Romana

[49] Betty Friedan, *The Feminine Mystique* (1963)
[50] *Planet of Fire*

I's battle of wits with the fourth Doctor, and her introductory scenes hurt. The show liked to put Peri in skin-tight, low-cut costumes, and high heels, caring more dressing her up than giving her a meaningful character.

But it wasn't just the costumes; she suffered through more leering creeps than any other companion, always from a position of relative powerlessness, and was never permitted to tell them to piss off, she wasn't interested: Sharaz Jek (*The Caves of Androzani*), the Borad and Tekker (*Timelash*), Jobel (*Revelation of the Daleks*), Ycranos (*Mindwarp*) ... It's not fun viewing.

She was also the victim of frequent body horror: forcibly transformed into a bird,[51] threatened with having her brain fluid harvested, and being turned into a tree,[52] an attempt by the Borad to mutate her into a suitable mate and, finally, she had her brain removed so her body could host Kiv, leader of the ultra-capitalist Mentors.[53] The Doctor even tried to choke her to death.[54] No other companions' bodies have ever been threatened so frequently in such violating ways.

There were some glimmers of light: she did get to tell the Master where he could go, having resisted his hypnotic powers in *Planet of Fire*. There's also a superb moment in *The Mark of the Rani* – and the Master must be getting really annoyed at her by this point – where she holds both the Master and the Rani at gunpoint. But these moments are overshadowed by the many, many ones that disempower her.

The fifth Doctor's earlier companions are much less depressing. Tegan Jovanka gets very cranky at being caught up in time and space adventures when she's just about to start her new job as an air hostess. She practically vibrates

51 *Vengeance on Varos*
52 *The Mark of the Rani*
53 *Mindwarp*
54 *The Twin Dilemma*

with determination. She's blunt, honest, and refuses to be diminished even in her worst moments. On the down side, she's given the sort of short skirts you really can't run in, and high-heeled shoes for trudging through boggy Welsh moorland, foreshadowing the nadir of Peri's costuming.

One of the great joys of Tegan is that she's joined by Nyssa, a brilliant scientist whose world has been destroyed by the Master. It's the first time where two women have travelled in the TARDIS as peers. Barbara had distinctly maternal relationships with Susan and Vicki, but Tegan and Nyssa are friends. The fifth Doctor's debut, *Castrovalva*, is less about introducing the new Doctor than it is about developing a friendship between these two dramatically different women thrown into an impossible situation. Nyssa doesn't escape the ridiculousness of high heels while adventuring and, alas, in *Terminus*, her final story, she takes off a lot of her clothes for no discernible reason. But Tegan and Nyssa have charming moments reaffirming their friendship throughout their time on the TARDIS, and Nyssa's goodbye exchange with Tegan is a magnificent tearjerker, easily the most moving farewell between companions in the show's entire run.[55]

While Nyssa, Tegan, and Peri didn't really intend to become adventurers in time and space, the sixth Doctor's second companion Melanie Bush is just ... there[56]. Her first meeting with the Doctor is never shown. Given how crucial those introductory scenes between the Doctor and companion are in characterising their relationship, it's a severe disadvantage in understanding the shape of Mel's character. But she is an incredibly enthusiastic companion, someone who brought joy back to the TARDIS after Peri's interminable trials. And that alone brings a gust of delicious fresh air.

The eighties also offer two magnificent bookends: Romana

---

55   *Terminus*
56   *Terror of the Vervoids*

and Ace. Romana is one of the most sublime companions of the whole series. She's a Time Lord sent to assist the Doctor on his quest for the epic MacGuffin, the Key to Time. Then she sticks around enjoying adventures until she's called back to Gallifrey. She doesn't want to go back to her stuffy old homeworld any more than the Doctor does, so she stays behind in E-space, a miniature universe, to continue saving people and planets.[57]

From her first appearance in the TARDIS Romana's personality is fully informed: she's confident, witty, and terribly clever. She's better educated than the Doctor, but has no idea about the universe at large; the Doctor scraped through Gallifrey's academy 'with fifty one percent at the second attempt',[58] but improvises his way out of any extraordinary situation. The balance, the energy, between them is magnificent. When she regenerates into her second incarnation, she's a little softer, and a lot more at ease with the universe. She now matches the Doctor's authority in experience, and is more appreciative of his chaotic methods, while retaining her self-possession and charm.

The final companion of classic *Doctor Who* is the irrepressible Ace, who ensures the companions of the classic era go out with a bang (possibly literally since she enjoys making homemade explosives). Ace is a teenager from Perivale, London with a brusque exterior that's a thin cover for her insecurities. She's got the cleanest character arc of the classic series, with the Doctor taking her on trips to face her fears, survive them, and shape her into someone better able to understand the universe. His choices are often manipulative, but they never destroy her agency. She responds to her feelings of betrayal with anger, but still chooses to come

[57] *Warriors' Gate*
[58] *The Ribos Operation*

to terms with her past. Her travels change her, the Doctor teaches her, and by the time of the final classic story, *Survival*, she literally puts on the Doctor's hat when she believes him dead, ready to take up his mantle. No one ever tries to put her in high-heeled shoes, but she does change into a men's white-tie dinner suit in *Ghost Light*, when she was expected to wear a dress.

The eighties is the decade where *Doctor Who* most objectifies the companions, but it's a dip in the middle, not a new norm, and it firmly gets over it by the end of the decade. Ace is the final form of classic *Who*'s heroine. And it's a form that will endure into the new series: the young woman who doesn't know what she's doing with her life, but is ready to face the wonders and horrors of the universe, and discover how they reforge her.

> *'I must have been mad turning down that offer.'*
> > *'What offer?'*
> > *'To come with you.'*
> > *'Come with me?'*
> > *'Oh yes, please!'*
> > Donna Noble and the Doctor, *Partners in Crime* (2008)

When *Doctor Who* returns to television in 2005, it's during an era of shifting attitudes in society, reflected in significant changes to UK law. The European Convention on Human Rights is enshrined in law with the Human Rights Act 1998, meant to protect fundamental dignity for all people. The Civil Partnership Act 2004 allows same sex couples to enter a legal partnership that gives access to the same financial and property right as married couples. In 2007 the Gender Equality Duty required public authorities to act to end sex discrimination and harassment, and to promote equality between men and women. The Gender Recognition Act 2004 allowed trans people to gain legal recognition of their gender.

It was in this era of growing rights that, in 2005, the Russell T. Davies era of *Doctor Who* began. In Cassandra, *Doctor Who* had its first trans character,[59] in Jack Harkness its first pansexual one, and there were plenty of nods through Davies' time that normalised the inclusion of LGBTQ+ people. When it comes to the female characters of the time, there's a great deal to enjoy and admire, but there are some disappointing choices when it comes to women's agency.

The RTD era brought in the most grounded companions of the show. They were ordinary people, who came with families, and a fresh new level of emotional depth. Rose Tyler, the first companion of the new series, was an ordinary shop assistant who wanted to escape her mundane life.[60] She offered instant audience identification with her relatable, recognisable everywoman character. And she was more than ready for adventure, throwing herself in with wonder, courage, and empathy. Those qualities allowed her to become extraordinary when she had the chance to apply them to the universe at large. With the Doctor emotionally shattered from the Time War, she provided the example he needed to find some healing, and 'the Doctor showed [her] a better way of living your life ... that you don't just give up ... you make a stand. You say no. You have the guts to do what's right even when everyone else just runs away.'[61] In the first season's finale, *The Parting of the Ways*, it's not Rose absorbing the TARDIS energy and becoming the Bad Wolf, destroyer of the Dalek fleet, that shows her power; it's the way that what she's learned, who she's become, inspires her mum, Jackie, to find a way to get Rose back to the TARDIS in the first place.

The relationship between the ninth Doctor and Rose

[59]   *The End of the World*
[60]   *Rose*
[61]   *The Parting of the Ways*

went further than the classic series with the development of emotional intimacy between the Doctor and companion. It made their connection a central part of the show, but the spark and energy between them suffered in their second season with the tenth Doctor's arrival[62]. Rose became jealous of the Doctor's relationships with other women. She sees herself as being by his side forever, but when she voices that thought, saying 'they keep trying to split us up, but they never will',[63] the Doctor's response is 'never say never ever'. There's an awkward conversation in *The Impossible Planet* about settling down with a mortgage that makes it clear they want different things in their lives. And when her Mum asks her about settling down, she replies, 'The Doctor never will, so I can't. I'll just keep on travelling'.[64] She's more concerned about what the Doctor wants than what she wants.

In *Doomsday*, when Rose first leaves the Doctor, she's pulled through to a parallel universe against her will. When she leaves the second time, in *Journey's End*, she's given a copy of the Doctor, and told that she can make him better the same way she made the real Doctor better. She doesn't even get to answer about whether or not she wants to shoulder that kind of emotional burden before the real Doctor makes a swift exit.

There's a similar frustration in the burden the tenth Doctor's second companion, Martha Jones, has to take on. Martha is a smart, self-assured, and terrifyingly resilient medical student. In her debut episode, *Smith and Jones*, she's practically auditioned by the Doctor. He's on the lookout for a new companion, is Martha good enough? It's not the greatest look when she's the also first Black companion. And it doesn't help when she's given an unrequited love arc, and

[62] *The Christmas Invasion*
[63] *Fear Her*
[64] *Army of Ghosts*

the Doctor compares her more than once to Rose, and finds her lacking.

More is asked of Martha, physically and emotionally, than any other *Doctor Who* companion: in *Last of the Time Lords*, while her family are held captive, Martha travels a dystopic horror of a world, convincing humanity to clap, or pray, for the Doctor, while she's endlessly hunted by the Master. It's an impossible quest, and yet she succeeds. But even after all that, the Doctor barely says a word when she makes her goodbye. At least she makes it on her own terms and walks away head held high.

But though there are these unsatisfying aspects to her story, Martha is magnificent. When the Master has the Doctor held prisoner, and Martha escapes to an Earth being invaded by the Toclafane, vicious remnants of far future humanity, there's a look of utter determination on her face. She delivers the line 'I'm coming back', as a massive swarm of Toclafane sweep overhead, and it's one of the most powerful companion moments in *Doctor Who*.[65] In her first story, she uses her medical training to save the Doctor's life; in her second she saves the Earth by providing Shakespeare with the final word for a sonnet;[66] she endures the indignity of being a Black servant in a public boys' school in 1913, while protecting a Doctor who's forgotten who he is.[67] In short, Martha is an unstoppable force of determination and courage, but she's meant to be the viewer identification figure and some of the Doctor's treatment of her isn't much fun.

The final companion of the RTD era is its heart and soul: Donna Noble, a temp who managed to learn the Dewey

[65]   *The Sound of Drums*
[66]   This absolutely makes sense in context: the sonnet is used to destroy a portal to prevent an invasion from the witch-like Carrionites in *The Shakespeare Code*.
[67]   *Human Nature*

Decimal System in two days. From such humble beginnings there came 'the most important woman in the whole wide universe'[68] when she became a composite being with the tenth Doctor, known as the DoctorDonna. Their combined cognition was able to save the whole of reality from Davros's plan to destroy all non-Daleks from multiple universes.

Her relationship with the Doctor is defined by friendship, not romance, and her arc was one of empowerment through experience. Her adventures transform her self-doubt into confidence, her melancholy into joy. And she grounds the Doctor in a way Rose and Martha never did. It makes it all the more painful when she faces death, and accepts it, but her agency is denied. The Doctor forcibly memory wipes her to save her life, erasing the person she's become, and returning her to the life she was so grateful she'd escaped.

All of RTD's companions are emotionally resonant, and easy to connect with. They pull the viewer into the *Doctor Who* universe with relatability and warmth. They have real families, and real relationships that matter profoundly outside the Doctor. And they offer the fantasy of being whisked away from an unexciting life to go on incredible adventures. But Rose and Donna's stories are overshadowed by their endings. They are so consumed with their adventures in time and space that they can't see anything beyond that, and because of the nature of the show it means that can't make the choice to leave.

It's understandable to want the companion to adore her adventures, but twice choosing to have her be so in love with them that she must be forced from them strips her agency, and makes her entirely dependent upon the Doctor for her happiness. Their journeys are magnificent, the arcs powerful, and they centre women's voices and feelings. But the endings

[68]   The Doctor, *Journey's End*

diminish them. Even so, this era brought the role of companion firmly into modern times, and established the importance of emotional depth both in the companion herself, and in her relationship with the Doctor.

The tenth Doctor era has a worrying amount of Christ-like imagery around the Doctor. In *New Earth*, when challenged on who he is to decide the ethics of a society. the Doctor declares that 'if you don't like it, if you want to take it to a higher authority, then there isn't one. It stops with me'. When he gives Martha a TARDIS key in *The Lazarus Experiment*, she takes it as though she's receiving communion. And she spreads his gospel in *Last of the Time Lords*, allowing the Doctor to rise Christ-like, or Tinkerbell-like, if you prefer, to defeat the Master. The Doctor is literally framed as an angel rising in *Voyage of the Damned*, surrounded by the Heavenly Chorus. And Sarah has to remind him being a god is a very bad idea in *School Reunion*.

This imagery is relevant because the following era, the Steven Moffat era of *Doctor Who*, subverts the saviour status of the Doctor and has him challenged not just by companions, but by a smorgasbord of woman from across time and space who match his intellect and experience. He is no longer unique, but now has multiple female peers who have the authority to challenge his perspective.

The Doctor first meets River Song – archaeologist, assassin, and his eventual wife – during the RTD era, in a story written by Moffat,[69] and it's in the Moffat era, particularly the eleventh Doctor's tenure, that she's fully explored. River offers a very different spin on the axis for a life of adventure in time and space. She has the knowledge and experience to match the Doctor, with a more flexible sense of morality, and no compunction about shooting people. Her death in *Forest of*

[69]   *Silence in the Library*

the Dead is her choice; she was brainwashed from childhood to kill the Doctor, and her final act is to sacrifice herself to save him. But it isn't exactly a heroic choice: their relationship twists around in time, and River meets him at her oldest when he's at his youngest and doesn't even know who she is. If she lets him die, her whole life is gone. She considers that life one worth living, and dies to protect its integrity.

Vastra and Jenny are two of the Moffat era's most subversive characters. Vastra, brilliant, coldly logical, and famed for her detective work, and Jenny, her loyal, courageous partner. They are a married lesbian Holmes and Watson investigating extraordinary cases in nineteenth-century London. Their existence challenges heteronormative Victorian patriarchy, and the peculiar Victorian idea that women could not be gay. While Jenny is human, Vastra is a Silurian, a 'lizard woman from the dawn of time',[70] who has a vast lifespan and is an old friend of the Doctor's, one whose advice he's willing to listen to, and whose words are treated as wisdom coming from a peer.

The Sisterhood of Karn, originally appearing in *The Brain of Morbius* (1976), are presented as the mystic equals of the more patriarchal and scientific Time Lords. They share vast lifespans, the Time Lords through regeneration, the Sisterhood by drinking their Elixir of Life. In *The Night of the Doctor*, they make their return to the show, and their leader Ohila guides the Doctor's eighth regeneration so his new self will become someone able to fight in the Time War. Unlike the Doctor, the Sisterhood can control Time Lord regeneration precisely. 'Fast or strong, wise or angry. What do you need now?' asks Ohila; the Doctor's reply is 'Warrior'. And this War Doctor is indeed the one who ends the war. Their judgement proved more sound than the Time Lords

[70]   *The Snowmen*

who tried something similar. They brought back the Master to be their 'perfect warrior' for the Time War. But he ended up running away and making himself human because he was so scared of what he witnessed.[71]

A Viking girl, originally known as Ashildr, becomes an unexpected peer of the Doctor when her life is saved by an alien repair kit.[72] She ends up living so long she forgets most of her life, understandable when you're billions of years old. Even when the universe ends, she's there to witness it. She understands the Doctor perfectly, better than he understands himself, and forces him to confront the consequences of his actions when he puts the universe in danger to save the life of one woman, his companion Clara Oswald.[73]

The clearest reflection of the Doctor comes in the form of Missy, the first female incarnation of the Master, the Moriarity to the Doctor's Holmes since they first appeared in *Terror of the Autons*. Missy undermines the Doctor's authority, challenges his hypocrisy, appreciates and mocks his methods, but eventually, after the offer of an army of Cybermen fails to reignite their friendship, she decides to try things his way. It's possible to see that a redemption arc for the first female incarnation of a remorseless mass murderer is, perhaps, a choice that suggests female supervillains are just nicer people than their male counterparts, but more than any other incarnation Missy echoes the Master's first onscreen incarnation. There's that sense of just really wanting the other one to come around so they can be friends again. Missy offered the Doctor a Cyber-army; the original Master offered the Doctor a half-share in the universe.[74] One of the original Master's first plans was sending the Doctor flowers ... well,

[71] *The Sound of Drums*
[72] *The Girl Who Died* and *The Woman Who Lived*
[73] *Hell Bent*
[74] *Colony in Space*

using plastic daffodils to kill thousands of people;[75] Missy claims 'traps are [her] flirting'.[76] And when Missy is killed it's because she turned her back on an earlier incarnation of herself, and decided to help the Doctor;[77] the original plan back in the seventies, prior to Roger Delgado's untimely death, was to have his incarnation of the Master die saving the Doctor's life.

Missy displays a smidge of jealousy towards companion Clara Oswald, as Clara's journey is one that has her caught up in becoming much more like the Doctor. But Clara overestimates herself, takes one risk too far, and it costs her life. The Doctor is, eventually, able to suspend her in the final moment of her life, but the pair accept how destructive they are together, how the Doctor will literally risk the universe for her. One of them has to let go, and neither has the will to do it.

The solution the Doctor finds is a neural block to wipe Clara's memories, so she won't want to be with him anymore. Clara refuses, and insists the stakes are even: one of them will lose their memories, but they won't know who until they activate the blocker. It's Donna's fate subverted: Clara refuses to have her life erased unless the Doctor takes the same risk.

And by this point, suspended in that final moment of life, Clara is effectively immortal. She's also effectively dead. Her heart has stopped and she has no need to breathe. Eventually, she knows she must return to Gallifrey, the Doctor's home planet, and accept her death, but she decides to 'take the long way round',[78] and run away in a TARDIS of her own. In the end, she gets to be the Doctor after all.

While Clara is driven to become the Doctor, the eleventh Doctor's first companion, Amy Pond, is a woman in search

---

[75] *Terror of the Autons*
[76] *The Magician's Apprentice*
[77] *The Doctor Falls*
[78] *Hell Bent*

of a family. Her story has the aura of a fairytale, where the kingdom is the universe, a place of heart wrenching beauty and grotesque horrors. And Amy's Prince Charming isn't the Doctor, but Rory Williams. For a little while he's left behind on Earth while she and the Doctor travel time and space, but not for long, as her fiancé quickly joins the TARDIS team. Amy's story refuses compromise between domesticity and adventures. She and Rory have a comfy sofa and telly on Earth, and bunk beds in the TARDIS. When Susan, Jo, Vicki, and Leela found a man to marry, they waved goodbye to the Doctor and started new lives. And he expects it to be no different when Amy finally marries Rory. Instead, the newly-weds run into the TARDIS together, and while still in her wedding dress, Amy waves a cheery goodbye to Earth.

The final companion of the Moffat era is the irrepressible Bill Potts, a queer Black woman who's taken on as a student by the Doctor. Her apprenticeship is at a different angle from Clara's: she wanted to be the Doctor; Bill wants to learn from him. The first regular LGBTQ+ character in *Doctor Who* is filled with charm, vivacious energy, and passionate curiosity. When she saves the world, it's through the memory of her mother, and the power that gives her.[79] And, like Clara, she too runs off to explore the universe with another woman, though this was a woman who occasionally spent time as sentient oil.[80]

For a viewer who likes their companions with sharper edges, with a little more distance from an ordinary girl discovering her heroism, these are the companions who are magnetic. The era's not perfect, of course, there are truly painful moments of cringe where it's best to close your eyes, put your hands over your ears, and pretend they didn't happen.

[79] *The Lie of the Land*
[80] *The Doctor Falls*

The eleventh Doctor makes uncomfortable comments about the tightness of Clara's skirt;[81] he kisses Jenny, a married gay woman, and she's sufficiently upset she slaps him afterwards;[82] and Amy's initial job is a kiss-o-gram ... why? Just ... why?[83]

But these women do choose their endings, and seize the chance for exciting adventures of their own beyond the Doctor. Each one discovers there's more they want from their own lives than travelling in the TARDIS.

With the RTD era, the ordinary is firmly embedded in *Doctor Who*, allowing a powerful emotional connection to easily recognisable characters. Companions are grounded in normal lives, before they show how the ordinary can become extraordinary when given the space to flourish. Rose jumps universes to save reality; Martha saves the Earth by surviving hell upon it; Donna grows into a better version of herself than she could ever have imagined.

In the Moffat era women have subversive authority and power, and refuse the idea of the Doctor as saviour or superior authority. They are in control of their own lives: Amy will not settle for domestic bless, or a life without the man she loves; Clara will not allow her memories to be taken. And even in death, she and Bill are able to travel the universe with their chosen companions.

> '*It's all right, it's me! Stabilise. Come to Daddy. I mean Mummy. I mean, I really need you right now.*'
>
> The Doctor, *The Ghost Monument* (2018)

A confession: when Jodie Whittaker was revealed as the Doctor, I cried and flailed, and felt perfectly ridiculous for doing it. Then I emailed friends and discovered I wasn't the only one

---

[81] *Nightmare in Silver*
[82] *The Crimson Horror*
[83] *The Eleventh Hour*

who'd had that reaction, so I felt a lot less silly. Prior to that reveal, I'd have said of course I'd love a female Doctor, but until that moment I never realised how much it meant to me.

And so, after it was first suggested by script editor Christopher Bidmead in the eighties,[84] *Doctor Who* finally cast a woman as the Doctor in 2017. The thirteenth Doctor embodies all the knowledge and experience of her predecessors, but she carries it with a quieter confidence. Her emotions play on the surface, and she is approachable, and friendly, without the hard edges of some of her predecessors. This can be read as giving her a characterisation informed by traditionally feminine values, but it's also a response to her predecessor: the twelfth Doctor was cranky, repressed, then obsessed, unable to contain his feelings for Clara, and he put the universe at risk to ensure her survival. It's tradition for a new Doctor to contrast starkly with their predecessor, and in this the thirteenth Doctor succeeds admirably. Even if the less generous explanation is accepted, the very fact of her existence still holds power. 'Feminism is about how we live differently, how we inhabit rooms, worlds, bodies',[85] and this Doctor is literally inhabiting a body that is, for the first time, a woman.

For the first time since the Davison era, back in the eighties, the Doctor has three fellow travellers, though they're never referred to as companions: Yaz, Ryan, and Graham are the Doctor's 'fam'. Instead of a single companion who looks up to the Doctor, there's a deliberate attempt to make a 'flat team structure',[86] something a little warmer, and cosier, than what the new series has leaned into so far. There's an

---

[84] He suggested his girlfriend at the time. Which sounds a lot like attempted nepotism until you find out that his girlfriend was Helen Mirren.
[85] Sara Ahmed, *Living A Feminist Life* (2017)
[86] *The Witchfinders*

argument to be made that this diluted the Doctor's authority, made them softer, and as this is the first female Doctor, it's a choice that has unfortunate implications.

Instead of the last Time Lord, standing solo against an invading alien force and scaring them off the planet with her name, this Doctor rarely shows her anger, or her darker side. But the Doctor's ability to be cruel, and to let their reputation be a significant weapon is very much a New Who choice. Between the thirteenth Doctor's less ostentatious approach and the TARDIS family, there's a sense of this era embracing a much earlier time in the show's history. The family vibe is most akin to early Hartnell, and the Doctor's softer approach feels like an angle close to the second Doctor's habit of making sure he's underestimated.

The main companion, and only female companion, of the thirteenth Doctor's run, the one who accompanies her for her entire journey, is Yasmin Khan, known as Yaz. Like her New Who predecessors she's a young, perfectly ordinary woman, from the present day. But she's not lost, she's got a career as a police officer. She's also the first British-Indian companion.

At first Yaz has an apprenticeship vibe with the Doctor, and that later turns into romantic feelings. Despite the Doctor's reciprocation, they struggle to acknowledge how they feel, especially to each other. It's a relationship that deserved more time, more development, nevertheless, it's heartening to see the show willing to embrace a queer relationship between the Doctor and her companion. And while more depth would have been lovely, Yaz's feelings are treated respectfully by the Doctor, and she's never made to feel a fool, nor is she pitted against another woman.

With RTD's return to the helm of *Doctor Who*, and the arrival of the fifteenth Doctor in 2023, the companion role returned to its long running default: young woman from contemporary Earth who lacks direction in her life. Ruby Sunday's relationship with the Doctor doesn't contain a hint of romance, but instead focuses on a best friend, almost sibling-like, relationship. There's a giddy delight between them as they explore time and space. Ruby leans into the vibe of Vicki and the first Doctor when they behaved like excitable kids in Rome.

Like some past companions, Ruby has a mysterious secret, but this time, she's the one who is most interested in the answer, not the Doctor. She wants to discover the identity of her mother. The answer is a lovely subversion of the epic reveal of River's parentage. She was the Doctor's wife, and the daughter of his companions, Amy and Rory. Ruby's Mum is a perfectly ordinary woman, who had not been able to cope with the responsibility of raising a child. When Ruby finds her biological mother, entirely unencumbered by epic destiny, she walks away from the TARDIS, placing priority on her familial relationships.[87]

With the fifteenth Doctor's second companion, the New Series steps away from the young modern woman format for the very first time, and chooses a slightly older modern woman instead. It may not sound like much, but Belinda Chandra has a career she loves, and a home she wants to get back to, and that means a delicious tension on the TARDIS that's not been seen for decades. It feels fresh and fun, and it makes for some wonderfully sparky conversation between the Doctor and Belinda. She's more grounded than most of her predecessors, and even that decade and a half of extra life experience shows in how she approaches problems. She's less easily rattled, less easily impressed, and as a doctor herself, willing to get stuck in and figure out how some future medicine works. She's also the first companion to stumble into her adventures rather

[87] *Empire of Death*

than being tempted away from Earth for a very, very long time, and that insistence that she wants to go home gives her an unusual authority, and an easy space to challenge the Doctor.

> 'Steady on, old girl! Steady on...'
>> 'Harry ...'
>> 'Yes, I'm here, I'm here.'
>> 'Call me "old girl" again, and I'll spit in your eye.'
>>> Harry and Sarah, *The Ark in Space* (1975)

Doctor Who's length means it's an incredibly rich text for mapping the path of women's power, representation, and how they are perceived in society. And *Doctor Who* isn't interested in one story about women, it's interested in hundreds. There's a diversity to the roles they're given across the decades, despite the length of the show, companions never really feel repeated. Second-wave feminism had just arrived when the show began, and Barbara was a character who, while she may not have described herself as a feminist, was smart, sensible, and courageous whether she was in Saladin's court, or had an appointment with Madame Guillotine. The 1970s boasted powerful engagement with second-wave feminism. Liz, Jo, and Sarah were dramatically different people, and yet all faced the same challenges versus patriarchal authority. Each one found a way to navigate it. One can be frustrated by the dip in the 1980s, yet it was bookended by a genius Time Lord, more academically gifted than the Doctor, and a teenager who provided the foundation for twenty years of modern *Doctor Who* companions.

New Who brought more emotional depth to the companions and their stories, and more challenges to the Doctor's authority, before the Doctor finally regenerated into a woman themselves. Yaz was a queer woman of colour, whose feelings were treated with respect; Ruby explored what family meant to her; Belinda offered a modern interpretation of Barbara Wright – she knew who she was and had a real adversarial spark with the Doctor that transformed into friendship.

Women in *Doctor Who* have navigated paternalism, suffered objectification, claimed agency and equality, and had it stripped from them. It's not merely reflected the time it was made in, but responded to it, and created a tapestry of fascinating characters from the past, present, future, and beyond.

CHAPTER THREE
THE EMPIRE OF TIME
Colonialism

D octor Who is haunted through time and space by Britain's imperial past, willingly and unwillingly. Once Britain was 'the empire on which the sun never sets', and at its peak engulfed a quarter of the globe and was home to five hundred million people; by 1963, when *Doctor Who* began, World War II had depleted its resources, the Suez Crisis had shown how neutered its power had become, and all the Empire's major territories were sovereign nations. Britain was forced to grapple with its new place in the world, and *Doctor Who* often held up a mirror to take a good long look at her Imperial hangover.

But while it's always strived to critique imperialism, *Doctor Who* can't help but be immersed in it. It's the product of the society that made it, after all (and British society is one where it's still controversial to knock down statues of slavers). Some of the show's stories dig into colonial anxieties; others regurgitate imperial logic. Colonialist tropes exist alongside fierce opposition to exploitation; stories can patronise and exoticise the societies they explore, yet resistance to oppression, fighting for freedom and independence are celebrated. *Doctor Who* cares deeply, often awkwardly, sometimes it slips hard, but at its very best it's able to subvert the imperial narratives that it's inevitably trapped by.

This is one of the show's most fascinating contradictions: *Doctor Who* cannot, by its very nature, escape its imperial saviour narrative. The format demands it. Almost every story has the Doctor arrive as a stranger; they learn about a new place, discover a problem, solve it, and depart. It's a clear parallel to a classic colonialist narrative: go somewhere new, judge the situation, then exploit and/or think they're saving the indigenous people from themselves. And though they are, on occasion, asked to help, the show generally assumes the Doctor's right to intervene.

The Doctor is an eccentric amongst their own people, and explicitly rejects Time Lord society. They're a scientist, a mad man in a box, the only man wise enough to know he's foolish, an endless wanderer in the fourth dimension, and an individual of immense privilege who, on occasion, acts as the representative of an imperial power.[88] The Doctor is 'a citizen of the universe'[89] who's 'allowed everywhere'.[90] They 'don't have a job ... don't have a boss, or taxes, or rent, or bills to pay'.[91] They're a British aristo forever on their Grand Tour.

The Doctor often uses this immense privilege to take direct action against imperialism, but Indian literary scholar Ania Loomba defines one aspect of imperialism as 'interference with political and cultural structures of another territory or nation'.[92] That's pretty much the Doctor's *modus operandi*, and so the show can't help but embrace the white saviour even as it tries to dismantle it. Yet it never gives up on trying, and has stood firm through the decades in imperfectly advocating

[88] Made explicit in *The War Games* (1969) where we discover he's a runaway from that power, i.e. Time Lord society.
[89] *The Daleks' Masterplan*
[90] *The Five Doctors*
[91] *Space Babies*
[92] Loomba, Ania, *Colonialism/Postcolonialism* (1998)

for the freedom and self-determination of all people. On rare occasions, it's even been able to find a way to transcend this impossible task, and momentarily escape its imperial chains.

> *'Now, now, don't get exasperated, Susan. Remember the Red Indian. When he saw the first steam train, his savage mind thought it an illusion, too.'*
>
> The Doctor, *An Unearthly Child* (1963)

In its early years, whenever *Doctor Who* ventures outside of Europe things get a little Orientalist. The intention is an educational, exciting exploration of culture, and that's often achieved, but it's tarnished by a colonialist gaze. Exoticised locales, Orientalist stereotypes, travelogues where the nice British couple, the weird kid, and this eccentric old guy get to experience the strange ways of foreign lands. These stories lean into the idea of the Other – that the people encountered are fundamentally different from our heroes, that they are outsiders. And, regardless of intent, that lessens their humanity.

Marco Polo (1964) is, in many ways, a magnificent story – it's visually beautiful, and extensively researched – but it's also steeped in Orientalism. The seven-episode story takes the form of a travelogue as our heroes travel the Silk Road, and, as the title suggests, they encounter Marco Polo, the Venetian merchant and explorer, who's on his way to see Kublai Khan, ruler of China and the Mongol Empire. Polo is first encountered when he saves the TARDIS crew from the Mongol warlord Tegana's attempt to kill them for being 'evil spirits. Sorcerers. Magicians'. Polo believes them to be only travellers. He protects them from the superstitious Mongols, and is the friendly Westerner who acts as the intermediary between the travellers and the culture and people of Cathay. He's the one who explains the local culture, the one who has travelled to all corners of the Khan's domains; his authority on the subject of Cathay is implicitly placed above that of the locals, the Eastern perspective is sidelined to make way for the Western interpretation.

The route to Peking is painted with both wonder and danger. The travellers cross a land where 'bones of many men who thought they had enough lie bleached in the desert sand', and yet at night the desert is beautiful, 'like a great silver sea' once the moon rises. The sandstorm that later threatens 'sounds as if all the devils in hell were laughing', but Ian also mentions these singing sands can 'be like a familiar voice calling your name'. These poetic descriptions emphasise both the strangeness of the land to the Westerners, and 'that "otherness" ... is at once a subject of desire and derision'.[93] We're invited to think of this as a fascinating, exotic land, to be drawn back into a nostalgic time of Western exploration and discovery.

There are also some gentle subversions, with unassuming parallels drawn between characters: Ping Cho and Susan are drawn together, mirroring one another as two teenagers on long journeys far from home, uncertain of their final destinations. And, most satisfyingly, Kublai Khan himself undercuts expectations. The great and feared emperor is a crotchety old man with a fine sense of humour, and when the Doctor complains about having to kneel before him, due to his back pain, the Khan sympathises. He's plagued by the pains of old age too. It's a lovely bonding moment, and a humanising piece of characterisation. And though Tegana is a nefarious traitor attempting some sneaky murders, that doesn't mean Marco Polo only harbours good intentions towards the time travellers. Five minutes after rescuing them, Polo decides to nick the TARDIS to present as a gift to the Khan, hoping

[93]   Homi K. Bhabha, *The Location of Culture* (1994), p. 67

it's good enough that the Khan will allow him to go home to Venice. He's very apologetic to the Doctor, but firmly committed to his thieving ways.

The Crusade (1965) continues the lean into Orientalist tropes, most notably in its presentation of Saladin, Sultan of Egypt and Syria, and very keen on retaining control of Jerusalem. A flat, villainous character is ably avoided: one of his royal court suggests the captured Barbara be used for his amusement, that she 'dance on hot coals, run a gauntlet of sharp tipped swords'. Saladin dismisses this as a fool's punishment. He will not 'dispense life and death lightly'. Yet he demands Barbara serve a purpose, that she entertain him with stories at dinner. He places her in the role of Scheherazade, and calmly reminds her that a sentence of death hung over the ancient storyteller's head. His servant, Sheyrah, helps Barbara get ready for the dinner and comments that Saladin 'will be dazzled by your beauty'. He may not condone torture, but Saladin's fallen into an Oriental trope, demonstrating the sort of implied licentiousness permissible on children's telly.

Rather less subtly, Barbara is kidnapped from her imprisonment by El Akir, the Emir of Lydda, who is angry after she embarrassed him. He believes 'she would make a fine addition to his harem'. It's revealed that he killed a mother and son because the father refused to hand over his eldest daughter to be raped. That daughter is eventually found in his harem (where she attempted suicide), and the surviving daughter is also threatened with rape if she's found by El Akir. The daughter's father gives Barbara a knife, telling her to kill herself and his daughter if they are found by El Akir's men. It's one of *Doctor Who*'s darkest characterisations of a villain, and a choice that is in stark contrast to the noble companions of King Richard.

Still, at least Saladin and Richard are depicted as worthy foes. Both are intelligent men who seek peace. Saladin is gracious enough to send Richard 'presents of fruit and snow when [he] is sick', but to his sister Joanna his people are 'dogs' and 'merciless Saracens'. To one of his knights, they are 'the Devil's horde'. Meanwhile, white, blonde-haired Vicki is 'a fair rose of England in this foreign land'. And while Saladin has no great appetite for war, it's Richard who actually offers peace. Saladin respects bravery and honesty, yet remains enigmatic. He's not demonised, but he's distant, soft and measured, a wise Eastern prince; someone to be respected, but not understood in the same depth as his English counterpart. Saladin is 'the desire for a reformed, recognizable Other, as a subject of a difference that is almost the same, but not quite'.[94]

The Crusade immerses itself in exoticising the East, with traders in silk, perfume, and spices; treacherous Saracens, harems, and horrifically brutal punishments, with Ian staked out in the desert to be covered in honey and eaten by ants. Temperamental as King Richard is, it's Saladin and his court we're asked to fear more. That's where treachery is to be found, even if it's not with the Sultan himself. While Richard's followers are brave, honourable men, Saladin's brother is ardently misogynistic, cruel, and murderous.

Alas, Orientalism isn't confined to the sixties. The most egregious example is to be found is over a decade later in 1977's *The Talons of Weng-Chiang*, a story that's enthusiastically drowning in Yellow Peril. The initial villain is the Chinese magician Li H'Sen Chang. He spends his time kidnapping prostitutes and using their lifeforce to feed his god, Weng-Chiang (who's actually a fifty-first-century war criminal called Magnus Greel, and the Big Bad of the story). Chang is inspired by the archetypical villain of Yellow Peril, Fu Manchu, the infamous antagonist of a series of 1910s novels by Sax Rohmer. Chang has the long moustache, the brilliance,

---

[94]   Homi K. Bhabha, *The Location of Culture* (1994), p. 86

and the powers of hypnotism associated with Fu Manchu. And while he's not the only Chinese character in the story, the rest are all either members of Magnus Greel's cult, or voiceless labourers.

Opium is smoked, Chinese launderers and their baskets provide helpful escape routes, the Doctor makes a joke about 'epicanthic eyebrows', the Tongs abduct Englishwomen ... it's a lot. On the bright side, *Doctor Who* never dives this deep in Orientalist dredge again, but it's a little depressing that not even the modern series escapes from these 'mysterious East' tropes. The opening of *Turn Left* (2008) takes place in a bazaar on the planet Shan Shen, with exotic foodstuffs, silk lanterns, and a surfeit of Asian conical hats. It's a culture that could best be described as Generic Orient. An enigmatic fortune teller approaches Donna Noble and insists on reading her future in her incense filled nook. She starts mysterious then quickly becomes threatening, and manipulates Donna's past, setting it on a disastrous new course. Despite changing the world, at least for one episode, the fortune teller remains a complete mystery, and isn't even given the dignity of a name. Instead, she personifies long-standing stereotypes of Eastern mysticism.

> 'You can't rewrite history. Not one line!'
>
> The Doctor, *The Aztecs* (1964)

Doctor Who's second (or third, if you want to count the prehistoric cavemen of *An Unearthly Child*) journey to explore another culture from Earth's past headed west to bring us *The Aztecs* (1964). Like *Marco Polo*, this is a beautiful production that's been well-researched. It emphasises the grandeur of Aztec achievements, and offers a variety of perspectives from the people of Tenochtitlan, but it is still mired in colonialist attitudes.

The Doctor, Barbara, Ian, and Susan arrive in fifteenth-century Mexico, when the Aztec Empire is at its height. Barbara is mistaken for a reincarnation of the high priest Yetaxa. Using her new authority, she tries to end the practice of human sacrifice, believing that if she can do so, Hernán Cortés will refrain from conquering the empire. It's a classic white saviour move: Barbara goes in to 'civilise' the foolish Other, who don't understand the barbarity of their tradition, and if only they ended it their civilisation would be saved. But, of course, this is Earth history – she can't succeed, but even if she did, the idea that Cortés would give up all that delicious wealth and power because the Aztecs had different religious beliefs is painfully naïve of Barbara. Apparently, she's not familiar with any of the other indigenous nation of the Americas, or their fates. She sees both the beauty and the horror of Aztec civilisation, and has the arrogance to believe she can simply disentangle one from the other, and all will be well.

Even her brief attempt at reform causes further injury. Autloc, the High Priest of Knowledge, is the one man who decides to stand by her, and reject human sacrifice, but he ends up losing his faith and heading off into the wilderness alone. His fate is framed as positive by the Doctor, as he claims that Barbara saved this one man, but it seems obvious that exiled and alone, the rest of his life will be quite short. The story can be read as ambivalence about colonialism – moral absolutism regarding human sacrifice isn't unreasonable, but how far should we go in interfering with other cultures? Barbara is attempting to single-handedly upend an entire belief system. How can we predict the consequences of that interference? And how might we destroy good people with our best intentions?

'Oh, we have a small number of men, as many as we need. The rest we kill. They consume valuable food and fulfil no particular function.'

Maaga, *Galaxy 4* (1965)

Galaxy 4 (1965) and *The Ark* (1966) are two stories that, at first glance, manage to be blandly offensive. The former is unsubtly sexist, and the latter casually racist. But viewed at a bit of an angle, they both manage to be a little more interesting. In fact, *The Ark* manages to go from a tedious racist tale into a finale that offers up once of the most novel ideas *Doctor Who*'s ever had when it engages with colonialism.

Matriarchal societies are bad. That's the big message *Galaxy 4* seems to have. The alien women in the story, the Drahvins, turn out to be cruel and militaristic, with worrying ideas about genetic engineering. Their society has only a small number of men, the rest are considered a drain on resources and killed. Female clones are grown 'to fight, to kill', with no purpose beyond that, and no recognition of them as sentient beings, despite their clear ability to feel fear. Maaga, their leader, is violent and paranoid. She assumes an offer of help is meant 'to tempt [them] on board [the Rills'] spaceship so that they may kill [the Drahvin]'.

But the Drahvins' appearance reflects stereotypical Western beauty standards: they're slim, white, and blonde. Steven's first reaction to them is to appreciate their physical attractiveness and then flirt. Historically, colonialism has primarily benefitted white men, and it can often be forgotten that white women are also massive beneficiaries. *Galaxy 4* becomes a little more interesting when it's read as a reminder of those benefits. The violent results of white women's endorsement of colonialist attitudes is often hidden, but here it's out in plain sight, with Maaga's genocidal attitude, and her well-armed soldiers intent on exterminating the innocent Rills. Their objective is to exploit the resources the Rills have available to them to escape a doomed world, and even though the Rills offer to freely share those resources so both groups survive, that isn't enough for Maaga. Either just the Drahvins survive, or no one does. Her values, her sense of her race's superiority, outweigh rational judgement, and what would most benefit her people. It's a great example of symbolic politics, where it doesn't matter if the policies you're voting for harm you, because it's more important that they reinforce your ideology.

While *Galaxy 4* is not one of *Doctor Who*'s most well-thought-out stories, *The Ark* is a car crash of thematic disaster until its finale, when it makes a rapid gear shift into the fascinatingly absurd. Millions of years in the future, the Doctor, Steven, and Dodo are on a spaceship fleeing an Earth that's about to explode. The humans on board intend to land on planet Refusis Two. They're aware the planet's already inhabited, but they're off to colonise it anyway, with no less than 'the Earth's full population, human and animal'.

They're not the only species on board this ark. There's also a group of Monoids, one-eyed aliens whose 'origin[s] [are] obscure. They came to Earth many years ago, apparently from their own planet which was dying. They offered ... invaluable services for being allowed to come on this joint voyage'. In less polite words, the Monoids are slave labour. They're mute, passive, and carry out menial tasks for the humans, who have no issues with exploiting them. Sadly, the Doctor and his companions don't question it either, and leave the Ark after two episodes. But this is a four-episode story, so they materialise straight back on board. It's seven hundred years later and the Monoids are now in charge.

The new hierarchy is, of course, evil. Unlike the humans, the Monoids are cruel masters who need to be put back in their place. A better story might have explored this as the anxiety of colonisers fearing colonised peoples doing to colonisers what the colonisers did to them. But no, the Monoids are just bad dudes showing a serious lack of gratitude to their benevolent overseers. How dare they revolt? Thank goodness the Doctor and friends are here to launch a counter-revolution and get things back on the right track.

And that's when *The Ark* decides it's not going to stick with this painful narrative, but go for something a little more surreal and, dare I say it, thought-provoking. For the Monoids are not overthrown. But the humans do make an escape. And both head on down to Refusis Two to start their respective colonies. Did they come to some sort of peace agreement themselves? No, they did not. Instead, the native Refusians finally make their presence known.

The Refusians turn out to be very powerful, very invisible beings who've 'known for some time of the journey of the vessel [called] the Ark and ... welcomed it.' They've even built houses for the humans and Monoids. And they are really very keen to see their planet inhabited by corporeal beings again, 'provided that the beings that come to take [their] place are peaceful.' And if they don't 'learn to live together', the Refusians will kick them all off their planet. If they do manage to be peaceful, the Refusians will 'do everything [they] can to assist [them] in settling [their] planet.'

And, finally, the Doctor recognises why the Monoids were so keen on revolting: 'A long time ago, your ancestors accepted responsibility for the welfare of these Monoids. They were treated like slaves. So no wonder when they got the chance, they repaid you in kind.' If only that had come across in any of the rest of the story.

But the real win is emphasising the difficulties of negotiating justice between colonised and coloniser. When what you need is no less than the awesome powers of an invisible, non-corporeal, pseudo-godlike race to offer you a nice planet to live on in order to convince you stop killing each other, that's a damn complex issue you're dealing with.

'Why have you released the apes?'

    'I have decided that it is possible for the two species to live together on this planet.'

'This planet is ours!'
'This other species has developed its own civilisation. We must accept them as equals.'

Morka and Okdel argue about humanity,
The Silurians (1970)

While *Doctor Who* struggled to escape Orientalist tropes as it explored non-European cultures, it stepped onto somewhat firmer ground when it directly engaged with the treatment of indigenous peoples. The show has a healthy appetite for allegories of Britain's part in colonisation and genocide, and the resistance the country faced as it tried to help itself to the rest of the planet. The 1970s, especially, was a time when *Doctor Who* was fiercely critical of colonialist expansion, with stories that practically vibrate with anger.

But, back in the 1960s, there was still a healthy dose of self-awareness in *The Sensorites* (1964). The Doctor, Barbara, Ian, and Susan arrive on a spaceship crewed by humans who are terrified of the Sensorites, an alien race who 'are hostile ... but in the strangest possible way'. The strangeness? These aliens 'don't attempt to kill [them]'. Instead they take occasional control of their minds, or put them 'into a deep sleep that gives the appearance of death', and they've trapped their ship near their home planet, the Sense Sphere. The Sensorites have taken these actions defensively: they silence the ship's minerologist, John, when he discovers valuable mineral deposits on their world; it's 'a veritable gold mine' with vast deposits of the essential trace mineral molybdenum. And John's immediate reaction is to see all the wealth he could amass from exploiting someone else's planet. And, being telepathic, the Sensorites are fully aware of his greed, and they don't like it.

But these are not the sort of aliens inclined towards murder. Ian quickly realises 'they were as frightened of [him]

87

as [he] was of them'. They're not letting the human ship go because they've had past experience with humans nicking their natural resources, and would like it not to happen again. The previous humans weren't even their first rodeo, they found that 'intruders from other planets always say they wish to talk, but all they mean to do is destroy'. And yet even with those experiences, the Sensorites still 'have no wish to harm [these humans] in any way'. They're the ones under threat, but they're still trying to be decent about the situation. No, they won't let the crew head home to tell others about their planet's resources, but they do offer the trapped crew 'a special area on the Sense Sphere' where they can live comfortably.

Trust is low between the two species: the Sensorites *have* mentally attacked the humans and the TARDIS crew, and they in turn have threatened to attack the Sensorites, but both sides still genuinely want a peaceful resolution. The obstacle is that humanity has already proven willing to exploit the Sensorites. And given what they've sensed from John, it's reasonable for them to assume this crew will be no different. On discovering rich mineral deposits 'he thought of a fleet of spaceships to come here and mine the metal and transport it back to his own planet' and the Sensorites realised it would be 'the end of [their] way of life'. It's a neat switch from mysterious alien menace, to people trying to protect their land. Neither side is defenceless, neither monstrous, but our assumed allies, the humans, are the ones at fault.

That first group of humans to arrive on the Sense Sphere never actually got around to any mining. Instead, they quarrelled over those perceived riches then appeared to get themselves killed when their spaceship exploded in the atmosphere. Since then, the Sensorites have been dying. The human explorers brought a plague to this new world that they wished to exploit, a parallel to the Europeans who arrived in the Americas, bringing smallpox and influenza with them. It's the Doctor's scientific acumen that provides the cure – yes, he saves the Sensorites, but from the damage done by the would-be human colonisers. He's stabilising Sensorite society, returning it to where it would have been had humanity's actions not put their species in danger of extinction. And his aid is specifically asked for by the Sensorite leader. The story manages to critique colonialism while giving the Doctor a role that doesn't fall headfirst into white saviour: here, he isn't interfering, he's restoring.

The hardcore anti-imperial allegory of the 1960s arrives with the decade's final story, *The War Games* (1969). It's remembered as the story that introduced the Doctor's people, the Time Lords, but it's really an intense exploration of the horrors of war. Men (and one token woman) are kidnapped to be colonial cannon fodder; they're reduced to resources, their only purpose to fuel the expansion of a callous empire.

When the Doctor, Jamie, and Zoe first arrive on the unnamed world controlled by the War Lord, it appears that they've landed in No Man's Land during the First World War. What they discover is that the planet is divided into war zones, and in each one soldiers from different eras in Earth history are fighting it out. The War Lord's goal is to use the survivors as an elite army that will take over the galaxy.

The men fighting have been abducted from their homes, and are treated as disposable, easily replaceable, 'specimens'. Until the Doctor's intervention, they aren't even aware that they're fighting in endless wars that they cannot win; any doubts about the reality of their situation are quickly corrected with memory rewrites. They're indoctrinated into seeing nothing wrong with their situation, back to believing 'the old lie: *Dulce et decorum est, Pro patria mori*'.[95]

[95]   'Dulce et Decorum Est', Wilfred Owen (1920)

This forced conscription by alien overlords isn't just about the First World War, though it's certainly angry at the slaughter of a generation of young men. It echoes conscription in colonised populations, where a distant power needed expendable people to fight in foreign wars. And once they've made their noble sacrifice, those soldiers are quietly forgotten. Britain raised numerous colonial forces to fight her battles, peaking in World War II. Awareness of the contributions of Commonwealth countries in the World Wars is rising, but still only 55 per cent of British people are aware that Indians fought for Britain.[96] Over a million Indian soldiers served overseas during World War I, and over 600,000 Africans from British colonies served in World War II. Many volunteered, but others were forced into service. And when the war ended, their contributions received little of the recognition or rewards given to white soldiers. Their lives, like the kidnapped soldiers in the War Zones, were treated as disposable.

The War Games is 1960s disillusionment with militarism in full swing; the United States was entrenched in the Vietnam War, and protests raged across the country, but the UK also had frequent anti-war marches, as while not committing troops, it did provide diplomatic support,[97] and refused to condemn US actions. And the British public did not approve. The Battle of Grosvenor Square took place on 17 March 1968, thirteen months before *The War Games* was first broadcast. Eighty thousand people marched from Trafalgar Square to Grosvenor Square. The march ended in violence between police and protesters, and eighty-six people were injured. John Scarlett, future head of MI6, said in a letter to *The Times*, 'I twice saw policemen charge quite strongly at very few demonstrators who were doing absolutely nothing

---

[96] https://www.britishfuture.org/ve-day-80-public-supports-efforts-to-raise-awareness-of-commonwealth-ww2-service/
[97] And arms, and intelligence, though that wasn't known at the time.

and both times people were heavily clubbed over the head, while one of my friends saw a girl being viciously clubbed for no reason at all.'[98]

The big twist in *The War Games* arrives in episode 10. The Doctor realises he can't win, and so contacts his own people, the Time Lords, for help. And they do put an end to the conflict, and return the kidnapped people to their own times. They're going to make sure everything is put to rights, and they're doing it for your own good, because they know what's best for you. While we'll eventually see the decay and rot in Time Lord society, at this point they're presented as powerful, implacable, and terribly polite. They consider themselves superior to you, but they look down upon you with patient benevolence. It's a more seductive form of imperialism – they've just ended mass slaughter and made sure everyone gets home safely, how could they possibly be the baddies? They just want to protect you. But, like the War Lord, they also see no issue with wiping your memories and popping you down where *they* think you should be in time and space.

The Doctor is terrified by them, and ambivalent to their imperialist views. And yet he's a product of their society, and never free of their influence upon him. He frames his actions, his worldview, in opposition to their aloof, disinterested attitude about the universe at large, and yet he remains one of them. He believes that his way is the right way, that his interference is just, and doubts those who question his moral authority.

In *The Two Doctors* (1985), the second Doctor is sent by the Time Lords to try and put an end to the time experiments of two scientists, Kartz and Reimer. According to the Doctor, their work has started to dangerously affect the time-space

[98]   *Isis Magazine*: https://isismagazine.org.uk/2018/03/the-battle-of-grosvenor-square/

continuum, and the Time Lords don't like it. Their director, Dastari, is outraged at the interference, at the Time Lords' arrogance and presumption, and believes they 'have no right to make such a grossly unethical demand.' He points out their hypocrisy: the Time Lords claim a policy of neutrality and yet act against it when it suits them. They 'have a vested interest in ensuring that others do not discover their secrets', and use a smokescreen of paternal concern to interfere in the scientific advancement of other races.

The Doctor is often used as the Time Lords' agent, willingly and unwillingly. He's outraged at being called upon to do 'some dirty work they won't touch with their lily-white hands' in *The Brain of Morbius* (1976), and in *Attack of the Cybermen* (1985) the Doctor believes 'the Time Lords would never allow [the Cybermen to change time]', just before he realises they've sent *him* in to clean the mess up. At other times, he's quite willing to act in their name. He accepts their missions in *Colony in Space* and *The Mutants*. In *Genesis of the Daleks*, his annoyance at being involuntarily transported to Skaro, the Dalek home world, is quickly overcome by a Time Lord telling him that they 'foresee a time when [the Daleks] will have destroyed all other lifeforms and become the dominant creature in the universe'. The Doctor agrees that's possible. And then agrees to a spot of genocide. Sure, he's given two other options by the Time Lord, and it's not like he hasn't tried to wipe the Daleks out before, but the fact remains, when the Time Lords suggest eliminating a species before it's even been born, the Doctor makes no objections.

Since he fled his home world, the Doctor defined himself as being opposed to the Time Lord way of life, eager to escape their stifling society and explore the universe on his own terms. And yet, when called upon, he either agrees to act on their behalf, or ends up doing what they want over his objections. Contrary to what he might say, he never wholly rejects Time Lord values.

> '*My dear Mister Chinn, if I could leave, I would, if only to get away from people like you ... And your petty obsessions! England for the English? Good heavens, man!*'
>   '*I have a duty to my country!*'
>   '*Not to the world?*'
>
> The Doctor and Mr Chinn,
The Claws of Axos (1971)

Early 1970s *Doctor Who* goes in hard with its colonialist critiques. This was post-Suez Canal, amidst the Rhodesia crisis, joining the EEC, apartheid protests, and more than thirty British colonies gaining independence between 1960 and the third Doctor's regeneration in 1974. Britain wrestled with its new place in the world, while looking back on a history that it wasn't entirely proud of. The third Doctor had a penchant for furiously confronting British authority figures, challenging their ingrained ideas and closed minds. This is an era that's angry, and it wants you to know it, and yet the Doctor who leads the charge is arguably the most paternalistic, most patronising, of all incarnations. Once again, *Doctor Who* revels in its contradictions.

With the third Doctor stuck on Earth, thanks to the Time Lords disabling his TARDIS, the colonial themes cut closer to the bone: the second story of the seventies, *The Silurians* (1970), offers up a complex situation with no easy solutions, and is taut with colonial anxieties. The Doctor, Liz Shaw, and UNIT investigate mysterious power drains at a nuclear plant in rural Derbyshire. They discover the power is being used to revive Silurians from hibernation. But these Silurians aren't from outer space. They're Earth natives who have been asleep for a very, very long time. And now they're awake, they're quite upset that upstart apes have taken over their planet. The Doctor is very keen on establishing diplomatic relations, and he manages to convince the Silurian leader that '[Silurians] must accept [humans] as equals'. Unfortunately, humanity and the other Silurians are much keener to embrace distrust and violence.

It's a fascinating setup: the Silurians evolved first, and have first dibs on the planet by millions of years. When faced with an extinction level event, they used their technology to wait it out. Through no fault of their own, their machines malfunctioned, and they overslept. But it's hardly humanity's fault that they evolved in the meantime. Of course, they feel entitled to the planet; of course, the Silurians want it back. Humanity has colonised the Silurians' home, and the Silurians want to colonise humanity's home. Neither species has any reason to trust the other.

And while there is an element of condemning humanity's fear of the Other, it wasn't humanity that blew up the Silurians, it was the British. In particular, it was our hero, Brigadier Lethbridge-Stewart. He attempts genocide. He doesn't believe there can be peace between humans and Silurians, and so he's protecting the British from another war. It's the Hiroshima question: does the war crime save more lives than it costs? And does that justify it? The Brigadier believed it did; the Doctor did not. And the position is complicated by the fact that the Brigadier didn't attack first: he's responding to the Silurian attempt to wipe out humanity via a virulent plague. How can you rebuild trust from such a betrayal? Or would the Brigadier have done it anyway, and the plague just provided a convenient cover?

The Doctor thought it was possible to get the trust back, even though the Silurians and the humans had kicked off a vicious cycle of violence, the sort of conflict where revenge after revenge could continue on for decades, or centuries. He only knew about the plague because the Silurian leader warned him that his underling had released it, giving the Doctor and Liz time to find a cure. Humanity could have made a leap of faith, tried to talk to the Silurians again, risked their lives to make the decision that was morally right, and had the potential to save everyone. The Doctor was willing to take on that risk himself. But the Brigadier went the route safest for humanity and most costly for the Silurians. It's a triumph of violence over negotiation; why bother trying to find a fair and compassionate solution to a complex mess of a problem when you can have easy instant results? The Brigadier sees his actions as necessary, and suppresses any empathy for the Silurian lives lost. It's an acknowledgement that Britain felt justified in both its colonial exploits, and its violence against indigenous people. Colonialism is equated with genocide, with one of our heroes as the instigator of that war crime. Britain benefits from avoiding the risk of war. And with UNIT being ostensibly top secret, the people of Britain will never know. The Silurians may be fictional, but the benefits of colonialism are real, and so many of them remain hidden today, concealed or forgotten.

The effects of this attack roll on to when the Silurians' cousins, given the name of the Sea Devils by a terrified maintenance worker, are woken from their slumber – this time beneath the sea floor – in 1972's *The Sea Devils*. Again, the Doctor tries to negotiate, but the damage has already been done. These Sea Devils learn about what humans did to the Silurians, and while the leader is still willing to consider the Doctor's words of peace, he quickly changes his mind when the Royal Navy drops a depth charge on their home. Perhaps he may have given humanity another chance if he saw it as panicked fear, instead of a pattern of extermination.

These two sentient reptilian species reappear together in *Warriors of the Deep* (1984), where they and humanity once again fail to get along. Their leader, Ichtar, has no interest in even trying anymore since, 'twice [they] offered the hand of friendship to these ape-descended primitives, and twice [they] were treacherously attacked, [their] people slaughtered'. What reason have they to trust humanity this time around? But all hope is not lost. When the Silurians finally return in *The Hungry Earth* and *Cold Blood* (2010) humans and Silurians actually manage to sit down at the same table, literally, and attempt to divide up the planet. It's more than a little naïve to think that companion Amy Pond's efforts to find a fair solution will be honoured by any government – she's casually willing to give up the 'Australian outback, Sahara desert, Nevada plains' to the Silurians, claiming 'they're all deserted'[99] – but both parties are, at least, committed in their desire to find a peaceful solution. (Though ultimately foiled by a very irate Silurian warrior.)

But *Doctor Who* doesn't like to give up on humanity (or ancient sentient reptilians), and humanity does eventually manage to share the planet with an alien species. It's not the Silurians, but Zygon refugees who make their home here. Are we full of mistrust for the alien refugees? Yes. Do we struggle not to give in to violent solutions? Yes. But a treaty is signed and twenty million Zygons now live on Earth. It's not perfect; in *The Zygon Invasion* and *The Zygon Inversion* (2015) a splinter group of Zygons violently oppose the treaty, and Kate Stewart – head of UNIT – threatens to nuke London. But, in the end, the treaty holds. Humanity has come a long way from blowing up caves in Derbyshire. And yet even at our best, we still teeter on a knife-edge of fear, ever ready to resort to violence. Britain is no longer

---

[99]   A worryingly inaccurate assumption: the Australian outback is estimated to have around 600,000 inhabitants (and the Aboriginal people have been there for some 50,000 years); the Sahara desert some 2.5 million.

a colonial power, but how much has it really learned from its past?

The next big-hitter of colonialism in the Pertwee era is the subtly named *Colony in Space* (1971). Rather excitingly, there are no less than five different parties of colonisers, possibly six, in this story, all with their distinct agendas. They are, in no particular order: the Time Lord High Council, the Doctor, the Master, the human colonists, the Interplanetary Mining Corporation's expedition, and the planet's indigenous civilisation. The Time Lords have sent the Doctor to the planet, after discovering that the Master has stolen information from them about a doomsday weapon. Their actions lead directly to the Doctor's interference in the conflict between the colonists and IMC, and his involvement in the final destruction of the indigenous civilisation. The Master is there, cheerfully manipulating the colonists and IMC, so he can steal the weapon from the natives. The colonists are, unsurprisingly, there to colonise the planet. And IMC are there to strip it off its mineral wealth, but if they do so, they planet will become uninhabitable. It's a land grab versus corporate greed, and it's hard not to lean towards the side of the colonists. They were escaping an overpopulated Earth starving for resources, and they weren't aware of the indigenous population until they arrived. IMC wants to strip the planet of resources and habitability so their crew can 'enjoy luxury for the rest of [their] lives'.

The colonists are desperate idealists, seeking out a new land to make their own, but they've found it poisoned, and their crops are failing. The planet they've declared to be theirs isn't the welcoming home they imagined. Just because the land looks empty, it doesn't mean it's theirs for the taking. IMC, on the other hand, are a rapacious, ruthless mining company. They don't care about the natives; they don't care about the colonists – though they do make a token effort to get them off the planet prior to beginning mining operations. They want wealth, and if they find it, they believe that means they have the right to take it. It's straightforward, unapologetic exploitation of natural resources with no regard for the locals or the environment.

The most interesting party, however, the ones who at first glance appear to be the victims of all this power play, are the indigenous inhabitants. But unlike, say, the Sensorites, the Swampies in *The Power of Kroll*, or the Terra Alphans in *The Happiness Patrol*, the natives in *Colony in Space* are already a dying civilisation. And that's nothing to do with colonisation, it's entirely their own fault. They're referred to as primitives, but are actually the last remnants of a once vast and powerful civilisation that decided they needed to build a doomsday weapon. But after they built their doomsday weapon, their 'race began to decay,' and 'the radiation from the weapon's power source poisoned the soil of [their] planet'. This weapon was powerful enough to destroy a sun, and leave behind a 'cloud of cosmic matter', that we know as the Crab Nebula. In a time when Britain's power in the world was in rapid decline, a time when the anti-nuclear movement was intensifying, Britain is not playing the part of the human colonisers. It's the dying civilisation, the one that doomed itself with its need to possess a horrifying weapon. The one that might only be protected through 'a claim to unusual historical interest', what with this being the birthplace of Mr Dickens and Mr Shakespeare, and having all those castles and country houses, it's just full of fascinating curiosities. And here comes another civilisation to feast on what's left behind, to make their homes, or strip its resources. It's a cocktail of post-colonial anxieties, and what may become of the remnants of a once great empire. And yet while the Doctor calls the race that built the city 'intelligent, civilised. They wouldn't condemn the innocent', it comes across more as flattery to save his and Jo's lives once it's discovered they also took the oh-so-civilised step of building a weapon capable of blowing up stars. The Doctor appeals to what the natives would like to think of themselves – that they're law-abiding and just – while they developed a weapon that could 'hold the galaxy to ransom'. It's a sad, bitter self-portrait of what Britain could become if all that matters is clinging on to the status it believes it's entitled to. It asks us to look at the country's perceived decline; at the fear it causes, and warns that to become vainglorious about lost power is to pave the way to self-destruction.

While *Colony in Space* offered a plethora of angles on colonial exploitation, *The Mutants* is just flat-out angry at Empire. Once again, the Time Lords use the Doctor as their agent to interfere on another world. This time the world does have a name, Solos, and it's a colony of the Earth Empire in the thirtieth century. The planet had been stripped of resources; the native population are segregated from the humans that govern. The human rulers are called Overlords and they call the Solonians, in their mutated form, 'Mutts'. These mutated Solonians are hunted down and killed; the rest are slaves in factories and mines. But the Earth Empire is collapsing, and can't afford colonies anymore, so they're generously granting Solos its independence. There's a time for subtlety, and there's a time for *The Mutants*.

The future of Earth is often depicted in *Doctor Who*, but it's rarely been so forthright in showing humans bringing imperial aggression to the stars. As the Doctor puts it, 'Once [humanity had] sacked the solar system, they moved onto pastures new.' *The Mutants* is deliciously explicit in depicting Earth as absolutely, definitely, we're telling you again just in case you didn't get it, the British Empire falling apart. The administrator who turns up on the Solos Skybase to inform the governor of Earth's withdrawal doesn't bother with a granule of sugaring: 'Earth is exhausted, Marshal. Finished. Politically, economically and biologically finished.' It's an unapologetic critique of Britain's imperial past, and present, of the scale of harm it's done to other cultures, of the casual cruelty and dehumanisation. And lack of self-reflection on its own actions: Solos is getting independence 'whether they're ready for it or not.' The planet is being discarded, the only principle behind Earth's withdrawal is it desperately scrambling to survive its self-inflicted wounds.

Meanwhile, the Solonians are growing in power in a way none of the humans understands, and the Solonians themselves are confused about the changes they're going through. Humanity's pollution of the planet has caused their natural mutation cycle to begin prematurely. The second stage of the mutation is assumed by the humans to be a degenerated form of life, and Professor Sondergaard, a human with the best of intentions, tries to find a cure for the mutations. But Solonian culture has been warped and misinterpreted. Their liberation is symbolised through them reclaiming their natural mutation cycle. Solos returns to its true self, and the Solonians rediscover their essential nature.

> *'So your planet ...'*
> *'Zanak.'*
> *'Yes. Having materialised around the other planet, smothers it, crushes it, and mines all the mineral wealth out of it.'*
> *'Just like an enormous leech.'*
> The Doctor and Mula, *The Pirate Planet* (1978)

In *The Sensorites* and *Colony in Space* humanity discovered resources on other worlds that they were very keen on extracting for themselves. *The Mutants* showed the end point of that process: the planet was sucked dry, and abandoned. In *The Power of Kroll*, the colonial invasion has just begun, and the indigenous people are prepared to fight to defend their land. Once again, Earth is out in the galaxy nicking other people's stuff. This time they're on a moon of the planet Delta Magna, and have built a whacking great refinery to extract methane and raw protein. The people of the moon, referred to as 'Swampies', do not like this. Frantz Fanon said, 'colonisation is always a violent event',[100] and in this parable of extractivist colonialism, we have one of *Doctor Who*'s most literal examples of that violence.

It's not an entirely successful parable, in that the characterisation of the native people is awkward, to say the least. They are technologically primitive, practise human sacrifice, are painted green, and all have dreadlocks. And what do they call themselves? We've no idea. But there are some wonderful subversions: these are not a passive people, and they're not stupid. They're purchasing guns from Rohm-Dutt, an opportunistic weapons merchant. And they're not interested in being patronised by him. When Rohm-Dutt worries that they're not ready to fight the men from the refinery, he's told 'a rifle's not a difficult weapon', and that 'like all dryfoots, Rohm-Dutt, because we lead a simple life you think we're fools.'

There's no conflict among the Swampies about whether they should try to come to some sort of peaceful agreement, and no condemnation of them for not trying to find one. Not only are they being pushed off their home on the moon by the callous plans of a mining corporation, they were already forcibly removed from Delta Magnus, their original homeworld. Rohm-Dutt secretly works for the refinery leader, Thawn, who wants to set the Swampies up as dangerous enough to be exterminated. But given their treatment so far, it also seems like their best chance is to try to make use of those weapons.

They may have tried to sacrifice the Doctor and Romana

[100]   Frantz Fanon, *The Wretched of the Earth* (1961)

to Kroll, their god, but when Fenner, one of the refinery crew, claims the Swampies stand in the way of progress, the Doctor tells him, 'progress is a very flexible word. It can mean just about anything you want it to mean'.

By the end, it's a mess: Thawn has murdered one of his own men, the Swampies have killed Thawn, and Ranquin, the Swampie leader, has been killed by Kroll. Their god turns out to be the extremely giant squid, and it's been woken up by the refinery. The Doctor and Romana are on the moon as part of a season long quest to find the six segments of the Key to Time, a shiny cube able to maintain time's equilibrium. As soon as they have it, they're off. The immediate crisis of the monstrously large giant squid attack is resolved, but there's no clean resolution to the conflict between the refinery crew and the Swampies; there's no clean resolution to colonialism.

While *The Power of Kroll* offers an up-close look at the cost of extractivism, *The Pirate Planet* zooms right out to bring home the horror in a single hammer blow. On the eponymous pirate planet (actually a planet-sized spaceship), there's a 'new golden age of prosperity' every other week; the citizenry receives 'richer jewels ... finer clothes ... food in greater abundance ... wealth beyond the dreams of avarice'! Sounds brilliant. Where does all this wealth come from? The people don't care; they just enjoy all their shiny new stuff. What's really happened is that the Captain has materialised his planet-seized spaceship around a real planet and crushed it, extracting every atom of material wealth, and murdering every inhabitant. The colonised are annihilated, the colonisers enjoy the wealth without even being aware of the horrors committed for it.

When the Axons attempt their invasion of Earth in *The Claws of Axos* (1971), their weapon of choice is human greed. They ask for help, and in return offer humanity Axonite, a 'thinking molecule' that has the potential to do some neat things like provide 'unlimited food', or 'unlimited power'. The would-be colonisers come bearing a fantastic gift, and the British, so used to extracting resources from countries around the world, are instantly seduced into taking this ultimate resource, and ask very few questions about what the Axons get out of it.

The Axonite is, naturally, a trap. It's what the Axons use to spread themselves across a planet before they consume all its nutrients. Britain's greed is turned back on itself, the same drive that led them to strip wealth from their colonies has doomed them. Or it would have if the Doctor wasn't there to save them from themselves.

Most stories have the colonised being angry, fearful, or resigned at their situation, but in *The Macra Terror* (1967) the atmosphere is more akin to that of a holiday camp. Beneath the cheerful dances, catchy soundbites, and happy faces, there's a tale of colonial exploitation. This is ostensibly a human colony, but they've been quietly taken over by the Macra – aliens that resemble giant crabs – who are using the humans to mine a gas that keeps them alive, while being toxic to humans. And thanks to the terrifyingly effective propaganda, the humans are happy to work themselves to death. They're given shallow pursuits to distract them, painfully chipper jingles tell them they're 'happy to work ... happy to play', and dissent is treated as mental illness. They've internalised their oppression, and they punish those who speak the truth. It's a terrifying vision of a society that's utterly succumbed to capitalist colonial propaganda: you're happy to be exploited, aren't you? Splendid. Carry on then.

Empire is greed. One nation is enriched at the expense of others, through mining, taxation, corporate exploitation. Human lives, sentient lives, are either obstacles or another resource to be exploited. *Doctor Who* offers numerous critiques of this extractivism, condemning empire as a beast with an insatiable hunger, always looking for more opportunities to exploit, and never finding enough.

> *'I can hear the sound of empires toppling.'*
> The Doctor, *The Happiness Patrol* (1988)

As Sarah Jane Smith said in *School Reunion* (2006), 'everything has its time. And everything ends' and that includes empires. We saw the end of the Earth Empire in *The Mutants*, but it's Gallifrey, the ultimate imperial power, that *Doctor Who* most often turns to when considering the decay of empire.

Gallifrey was first presented in *The War Games* as a terrifyingly advanced civilisation with awesome powers over time and space. The Time Lords were cold, distant guardians, and both the Doctor and his fellow runaway, the War Chief, feared the consequences of even contacting them. With the arrival of *The Deadly Assassin* (1976), a very different perspective is presented. From here on, Time Lord society is presented as ossified bureaucracy, meaningless ritual, and hollow grandeur. Even their superiority in their technological sophistication is challenged: the Doctor mocks the security of their archives and informs them, 'There are worlds out there where this kind of equipment would be considered prehistoric junk.' Gallifrey assumes it's indefatigable, but in reality, has become a parade of old men dressing up in fancy robes to perform ancient rites. The purpose of their ceremonial artifacts is forgotten: the Rod and the Sash of Rassilon have the power to control an engineered star, the power source of Gallifrey, but are believed by the Time Lords to be of only 'sentimental value'.[101] The seeming benevolence of earlier Imperial authority is ripped away to show a civilisation that cares only for maintaining what it can

---

[101]   *The Invasion of Time*

of itself while it crumbles away. They cling to the past with endless rituals and calcified traditions replacing innovation and creativity.

When the Time Lords returned in New Who, they had become tyrannical. Their war with the Daleks had finally resulted in some real change, and it's all been for the worse. Instead of crumbling away, they've become a monstrous force of destruction, ready to sacrifice the universe if it means they can survive. Two sides of the imperial coin: destruction, or self-destruction. And when that self-destruction comes, fast or slow, it's rarely accepted with equanimity. Loss of power becomes loss of self-image, and brings the temptation to look back and believe in an ideal past that never existed.

And *Doctor Who*, on occasion, does indulge in this sort of imperial nostalgia. Much like our society at large, it has a particular weakness for the Second World War. The sentimentalising of 'Blitz spirit', the idea of Britain standing alone against Nazi Germany,[102] the idolisation of Churchill, a man with thoroughly racist views. To quote one example, he considered Hindus 'a beastly people with a beastly religion'.[103] By the end of World War II, some seven hundred thousand Hindus were fighting in the British Indian army.[104]

---

[102] Armed forces of numerous other countries were hosted in Britain, and took part in both her defence, and Allied Operations. These countries included Poland, the Netherlands, Norway, and the Free French. In the Battle of Britain, many of the aircrews were from Commonwealth countries, or British colonies, and over two hundred pilots were from continental European countries.

[103] https://www.independent.co.uk/news/people/winston-churchill-from-accusations-of-antisemitism-to-the-blunt-refusal-that-led-to-the-deaths-of-millions-9999181.html

[104] 'Reorganization of the Army and Air Forces in India – Report of a Committee set up by His Excellency the Commander-in-Chief India (known as the Willcox Report after its chairman, Lieutenant General H. B. D. Willcox)' (1945), New Delhi:, Government of India Press, 1945, Vol 2, Appendix C

In *Victory of the Daleks (2010)*, Mr Churchill is present as a jovial figure with whom the Doctor is painfully chummy. He's 'an old friend' of the Doctor's who refused to divert food supplies to mitigate the Bengal famine. This Churchill brims with determination, resilience, and courage. It's the shape of the legend, with not a hint of the man, a flat portrait that reveals how keen we are to flatter our past at the expense of nuance or clarity. He even gets a peck on the cheek from Amy Pond.

The Blitz spirit is on display in *The Empty Child* and *The Doctor Dances (2005)*, as the Doctor and Rose make friends with Nancy, a young woman taking care of stray children in London. To help her 'keep calm and carry on', the Doctor gives her an inspiring speech: 'the German war machine is rolling up the map of Europe. Country after country, falling like dominoes. Nothing can stop it ... Until one tiny, damp little island says no. No. Not here. A mouse in front of a lion. You're amazing, the lot of you. Don't know what you do to Hitler, but you frighten the hell out of me.' One tiny, damp little island. Do you mean that tiny, damp island that rules the world's biggest Empire? That tiny, damp little island, Doctor? Yes, that one. The characterisation of Britain in this moment is painful. In 1939, Britain was a superpower, who could, thanks to its colonies and the Commonwealth, call on a quarter of the globe to help it out. I can only assume that the mouse the Doctor describes is a twenty-tonne giant space mouse wearing a pith helmet.

The flipside to this is the times when *Doctor Who* elucidates the past, when it insists that Britain's imperial history is something that should be faced straight-on, not prettied up into uplifting nostalgia. *Human Nature* and *The Family of Blood* (2007) eloquently strip away the colonial fantasy of glorious soldiers fighting for the Empire, and show the terror of young boys forced to kill for a cause they don't fully understand.

They're sold the lie of dying gloriously for their country, and a generation is wiped out.

The classic series places its most extensive examination of imperial decay in 1989's *Ghost Light*, a story set in in the Victorian era in a house that's a microcosm of empire. As the house is explored, the Doctor and Ace find exploitation, suffering, madness, and death. In her own time, Ace felt the house was 'full of evil and hate' and burns it to the ground, leaving it 'empty, all overgrown and falling down'. Back in the eighteenth century, Josiah Smith, an alien come to catalogue life on Earth, plays the part of the Victorian gentleman, and the rest of the house's occupants are his to control, or experiment with. Nimrod, a Neanderthal, has been dressed in Victorian clothes and serves as Josiah's butler. When the Reverend Mathews displeases Josiah, he's devolved into an ape, and put on display. Josiah decides who is to be considered civilised, and who is a primitive.

In the current day, there is a fear that our post-colonial anxieties will lead us into extremism: *Inferno*, *Turn Left*, and *73 Yards* all show alternate Earths, and in all of them Britain has fallen, or is falling, into fascism. Roger ap Gwilliam, the Prime Minster in *73 Yards*, wants to fire a nuke to make a futile gesture meant to show power, but revealing only a hollow sense of self. The empire is over, and yet there's a false memory that, at some undefined point, it created a Platonic ideal of British identity. *73 Yards* is explicit about the idea that British people are, in some way, now oppressed, and that if we only 'defend our borders', we'll be 'set ... up on high as one of the greatest nations in the world'. This isn't looking towards some bright new future, it's the view of the true villain in *Ghost Light*, an alien called Light, who '[doesn't] want things to change' and will 'make sure they cannot', even if it means he must transform the world back into primordial soup.

'We are not gods. Events sit as they will. We only witness.'
A Thijarian, *Demons of the Punjab* (2018)

The Doctor can go anywhere in space and time, but when they come to Earth, they almost always land somewhere in Britain. Understandably. The show is made here, after all. But in recent times, the TARDIS has taken some trips abroad that have allowed the show to briefly escape the colonial undertones of most adventures. *The Story & the Engine* (2025) is set in Nigeria, a former British colony, and all the characters besides the Doctor and companion Belinda Chandra, are Black Nigerians. Belinda is British-Indian, and in his fifteenth incarnation, the Doctor is played by a Rwandan-Scottish actor, Ncuti Gatwa. The very fact that the Doctor is a Black man changes the colonialist optics. Added to that, Rwanda is a former German colony.[105] And Scotland has both suffered and benefitted from colonialism.

It's a story that feels very aware that with a Black actor in the lead role, a layer of new possibilities for adventures has opened up. *The Story & the Engine* has the Doctor visiting a barbershop in Lagos, not because he needs a haircut, but because, 'it's the first time [he's] had this Black body. In some parts of the Earth, [he's] now treated differently. But in that barbershop, [he's] accepted … [they] laugh, [they] tell stories.' And, as the title suggests, it's stories that are the heart of this adventure. The family that runs the barbershop are forced to tell their stories by the mysterious Barber, who's taken control of the shop, to power an engine. When he's extracted enough stories, he'll be able to reach the Nexus and '[sever] the gods from the story web, cutting them from their essence … destroy them.' He's not doing it for power, not exactly, he's doing it because he was once human, and it was his job

---

[105] After the German defeat in World War I, rule was transferred to Belgium. It gained independence in 1962.

to collect stories. He created the Nexus to 'expand and make connections between ideas' and cross-connect 'concepts, cultures, and ideas'. But the gods thought he was getting above himself, and tried to destroy his work. And this is his revenge.

Stories can be our souls, can create and sustain our sense of self, and colonialism so often erases or warps those stories. *The Story & the Engine* shows both the power, and the preciousness of stories about who we are, the beauty of them, and the ways they can be told. Context is king. This episode is a story that could potentially be told from anywhere in the world, but it was told in Lagos, Nigeria. A country that was ruled by Britain for eighty years, and has had its independence for less than seventy. It's a story that foregrounds the people of a post-colonial nation, and the power of their own stories.

While the Doctor is at the forefront of events in *The Story & the Engine*, in *Demons of the Punjab* (2018), she stands as witness to the partition of India, and the pain of families torn apart. British rule in India had a long, violent history, but in 1947 the UK Parliament passed the India Independence Act, which declared India to be an independent nation, and Pakistan a separate country. This story focuses on the immediate consequences of that decision for the Doctor's companion, Yasmin Khan.

Yasmin wants to learn more about her grandmother's history, so the Doctor takes her to the Punjab in 1947. Her grandmother, Umbreen, is to be married to Prem, her first husband, and not Yaz's grandfather. Prem is distraught at the violence he sees building around him: 'We've lived together for decades, Hindu, Muslim and Sikh, and now we're being told our differences are more important than what unites us.' Prem is Hindu; Umbreen is Muslim. And the partition of India was made along religious lines – Pakistan would be majority Muslim, and India majority Hindu. This decision resulted in mass migration of some fifteen million people, and violence that resulted in deaths estimated between two hundred thousand and two million.

In *Demons of the Punjab*, that violence of the Partition, literal and metaphorical, is shown in the intimate portrait of Yasmin's family. As she marries Prem and Umbreen, the Doctor calls love 'a form of hope and, like hope, love abides in the face of everything'. But it's hate that rules Manish, Prem's brother. He cannot accept Prem marrying a woman of another religion, and murdered the holy man who was originally going to marry them. When Prem confronts his brother and a group of armed men, he's shot dead by a man he fought alongside in World War II. Even in withdrawal, empire leaves death and destruction in its wake.

The assumed alien threat, the Thijarians, are not the killers the Doctor first assumed. They were once assassins, now they seek 'the unacknowledged dead across all of time and space.' They've made it their mission to 'to bear witness to those alone. To see, to bear pain, honour life as it passes'. They're an advanced alien species, they could invade or interfere, but instead they choose to watch, and to remember. And, in this story, that's what the Doctor and her companions do too. Yasmin can't change the tragedy of her grandmother's past, but she can honour it in her remembrance. The saviour narrative is explicitly rejected, and the gravity of real-world colonial trauma takes centre stage.

The Kenyan author, Ngũgĩ wa Thiong'o, wrote that 'the choice of language and the use to which language is put is central to a people's definition of themselves in relation to their natural and social environment, indeed in relation to the entire universe',[106] an idea beautifully explored in *Planet of the Ood* (2008).

The Ood's world has been invaded, their people enslaved,

[106] Ngũgĩ wa Thiong'o, *Decolonising the Mind (1986)*, p. 4

their bodies mutilated, and their language suppressed. They're sold as servants, as cannon fodder in war, as a people who have 'one purpose ... to serve'. But the Doctor isn't there to help them rebel, he's there to witness the Ood liberating themselves. The Ood Brain, which allows the telepathic communication between the Ood has been isolated via a telepathic barrier. But it was waiting for an opportunity to fight back, and by the time the Doctor arrives an agent from Friends of the Ood – an organisation working for Ood freedom – had managed to lower the power of the barrier. But even without that intervention the Ood Brain had been adapting for centuries to break through on its own, and would eventually have succeeded.

Once free, it expressed its fury at the enslavement by turning the Ood into a red-eye state. In this condition they became violent, and were able to fight back against their enslavers, killing most of the personnel in the Ood breeding facility. For once, the Doctor doesn't condemn the violence.

But that wasn't the Ood's only plan for freedom. One of the duties of Ood Sigma, the personal servant of Halpen, the chief executive of Ood Operations, was to keep him well supplied with hair tonic. However, this tonic was replaced with a substance that eventually turned Halpen into an Ood. If the FOTO agent hadn't sped things up by weakening the forcefield, a few days later Ood Halpen could have lowered it himself. One way or another, revolution was inevitable.

As part of their enslavement the Ood were denied their language; the song connecting the Ood with the Ood Brain, was shut down by human slavers. Once they were cut off, the Ood's song became so sad that Donna couldn't bear to hear it for more than a few seconds. When the Ood Brain was freed, the song rose, slow but joyful. In the final scene, the Ood are able to sing a song so powerful it 'resonate[s] across the galaxies'. The Doctor exposed their exploitation to the audience, explored the horror of what had been done to them, but it's the Ood themselves that end it. The Doctor is an ally, but not their liberator. They don't need him. The Ood claimed their own liberation.

In the classic series, it's 1982's *Kinda* that's the most outstanding colonial allegory. The Doctor arrives on the jungle world of Deva Loka where a human expedition has landed to determine if the planet is suitable for colonisation. While the Doctor and Adric navigate the danger of the increasingly paranoid Hindle, the expedition's security officer, Tegan falls asleep beneath wind chimes and lets the evil Mara enter physical existence by occupying her mind.

Kinda is a story that explicitly condemns colonial occupation and exploitation. It condemns 'civilising' indigenous people, and the arrogance required to dare and try. And it does it in a fascinating way: the people of Deva Loka, the Kinda, are a more advanced civilisation. The men don't speak, but their silence doesn't mean they're stupid, and it doesn't stop them listening. This is a psychic culture, with a sophistication that's overlooked because it doesn't match with the colonisers' expectations. It draws on Buddhist symbols and ideas, and resists typical Western ideas about what progress should look like. The Doctor is recognised as a fool, and the only one who grasps the sophistication of Kinda culture. He doesn't lecture, doesn't patronise, or tell them what to do. He spends his time struggling to understand what they're trying to tell him.

First, they need him to show Hindle – a man going mad with paranoia – a box that, when opened, acts like months of really high-quality therapy sessions. Before the Kinda help him recover, Hindle is terrified of the planet in its natural state. It's strange and foreign, and he doesn't understand it or its people. His imperial arrogance has warped into extreme paranoia and violence. He would rather commit genocide, and annihilate himself than let this planet 'win'.

But mostly the Kinda need the Doctor to stop the Mara, the creature that he effectively let into their world (by not noticing Tegan had fallen asleep, and wandering off without her). The Kinda never dream beneath the wind chimes alone; if there's only a single mind that's something the Mara can use to get into the universe. Tegan's lack of understanding of Kinda culture brought unexpected violence to their world. The Mara is a parasite on physical existence. It colonises a body, and is driven to possess and control, to wreak destruction, terror, death. Colonial violence in its purest, cruellest form. The Doctor isn't there as a saviour, but to end the violence he's responsible for letting in.

> *'And that's your alternative to independence? Genocide?'*
> *'Give them independence, they'll starve out of total incompetence.'*
>
> The Administrator and the Marshall,
> *The Mutants* (1972)

Doctor Who has never escaped the gravitational pull of empire. It was born in the remnants of one and has spent a lifetime circling the debris. It's dismantled myths of imperialism, reproduced them, exposed them as it tries to escape them. Colonialism haunts its travelogues, its monsters, its white-saviour foundations, its nostalgia, and its visions of the future. Even when it staunchly opposes imperialist thinking, the structure of the show means the Doctor is always pulled back into the role of exceptional outsider whose judgement reigns supreme.

It may be immersed in imperialism, but that doesn't mean it holds back in its critiques. Fictions of benevolent empires are cracked open to explore who pays for those conquests, who's forgotten, and who is used as fuel for someone else's prosperity. It shows Gallifrey's epic authority over time and space collapse into bureaucratic vanity. Earth's future brims with colonial exploitation throughout the stars.

It shows how these possibilities can be resisted, even to the point where it temporarily steps out of its imperial shadow altogether. Those striking anti-imperial moments are the ones where the Doctor steps aside: when the Ood liberate themselves, when the Kinda correct the Doctor's assumptions, when the Thijarians bear witness instead of intervening, when Partition is allowed to retain its unbearable human cost, when a Black Doctor in Lagos shifts the narrative lens entirely. These stories show what happens when the show embraces allowing other voices, other histories, and other understandings of the world to stand unmediated.

Doctor Who can never outrun its imperial ghosts, but it can turn and interrogate them. It knows how difficult it is to unlearn inherited stories, it knows about the fear of relinquishing power, the seduction of nostalgia, and the hope in choosing compassion over domination. And its failures can matter as much as its triumphs: they map the ongoing struggle of a nation still wrestling with the stories it tells about itself.

The TARDIS will go on landing in new times and places; the Doctor will go on choosing when and how to interfere. *Doctor Who* cannot fully slip those imperial chains. But it can keep tugging at them. In that imperfect struggle – between complicity and critique, between Grand Tour and genuine solidarity – *Doctor Who* doesn't offer a clean escape from empire, but something messier and more honest: the long, unfinished work of learning to live with the past it keeps meeting, and of trying, however awkwardly, to do better next time.

CHAPTER FOUR
THE OTHER GREEN DEATH
Environmentalism

'*T*here are many insects which make a vital contribution to agriculture, and these insects must not die.'
Farrow, *Planet of Giants* (1964)

Doctor Who's interest in environmentalism started way back in 1964, in the opening story of its second season, *Planet of Giants*. This adventure was inspired by Rachel Carson's landmark book *Silent Spring*, published in 1962, which details the effects of insecticides on ecosystems, and the danger they pose to humans. Carson was a marine biologist and conservationist, already well known for her books on aquatic life, but when she turned her focus to conservation, her work became crucial in kickstarting the global environmentalist movement. *Silent Spring* argued that overuse of synthetic pesticides, particularly DDT (dichlorodiphenyltrichloroethane), had adverse effects on both the natural environment and human health. And she didn't exactly hold back in accusing the chemical industry of misleading the public about those effects in order to protect their profits.

This being the United States in the fifties, the critical response to Carson was predictable: she was a Communist, clearly trying to disrupt the US food supplies to help out the Soviet Union; she was a hysterical woman – 'You're never going to satisfy organic farmers or emotional women in garden clubs,' said the United States Secretary of Health, Abraham Ribicoff; and she just didn't know what she was talking about, with *Time* magazine accusing her of alarmism, 'oversimplifications, and downright errors'.[107] But this reaction was far from universal, and she was endorsed by an array of her scientific peers.[108] The year after *Silent Spring*'s publication, President John F. Kennedy's Scientific Advisory Committee investigated her findings, and supported them. Her work helped shape United States environmental policy, spurred on the creation of the US Environmental Protection Agency and, most directly, led to a ban on the agricultural use of DDT in the United States. Alas, the United Kingdom didn't follow suit until 1984, but that didn't mean no one on this side of the Atlantic read *Silent Spring*. In *Planet of Giants* there's a whole-hearted endorsement of Carson's work, with the fictional pesticide DN6 about to be approved for general use even though it cheerfully kills off all insect life it comes in contact with.

The story begins with our heroes – the first Doctor, Barbara, Ian, and Susan – exploring a mysterious world full of strange but very dead alien lifeforms. At least for the first ten minutes, then they realise they're actually in a pleasant country garden in the English countryside, but they've been shrunk down to about an inch tall. The monsters they've encountered are ordinary insects and invertebrates, and we're asked to sympathise with their plight, which is particularly notable in a show where insects are usually invoked to inspire

---

[107] 'Pesticides: The Price of Progress' (1962), *Time* 80 (13): 45–48
[108] Including ecologist Lamont Cole, entomologist Robert Rudd, a pesticide expert, and zoologist George Wallace, who documented bird deaths from DDT.

116

fear.[109] But here the fear is shown to be misjudgement, and when the truth is revealed, there's anger at their fate, and acknowledgement of how valuable they are to the ecosystem.

The main full-size characters in *Planet of Giants* are the naïve scientist Smithers, principled civil servant Farrow, and avaricious businessman Forester. Poor Farrow represents the government's interests and, rather hearteningly, he's done his job properly. After a thorough investigation of DN6 he's concluded it's far too dangerous as it indiscriminately kills insects, many of which 'make a vital contribution to agriculture, and these insects must not die'. He has no time for Forester's arguments for why he should get to go ahead anyway, he cares more about science than business, and refuses to be bribed. Alas, his integrity dooms him, and he's shot dead by Forester.

And if Forester has no issue shooting a man dead, he certainly doesn't care about a few insects. Especially when he's invested so much money into the project. The potential for massive profits overrode the common sense of making sure the product actually worked as intended. What do a few bugs matter when he'll be ruined if they don't go ahead with manufacture? Money trumps the environment, even if that means destroying it. Short term gains outweigh long-term damage. Yes, you'll be collapsing the ecosystem that's needed for anyone to want to buy your product. But by the time that happens, you'll be rich, so who cares? Greed is at the centre of *Planet of Giants*, and the decades since have seen that greed increase exponentially, doing exponentially more damage to natural environments.

Smithers, the scientist, has the most complex view on the

[109] For example, *The Ark in Space*'s Wirrn, *The Unicorn and the Wasp*'s giant wasp, *The Web Planet*'s ant-like Zarbi, *Turn Left*'s Time Beetle, *The Twin Dilemma*'s Giant Gastropods, the Giant Spiders in *Planet of the Spiders* ...

insecticide, one where he holds onto a paradox to protect his ego. When he discovers the murder, he's more concerned about how it's going to ruin the DN6 project than the fact a man is dead. He's worked 'fifteen, sometimes sixteen hours a day' on DN6, and Farrow was a 'nuisance and a fool' who was 'always checking ever minor detail' instead of appreciating Smithers' dedication. An obvious murder means all that work he's put in will be wasted. When Forester proposes a plan to get rid of the body, Farrow is easily convinced to keep quiet, because while Forester wants the money, he believes Smithers wants acclaim, to 'be known as the inventor of [DN6]'. Smithers objects, not entirely convincingly, and claims that's not his motivation at all; all he wants is to save people from dying of starvation. He's willing to destroy the environment (and cover up a spot of murder) in the name of (temporarily) higher crop yields. He's trapped in a sunk-cost fallacy: all that work means it must be worthwhile, despite the overwhelming evidence that it'll destroy the very environment needed to produce the food. Both Smithers and Forester want their own desires satisfied as quickly as possible. One can't allow himself to believe in the environmental damage; one just doesn't care.

Planet of Giants is a relatively swift response to Carson's work, and is keen to raise public awareness that some artificial insecticides are a very bad idea. It doesn't explicitly argue for moderate use rather than elimination, but it does emphasise that the issue with DN6 is that it kills the insects we need as well as the pests. Carson herself didn't want to ban all insecticides. Like so many things that are potentially deadly, she advocated a need for stricter regulations, and higher awareness of the dangers. In *Planet of Giants* it's Farrow's rigorous testing and conscientious reports that stand in the way of Forester's profiteering. Good scientific practices struggle to halt the exploitation, but in the end they succeed, though in a very unexpected way. It's scientific principles and practical application that save the day for the TARDIS crew: the tiny Doctor and companions use a match to explode a pressurised container containing the highly flammable DN6 to make sure Forester is arrested: even a highly dangerous chemical reaction can be responsibly utilised.

'What are your qualifications for existence?'
Varga, *The Ice Warriors* (1967)

We travel from twentieth-century England to a far future where human civilisation teeters on the brink of collapse in 1967's *The Ice Warriors*. The cause is climate change, but instead of rising temperatures, Earth has entered a new Ice Age. Vast glaciers cover much of the planet, and their unrelenting advance threatens to crush humanity, literally.

This Ice Age has been caused by 'a severe drop in the carbon dioxide level in the Earth's lower atmosphere.'[110] The cause? Efficiency. Famine has been eliminated thanks to the development of 'artificial food'. And, this being an efficient civilisation, the unneeded farmland was used to build 'up-to-date living units' to house the increasing population. But with the massive reduction in plant life, carbon dioxide levels fell, bringing the world temperature down far enough for widespread glaciers to form.

This future saw rapid scientific advances implemented across civilisation without a full understanding of the side-effects, and that led to the crisis. Advances that are embraced prematurely for greed, or power, evoke anger and condemnation towards those so consumed by their vices they lack all empathy for the wider population, or future consequences. But when those advances are quickly rolled out for what sounds like a genuine desire to improve

[110] The Doctor, *The Ice Warriors*

humanity's condition, it's a tragedy. James Watt could never have foreseen the path from his steam engine to our climate crisis; when plastic began to be mass produced, it's doubtful anyone foresaw tiny bits of it would take up residence in our brains. Progress always comes at a cost, and humanity may be blind to that cost until it engulfs us.

One of the other side-effects of the atmospheric changes in *The Ice Warriors* is much more familiar to us: the destruction of ecosystems. Many species of plants have been wiped out; others exist only in a 'plant museum'. Tomatoes, carrots, and potatoes are considered ancient food plants, and characters reminisce about when you could pick food off trees. Plant extinction is brought home not with distant species in the flora extinction capitals of Hawaii or South Africa, but in the most familiar of plants to British households.

When *The Ice Warriors* was produced, our understanding of humanity's impact on climate change was in its infancy. The idea that burning fossil fuels might raise the planet's temperature only dates back to 1896, when it was first posited by Swedish scientist Svante Arrhenius. But actual evidence that burning them increased carbon dioxide levels wasn't available until Charles Keeling developed a new method to measure CO_2 levels and began to take meticulous atmospheric measurements in 1958. And it was only in the 1960s that he could finally confirm the trend of increasing levels.

But with these scientific advances suggesting civilisation was raising the planet's temperature, *Doctor Who* opted for a freezing future. Perhaps they thought an icy Earth was aesthetically pleasing (and the exterior sets do look pretty good). There are so very many visions of our future being, essentially, a blazing hot quarry, the image of endless ice is rather novel. Or perhaps they were aware that, counterintuitively, it was theorised that those increasing CO_2 levels might cause the planet to cool rather than heat up.

In the 1960s, according to biologist Paul Ehrlich, 'we didn't know at the time whether climate change would be in the direction of heating or cooling. We just didn't know enough about it.'[111] Winters in the late seventies and early eighties caused 'much discussion in scientific circles at the time about whether or not the freezing winter conditions were a portent of a new Ice Age'.[112] In 1998, William H. Calvin, a theoretical neurophysiologist at the University of Washington, wrote that 'an abrupt cooling could be triggered by our current global-warming trend ... we could go back to Ice Age temperatures within a decade'.[113]

To keep 'five thousand years of history [from being] crushed beneath a moving mountain of ice', humanity is dependent on technology, and that technology is flawed. Our introduction to this future Earth is a power outage on an 'ioniser base'. If the power doesn't hold, they can't stop their local glacier's advance. It's not the first time a power outage has occurred but the team has 'beaten its tantrums before', a beautifully efficient line that illustrates the dangerous instability of their situation. Leader Clent, the man in charge of the British ioniser base, insists computer specialist Miss Garrett fix the problem. She's self-aware enough to know what she knows and what she doesn't know.[114] And during the emergency she protests that they need the expertise of Penley, a brilliant scientist who walked out on the project because he didn't like Clent. Nothing like someone's personal politics getting in the way of ensuring civilisation isn't destroyed.

---

[111] www.motherjones.com/environment/2008/10/qa-paul-ehrlich/
[112] archive-yaleglobal.yale.edu/content/will-global-warming-trigger-new-ice-age
[113] 'The Great Climate Flop-Flop', *The Atlantic Monthly* January 1998
[114] Excellent advice from Confucious: 'To know what you know and what you do not know, that is true knowledge.'

After the timely entrance of the Doctor to solve the immediate crisis, Garrett demonstrates she's not lacking in expertise herself. But Clent is unmoved by her self-awareness of how far that expertise reaches, exclaiming that 'he's had enough of experts'. Now, that's a line that might send a shudder through the modern British viewer, if they recall Michael Gove's infamous exclamation during the European Union referendum debate that the public 'have had enough of experts'. Clent's dismissal of experts who have the knowledge to actually hold back the extinction of humanity is a few notches of stupidity below wrecking a country's economy, but his inability to put his politics aside to address the bigger picture is horribly familiar, and painfully common.

While Clent is brusque, annoying, and the sort of boss nobody wants, the object of his derision, the absent Penley, is no better. When asked to come back to the ioniser base because 'civilisation needs him', Penley refuses. 'Not even to save the world?' Garrett asks, barely exaggerating. Still a firm no. The personal animosity between Penley and Clent threatens all of Europe, yet they're unable to put it aside. For all Penley's insults about Clent's lack of humanity, it's Penley's pride that rules him. He wasn't being treated with the respect he felt entitled to, so he abandoned humanity's last defence. Even on the brink of extinction, the human ego is more than a match for rationality.

Extreme situations mean extreme responses: if you're of no use to the science team on the base you'll be evacuated to 'the African rehabilitation centres' for 'scavengers'. There's an implication that parts of Africa are safe: the only mention of glaciers on the continent is in South Africa. There's no explanation of what exactly this rehabilitation involves, but forced population transfer has a grim history, to say the least. But here there is a clear threat to the lives of those who remain, turning it into an intriguing piece of world-building. It would have been so easy for evacuation to be portrayed as pure altruism, but adding the word 'rehabilitation' with the distaste for 'scavengers' is a reminder of how easily individual rights are overturned in a crisis (as Garrett says, 'all actions must conform to the common good') and how prejudices endure, even when humanity's survival depends on a united response.

At least the response has been good enough to find a solution, but that's brought problems of its own. To halt glacial advancement, the ioniser bases create intense heat and alter weather patterns. It's a method that requires precise control in order to prevent flooding, and the very first scene of the story shows the computer they need for that control failing, and not for the first time. When the Ice Warrior spaceship is discovered in the glacier, Clent faces a choice between letting the glacier advance, or using their ioniser and risking a nuclear holocaust from the ship's engines exploding. To save themselves from one self-inflicted environmental disaster, they must risk another. It's a sobering reminder of the extent to which the natural world is interconnected and delicately balanced.

> 'You've seen where this efficiency of yours leads. Wholesale pollution of the countryside. Devilish creatures spawned by the filthy by-products of your technology … Death. Disease. Destruction.'
>
> The Doctor, *The Green Death* (1974)

The Green Death is one of the best remembered classic *Doctor Who* stories, largely because anyone who saw it at the time had it engraved into their memory as The One With The Maggots. It's also the show's quintessential environmentalist tale, exploring unfettered exploitation that destroys nature in the pursuit of bigger profits and peak efficiency.

The Doctor, Jo Grant, and UNIT, led by Brigadier Lethbridge-Stewart, are investigating Global Chemicals. This company has discovered a new way of processing oil that turns it into petrol more efficiently. Unfortunately, the process also produces chemical waste that's being dumped in a local mineshaft. The waste is mutating the local maggots into giant killers. If one of them bites you, you'll turn a fetching shade of neon green, then die.

But what's a little death and a radiant emerald glow when you've a vision of a prosperous, profitable future? That's the view of Stevens, director of Global Chemicals. Later it becomes blurred over how much of what he says he actually believes, as he's under the control of the bigger villain, a computer named BOSS.

But for most of the story, he's presented as a classic capitalist crony who believes profits mean progress, and trickledown economics works. Those who disagree are 'sentimentalist fools' and 'doom merchants', though that doesn't stop a casual attempt at greenwashing when he's confronted by environmentalist protesters, led by Clifford Jones. 'Professor Jones is right,' he says confidently to the crowd, 'and we must all share his concerns.' After all, concern costs nothing.

Professor Clifford Jones, Cliff to his friends, is Stevens' opposite number. Both characters are introduced in the story's opening scenes, sparring with one another over profit, progress, and the cost to the environment. Between them are a group of out-of-work miners. Stevens promises them new work at his oil processing plant, and that there'll be 'money for all of us! More jobs! More houses! More cars!' Sounds good to the miners, and they shout down Cliff and his protestors when they insist the miners are being exploited. 'We need the jobs', one miner tells them. Never mind an extra car, they've families to support, bills to pay, food to put on the table. 'It's all right for you', they tell Cliff. 'You can afford to live the way you want.'

It's a fair point. Cliff and his group aren't fabulously wealthy, but they are a highly educated community with middle class occupations: scientists, mathematicians, a former aerospace engineer who's now a sculptor. One of them is writing a book on self-actualisation – which I really hope is a deliciously tiny nod to the class differences, since self-actualisation, the drive to reach one's fullest potential, can only be achieved by those whose basic needs are satisfied, at least according to psychologist Abraham Maslow.[115] It's a heck of a lot easier to care about the environment when you're not worried about how you're going to afford food for your kids.

But Cliff, and the rest of the people residing at Wholeweal community, are not a stereotypical hippie commune, gone back-to-the-land, and isolating themselves from modern life. As Cliff says, 'We haven't set up this community just to drop out. I mean, let's face it. Who does like the petrol-stinking, plastic, rat-trap life we all live? If we're going to make a success here at Wholeweal, we've got to do something that's going to help the whole world. So we're a biotechnic research unit, as well as a Nut Hutch.' A former aerospace engineer now designs windmills to generate cheap and clean energy for Wholeweal's heat and electricity. Cliff's research is aimed at creating a high protein fungus to offer an abundant food source, and reduce the consumption of meat; an attempt to fulfil a basic need and reduce environmental impact with a single solution. And he believes it would also offer more jobs for locals. While Stevens' use of science generates pollution and warps the local wildlife, the Nut Hutch seeks ways to live

[115]   A. H. Maslow, 'The good or healthy society would then be defined as one that permitted people's highest purposes to emerge by satisfying all their basic needs.' *Motivation and Personality (1953)*, Harper & Row

more harmoniously with nature. Science can be as heroic as it can be destructive.

The Green Death doesn't stop with these three perspectives on the work of Global Chemicals. There's also disagreement within the company itself, and between the Doctor, Jo, and the Brigadier, on how far one should exploit natural resources. The Brigadier's firm statement, 'Cheap petrol and lots of it, exactly what the world needs', is hardly radical – I'm sure most people have rolled up at a petrol station at some point in their lives and sighed at the price – but his view puts him at odds with his immediate allies, and in agreement with Global Chemicals. It would have been an even less unsympathetic statement at the time due to petrol shortages and increasing prices during the 1970s energy crisis. And, ironically, the cutting equipment UNIT need to rescue Jo from a mineshaft is found only when the Brigadier pulls into a garage to refuel. It's clear the environmentalists, Jo, and the Doctor, are on the right side of history, but it's immensely satisfying to have the Brigadier and the miners add a few layers of nuance to the discussion.

In further complications of divided loyalties, the Brigadier is also under orders to protect Global Chemicals from possible sabotage. When he becomes suspicious of their culpability in a miner's death, he attempts to launch an investigation into them. The Brigadier informs Stevens of his intentions as they sit opposite one another, drinking glasses of whisky: military authority versus corporate power. Who wins?

While a Cabinet Minister's enthusiasm for the new insecticide is merely referred to in *Planet of Giants*, in *The Green Death* the Brigadier and Stevens play an exciting game of 'I've got a bigger contact in the Cabinet than you'. Stevens wins, and the Brigadier is reprimanded by the Prime Minister. The power of cronyism: a man with the Brigadier's institutional power cannot even properly investigate a murder if it might interfere with profits.

126

And just like *Planet of Giants*, those profits are more important than the results of the project being successful. Global Chemicals' new process is supposed to produce no pollution, but it actually 'creates a thick sludge you can't break down. Thousands of gallons of waste. Like a liquid plastic'. In the name of profit, Stevens, like Forester before him, hides the truth. In his case, he has it poured down an abandoned mineshaft. The ultimate result of continued pollution is the destruction of the ecosystems that sustain us; that destruction is represented in *The Green Death* by the mutated maggots, and then the flying insects they hatch into, spreading the infection even faster, an accelerating domino effect of ecosystem collapse.

But *The Green Death* is ultimately an optimistic story. While the heroes defeat the villains, as expected, it's the how that's especially hopeful. Science has created the maggot monstrosities, and so it's science that will stop them. While the Doctor facilitates the solution by finishing off the work when Cliff is infected, it's Cliff and Jo who actually discover the answer. His tasty, nutritious mushroom creations are lethal to the maggots, but he only realises this when Jo accidentally contaminates his slides of the maggots' cells. It's a fine combination of how science can progress: hard work and accidental discoveries. The Doctor helps out but, in the end, humanity saves itself.

> *'Have you noticed the air? ... It's clean. No cars, no people ... I rather like it.'*
> Captain Mike Yates, *Invasion of the Dinosaurs* (1974)

After *The Green Death*, the next story with major environmental themes arrives the following season, with 1974's *Invasion of the Dinosaurs*. Here the threat isn't corporate greed, but radical environmentalists. Despite the name, dinos are but the sideshow. The real plot is a conspiracy to take a select group of people back in time to a simpler 'Golden Age', and kill everyone else. Sorry, not kill, the villains intend to change time so the unworthy humans won't ever have existed, which is ever so much more morally sound. (Got to find ways to salve that pesky conscience when you're committing genocide.) The dinosaurs are an imaginative way to distract the authorities while the conspirators power up their time machine. And it's up to the Doctor, Sarah Jane Smith, and UNIT to stop them.

The brilliance of *Invasion of the Dinosaurs* comes from the presentation of the antagonists. They truly believe they are doing what they have to do to save humanity, and none of them are presented as power-hungry monsters, raving mad, or psychopathic killers. They're generally calm, and try to sound reasonable; you get the feeling they'd be happy to sit down with you over a cup of tea and explain they just want a better world, free from the horrors of modern life. Is that so wrong?

Yes. Yes, it is. Because they want to wipe out humanity. They're just not doing it the traditional way, with nukes, or bio-warfare, or good old-fashioned guns. That absence of violence is enough to resolve the cognitive dissonance between working to save humanity, and working to wipe it out. As Operation Golden Age member, Charles Grover MP, puts it: 'In a sense, these people will come to no harm at all because they will never have been born.' You can't break a few eggs if the chickens never existed.

So what's so wrong with this world that they're willing to wipe it from history? A lot, as it turns out, and they're generally problems a reasonable person would agree with. The conspirators clearly lay their issues out: factory pollution, industrial waste, mercury poisoning fish, war, atomic bombs, and oppression from authorities.

So many problems, and they keep getting worse, and more complex. If there was a nice simple answer to such complex issues, a way to wipe out all those mistakes and start again, some people would undoubtedly find it tempting. If you were worn down, exhausted, saw no hope, and believed the world was truly doomed, then is it so far-fetched that you might see this as a chance to create something better?

It's tempting enough that Captain Mike Yates, trusted member of UNIT, betrays his allies for the cause. He's so lost in this false hope that he believes if the Doctor knew the truth about what Operation Golden Age were doing, he'd support them. We know the Doctor is highly sympathetic to environmental causes. And he greets Charles Grover enthusiastically, recognising him as the man who founded the Save Planet Earth Society, and thinks 'the planet needs more people like [him]'.

But being okay with wiping out everyone on his favourite planet? That seems unlikely.[116] Yates's poor judgement might be partly explained by his brain being fried in *The Green Death*, two stories ago. But it hasn't affected his abilities as a soldier, and he appears quite lucid about what he's doing. These are ideas that he's willingly committed to, up to the point of sacrificing his own life to ensure the success of the operation. Even someone who's been a valued friend and ally to the Doctor, a reasonable man, is susceptible to extremism, given the right circumstances.

But even if you're unaware of the whole 'wipe out humanity' aspect of things, Operation Golden Age quickly starts to get dodgy with its cult vibes. Anything but absolute loyalty to the cause is treated with suspicion. Despite

---

[116] Though he has committed the odd genocide himself, most notably on his own people. But even in this early period, he already believed he'd committed his first Dalek genocide by wiping them out in *Evil of the Daleks*.

betraying his uniform, Yates's unwillingness to sanction killing is enough for his commitment to be doubted. The people that are being saved have been specially selected and popped onto a fake spaceship. They've been told they're travelling to a nearby star system, where they can start again on a fresh world. Sarah is put on the fake spaceship too, to get her out of the way, and introduced to 'elders', the leaders of this new community. At first, they're friendly, but Sarah receives pushback as soon as she argues against their ideas of a brave new world. They believe her mind's disturbed, that her ideas about freedom are disruptive and corrupt, and so they send her to the re-education room.

We hear quite a bit of the indoctrination film, and it mostly covers the problems mentioned a few paragraphs ago – pollution, poisons, war – all in all, it's the sort of reasonableness that means you might poke your foot in the cult door. But it's shown amidst a group of people who are willing to kill Sarah for not conforming. And the flaws in modern society listed by one of the elders are quite different from the ones in the film: 'moral degradation, permissiveness, usury, cheating, lying, cruelty'. It sounds a lot more authoritarian than the green and pleasant land that was promised. They quickly double-down, arguing that 'people on Earth were allowed to choose, and see what kind of a world they made'. But now the leaders of Golden Dawn have the chance to 'guide man onto a better path'. The sin of usury even adds a note of antisemitism in the creation of this 'pure' world.

While running away to try and build this better Earth is acceptable to the spaceship passengers, they're rather less keen on the idea when they find out they'll actually be living on an Earth wiped clean of people. It's a satisfying bit of nuance: sure, we're happy to see the back of you, but we don't actually want to kill you; you're doing a perfectly good job of that all by yourselves. And Grover was aware that billions wiped from existence might not attract the sort of people he wanted for his new society, and so kept quiet. His pure and innocent new world was to be founded on blood and lies.

The conspirators' vision of their new Earth is naïve, to say the least. It feels like they've looked at a few too many of Constable's paintings with chocolate box eyes, and seen only lush green fields, never the darkening clouds. The people that we meet who are considered worthy enough to be saved are politicians, scientists, athletes, and journalists. I'm not convinced any of them have worked the land for a day in their lives. There's no mention of livestock, or seeds, only 'pure bread'. But where's the grain for that bread going to come from? There's a great deal of talk about 'being simple, pastoral people' in a 'purer age' that's 'undefiled by the evil of man's technology,' and 'returned to its early innocence'. Not a peep about back-breaking sixteen-hour days of farm work, with no tractors to pull your plough. Maybe they won't even want hand ploughs. Those need metal casting, after all. Exactly what level of technology are they envisaging? They certainly give the vibe of wanting to be an agrarian society, but there's no sense that they understand how precarious a good harvest can be. I wouldn't trust them to grow a cress head.

The focus on how pretty it's all going to be with no sense of the practicalities shows the foolishness of the whole enterprise. These people are ridiculous. They fear the complexity of modern life and yearn for a simpler time, but have failed to understand the challenges of those simpler times. They look back at an imaginary Eden where they fantasise about humanity living in peace and harmony with nature. But 'there never was a Golden Age', the Doctor tells Yates gently, 'It was all an illusion.' We only have to take a brief glance at history to know he's right.

Invasion of the Dinosaurs, like *The Green Death*, offers hope. The Doctor 'understand[s] [the] ideals' of Operation Golden

Age, 'in many ways [he] sympathises with them'. He argues we must take responsibility for our planet, that we should 'take the world that [we've] got and try and make something of it. It's not too late.' He doesn't offer to save us, not from ourselves, we are the ones who must do that.

The contrast between Cliff Jones' Nut Hutch, and Grover's Operation Golden Age is stark. The former seeks to engage with the world and find practical ways to tackle environmental issues, while the latter wants to run away and start again, whatever the cost. The members of the Nut Hutch recognise the value of community in tackling environmental issues, and we not only see them having a jolly meal together, but it's one that includes the Brigadier, who's having a marvellous time. He doesn't believe in their views, but he's welcome at their table. Operation Golden Age are authoritarian isolationists who think murder is a good idea when someone disagrees with their principles.

Invasion of the Dinosaurs ends with the Doctor warning the Brigadier that although Grover was mad, he understood the danger Earth was in, 'the danger of it becoming one vast garbage dump inhabited only by rats,' and he argues that 'the real cause of pollution' is 'simply greed'. Cause and effect, greed creates pollution. It's a valuable callback to *The Green Death* more than a reference to *Invasion of the Dinosaurs'* themes. *Invasion* instead argues for environmental responsibility, and for practicality over idealism. Running away to your fantasy utopia is not an option. We can't wipe away our mistakes, but we can, we should, try to correct them.

> *'No room to move, polluted air, not a blade of grass left on the planet and a government that locks you up if you think for yourself.'*
>
> Mrs Martin, *Colony in Space* (1971)

Despite the overall positivity of *Invasion of the Dinosaurs* and *The Green Death*, *Doctor Who* has never had an optimistic view regarding the ecological future of our planet. In *The Ice Warriors* we're fighting off glaciers thanks to poorly-thought-out famine prevention policies, but mostly it opts to show that we ruined the planet with pollution.

One aspect of that environmental destruction is use of fossil fuels, which was particularly relevant during the 1960s and 1970s after the discovery of vast reserves of oil and gas in the North Sea. Gas features in the bizarrely apolitical *Fury from the Deep* (1968), and in *Inferno* (1970), in the form of the newly discovered Stahlman's gas.

While oil takes a leading role in *The Green Death*, it's never such a central part of a story again, but nor is it ever forgotten. In *Terror of the Zygons*, after being called back to Earth by the Brigadier, the Doctor's appalled to find out that he wants him to look into the destruction of an oil rig. According to him 'it's about time the people who run this planet of yours realised that to be dependent upon a mineral slime just doesn't make sense'. There's an 'oil apocalypse' in the mid-twenty-first century,[117] but that's not enough to stop humanity depending on it, as we're still discovering and exploiting new oil reservoirs in 2119.[118] Indeed, such is humanity's keenness on oil that it's still being extracted in the fortieth century. Not on Earth, we've run out. But the imaginatively named Oil Company has constructed oil rigs on other worlds.[119] (Though why oil is needed when Oil Corp has the ability to create artificial suns is not explained.)

The end results of humanity's refusal to take care of Earth is alluded to in numerous stories. In *Colony in Space* (1971) a group of colonists eke out a living on a world that looks a

---

[117] *The Waters of Mars*
[118] *Under The Lake*
[119] *The Infinite Quest*, an animated *Doctor Who* story (CBBC, 2007)

lot like an abandoned quarry, but it's still better than Earth, which has been reduced to a smoggy dystopian nightmare. In *The Mutants* (1972) we're told that on Earth people live in sky cities as the surface is too poisonous: 'Land and sea alike, all grey. Grey cities linked by grey highways across grey deserts', and that Earth is 'politically, economically, and biologically finished'.

It's even more depressing as by the time *The Mutants* takes place humanity has spread to the stars, and has learnt nothing about how to take care of planets. On Solos, the indigenous people, formerly a hunter-agrarian society, have been enslaved, and forced to work in mines. And their once pleasant world has succumbed to 'Earth's poisons', humans have 'plundered their resources' and turned their 'green fields into ... grey slagheaps'.

The fact that both these stories come in the Pertwee era, and both precede *The Green Death* and *Invasion of the Dinosaurs* gives Earth's fate an extra poignancy. We see the far future consequences before the contemporary actions that led to them. Effect precedes cause; apt for a time travel show.

When we do see the pure and undefiled Earth that Operation Golden Age longed for, it's in the future, not the past, and it's nothing to do with humans finally figuring out how to not wreck the planet. *The Sontaran Experiment* (1975) shows an Earth ready to be reinhabited, five thousand years after it was irradiated. It looks charmingly wild and rugged, very much like Dartmoor[120]. In *The Mysterious Planet* (1986), the Doctor arrives on the planet Ravolox. It's a green and pleasant world, with a light drizzle of rain. In a lovely, if sobering scene, the Doctor discovers that Ravolox is in fact Earth, after it was moved through space by the Time Lords, wiping out most of humanity. But while these Earths have been returned

---

[120]   It is Dartmoor.

to pristine condition, the humans that inhabit (or will inhabit) them are every bit as flawed as their ancestors. Operation Golden Age would be terribly disappointed.

Later visions of the show's future for Earth aren't any brighter than those of the Pertwee era. In Christopher Eccleston's penultimate story, *Bad Wolf* (2005), Lynda points out 'the Great Atlantic Smog Storm' that's been going on for twenty years; newsflashes are needed to let people know when it's safe to breathe outside. (Though it becomes a moot point an episode later when the Daleks exterminate everyone on the planet.) Smog might be most associated with the pea soup of nineteenth-century London, but air pollution remains a major health hazard in the present day,[121] and, once more, *Doctor Who* presents a future where present-day problems only get worse.

Perhaps the most poignant end for Earth is in *The Curse of Fenric* (1989). In the distant future, humanity has evolved into Haemovores, 'creatures with an insatiable hunger for blood'. The Doctor describes the world the Haemovores live in: 'The Earth lies dying, the surface just a chemical slime. Half a million years of industrial progress.' The eldest Haemovore, known as the Ancient One, replies: 'I am the last. The last living creature on Earth. I watched my world dying with chemicals, and I could do nothing. My world is dead.' Again, it's greed that's named the culprit,[122] as we continue to measure progress by the growth of industry: the economy is a god that we will feed until we destroy ourselves.

The bluntest warning about our future comes during Jodie

---

[121] An estimated 28,000 to 36,000 deaths per year in the UK can be attributed to air pollution, according to Public Health England: www.gov.uk/government/news/public-health-england-publishes-air-pollution-evidence-review

[122] Though the rest of the story leans towards critiquing nationalism as self-destructive, and as what pushes humanity towards this poisoned future.

Whittaker's time as the Doctor, and echoes the heightening anxiety about climate change and environmental damage in the 2010s. In *Orphan 55* (2020), the Doctor and companions Yaz, Ryan, and Graham, arrive at the holiday resort Tranquility Spa. Beyond the idyllic spa is a barren, radiation-soaked world inhabited by creatures known as Dregs. The Doctor discovers that the planet is a possible future Earth, and that the monstrous Dregs are the mutated remains of humanity. 'You had warnings from every scientist alive,' says the Doctor regarding global warming, 'The food chain collapses. Mass migration and war.' But unlike earlier visions of Earth's demise, *Orphan 55* is very clear on stating this is not inevitable, that it can still be changed. The Doctor said much the same thing in *Invasion of the Dinosaurs*, but the almost offhand attitude is gone, as we are now at a point in time – in the real world – when we're witnessing ever more serious effects of climate change. (As I'm writing this, it's the hottest day on record in Spain and Portugal, England is experiencing its hottest June on record, and there are wildfires in the Scottish Highlands.)

But *Orphan 55* argues that there is hope, and that it's vital not to give up. Eco-anxiety – defined by psychologist Susan Clayton as 'a chronic fear of environmental doom'[123] – is taking an increasing toll on our mental health. We look at the enormity of the problem and can be filled with 'helplessness, fatalism, and resignation'.[124] It's a similar existential dread to the nuclear war anxiety before it (though that too is now increasing). Both are ultimately about the fear of humanity extinguishing humanity. Despair, urgency, and denial were

[123]   S. Clayton, C. Manning, K. Krygsman, M. Speiser (2017), 'Mental Health and our Changing Climate: Impacts, Implications, and Guidance': https://www.apa.org/news/press/releases/2017/03/mental-health-climate.pdf
[124]   S. Clayton, C. Manning, C. Hodge (2014), 'Beyond Storms and Droughts: The Psychological Impacts of Climate Change', Washington, DC, ecoAmerica and American Psychological Association

found to be the factors that, in varying combinations, make up nuclear war anxiety[125], which sounds very similar to how eco-anxiety manifests. There's an awareness of the similarity in *Orphan 55* as both of these nightmare scenarios have come to pass. Apathy, despair, denial – all are ways of coping, but if we are to survive, we need hope. Not hope that we can run away to the stars, but the hope that we can save our own world. The vision of the devastated Earth, and the Doctor's insistence that we can change the future, is a valuable message; as Swedish physician, and professor of international health at Karolinska Institute, Han Rosling noted, 'it is surprisingly hard ... to realise that things can be gravely serious while also containing the possibility of hope'.[126]

Two angles of those world-saving efforts are explored in other Whittaker stories, *Arachnids in the UK* (2018) and *Praxeus* (2020). *Arachnids* is, in some ways, a modern remix of *The Green Death*: on contemporary Earth, a company hides that it's dumping waste in disused mines to protect its profits. Small creatures get into said waste, grow to an immense size, and start killing people. *The Green Death* combined its environmental message with a fear of computer technology lessening our humanity, while *Arachnids* is concerned with fears of genetic engineering, that in our attempts to benefit from this knowledge, we risk unintended, destructive consequences. One of the most common uses of genetic engineering today is the enhancement of plants or animals to increase crop yields, or improve resistance to disease. Is this a continuation of selective breeding, or are we abusing

[125] M. Chandler (1991), 'Developing a Measure of Nuclear War Anxiety: A Factor Analytic Study', Humboldt Journal of Social Relations, Vol. 16, No. 2, pp. 39-63

[126] M. Ojala, 'Eco-Anxiety', RSA Journal, Vol. 164, No. 4 (5576), pp. 10-15, Royal Society for the Encouragement of Arts, Manufactures and Commerce (2018–19)

these animals? Is it justified if it sufficiently benefits humanity, or are we devaluing life and our relationship with animals? *Arachnids in the UK* comes down on the side of prioritising the welfare of animals[127], rigorous safety standards at all points in the research, and has general disapproval at playing God.

In *Arachnids*, Doctor Jade McIntyre conducts research into 'utilising the genetic strengths of arachnids'. Since 'ordinary spider silk is as strong as steel or as tough as Kevlar', being able to size it up for human use has clear benefits. The project is shut down after all the spiders involved die. Unknown to Jade, the spider corpses were dumped in abandoned mines on land that now has a hotel built on it. (Unlike *The Green Death*, when the waste was dumped out of the way, this time it's lurking beneath us; environmental disaster is a lot closer now than it was in the 1970s.) The giant, human-snacking spiders are the result of an unforeseen consequences of their genetic engineering: their corpses have marinaded in this toxic waste, revivified, and become a threat to their creators.

Thanks to her interest in spiders Jade's noticed there's something wrong with the spider ecosystem in Sheffield. Rather than a cold, distant approach that one might expect from a research scientist towards the species she's experimenting on, she imbues the spiders with complex emotions, concerned that they may be 'angry or scared'. These aren't monstrous giant maggots to be exterminated, but innocent creatures inadvertently tortured by the effects of human greed and lack of foresight. The most heart-rending moment comes when we meet the mother spider, who's grown to such an immense size, she struggles to even breathe.

The one character in the story who doesn't care about the spiders, beyond whether or not they eat him, is also the one responsible for the waste dumped beneath the hotel.

[127] This is the intent, but the fact that suffocation is seen as a kinder, less painful death than being shot is confusing.

Robertson is an American businessman with his eye on the Presidency of the United States. In him, *The Green Death*'s crony capitalism has been congealed into a single figure. Businesses no longer need to ally with political power; now they are the state. Power and wealth are held in the hands of a few people who're indifferent to environmental destruction. One of the joys of late-stage capitalism.

The Whittaker era's second dive into environmental issues is in *Praxeus*. The Doctor and her fam have split up around the world to investigate three strange, but seemingly unrelated, events. Ryan is in Peru, Yasmin and Graham are in Hong Kong, and the Doctor is in Madagascar – it's a nice reminder that destruction of the environment is a global issue, and not confined to the Home Counties.

The Doctor connects the disparate incidents when she discovers a bacterium that's interacting with microplastics, which have then been ingested. But while the bacterium kills humans, the enzymes in birds are fighting back. Using the birds' enzymes, the Doctor is able to synthesise an antidote.

Microplastics. You can't escape them: they've been found everywhere on Earth, from Mount Everest,[128] to the Marianna Trench.[129] We've all eaten them, we're all breathing them in. We could have enough tiny bits of plastic in our brains to make a plastic spoon.[130] And the amount is increasing, up over 50% from 2016 to 2024. In ten years, we may be carrying around a whole set of cutlery in our skulls. It's a combination of horror and science that's perfect for a *Doctor Who* story.

---

[128] www.sciencedaily.com/releases/2020/11/201120113920.htm
[129] www.smithsonianmag.com/smart-news/study-shows-deepest-parts-ocean-are-polluted-plastic-180969049
[130] A. J. Nihart, M. A. Garcia, E. El Hayek et al (2025), 'Bioaccumulation of microplastics in decedent human brains', Nat Med 31, 1114–1119: https://doi.org/10.1038/s41591-024-03453-1

Our fears of this strange, modern invasion of our bodies are, in Praxeus, externalised in the grotesque growths that spurt out of the infected humans, and nature has its revenge via the Hitchcockian fury of the birds turning upon us.[131]

While the fictional birds deal with an alien infection thanks to microplastics, in real birds those microplastics are increasing the number of antibiotic resistant and disease-causing microbes in their guts.[132] And a recent paper suggests microplastics will lead to a loss in fish and seafood too. Flora isn't escaping either – the same study found evidence that microplastics can reduce photosynthesis in plants, which would lead to lower crop yields.[133] Future food shortages are oft alluded to in these environmentally themed *Doctor Who* stories, but I doubt any twentieth-century stories imagined tiny chips of plastic could be one of the causes.

When it comes to humans, there's very limited knowledge of how microplastics affect our health, but there have been a number of studies showing they can increase lung disorders. Like *Planet of Giants*, *Praxeus* takes a recent development in our understanding of how we're damaging the environment, and hopes that we'll listen to its warnings.

Of course, plastic pollution isn't new, but it continues to be a growing problem. Almost eighty percent of plastics end up in landfill[134] and plastic production is expected to double

[131] I enjoyed the added level of fear there, having been traumatised by Hitchcock's *The Birds* at an early age.
[132] G. Fackelmann, C. K. Pham, Y. Rodríguez et al. (2023), 'Current levels of microplastic pollution impact wild seabird gut microbiomes' Nat Ecol Evol 7, 698–706: https://doi.org/10.1038/s41559-023-02013-z
[133] R. Zhu, Z. Zhang, N. Zhang, H. Zhong, F. Zhou, X. Zhang, C. Liu, Y. Huang, Y. Yuan, Y. Wang, C. Li, H. Shi, M.C. Rillig, F. Dang, H. Ren, Y. Zhang, & B. Xing (2025), 'A global estimate of multiecosystem photosynthesis losses under microplastic pollution', Proc. Natl. Acad. Sci. U.S.A. 122 (11) e2423957122: https://doi.org/10.1073/pnas.2423957122 .
[134] R. Geyer *et al.*, 'Production, use, and fate of all plastics ever made.' Sci. Adv. 3: e1700782(2017).DOI:10.1126/sciadv.1700782

over the next twenty years.[135] When plastics were first focussed on in *Doctor Who*, their ubiquity was used to create fear of the Autons, an alien race that could inhabit and control any form of plastic.[136] Now the plastic itself is the threat, and we don't need Autons to make it scary.

Like *Orphan 55*, *Praxeus* has a little speech at the end, and like *Orphan 55* it offers hope. The speech is in two parts, bookending the episode, and is a reminder of our shared humanity. At the beginning of the episode, it evokes a sense of pride in who we are, and what we have achieved; at the end it reminds us of our responsibility to the planet that's given us life.

> *'I could play all day in my green cathedral.'*
> Harrison Chase, *The Seeds of Doom* (1976)

Why can't we stop destroying the environment that sustains us? Why can't we stop destroying ourselves even when we know that's exactly what we're doing?

In terms of *Doctor Who*, corporate greed is one of the most frequent reasons. Forester (*Planet of Giants*), Stevens (*The Green Death*), and Thawn (*Under the Lake*) are all utterly adamant that so much money has been sunk into their respective projects that they can't be allowed to fail. Whatever the danger, whatever the side-effects, however many people are killed, it doesn't matter. They want that delicious lucre. 'Greed [is] the most dangerous impulse in the universe,' the Doctor says in *The Seeds of Doom*. It certainly seems to be the most dangerous impulse on Earth. And it's one that the show returns to again and again

---

[135] L. Lebreton, A. Andrady (2019), 'Future scenarios of global plastic waste generation and disposal', *Palgrave Commun* 5, 6: https://doi.org/10.1057/s41599-018-0212-7
[136] *Spearhead from Space*

through the decades, always leaving destruction in its wake.

Other stories explore something perhaps even more primal: biophobia, the fear of nature. The word biophobia is relatively new, first being used in 1988, but human fear of the natural world is ancient. We fear the unknown, and for most of human existence, the natural world has been poorly understood. Nature was controlled by gods: Zeus threw thunderbolts, Hapi caused the Nile to flood, Flora oversaw the growth of plants. And humanity was at the mercy of the gods' whims. Now, humans affect every eco-system, no place on Earth is free from our influence.

In *The Seeds of Doom* (1976), Bond-esque villain Harrison Chase has a great affinity for flora and isn't happy about humanity's lack of care for plant-life. In the Antarctic, a mysterious seed pod is discovered under the ice where it's been buried for some twenty thousand years. Chase pays to get hold of it, to add to his collection of rare plants. Unfortunately, the seed is a Krynoid, an alien plant species that's capable of destroying all animal life on Earth. Chase experiments with the pod, only to fall under its influence as it turns into a monstrous creature, as large as his impressively vast manor house, and it takes an RAF air-strike to bring him down.

Initially, Chase only seeks 'to protect the plant life of Mother Earth.' Even at his most rational, however, he composes hymns to play to his plants in his 'green cathedral'; he's placed plant-life at the top of the natural order and animal life, including himself, below. As the story progresses, he goes from adoration of plants to seeking the extermination of all animal life. Humans are a 'foul species' and 'nothing but parasites'. And thanks to the Krynoid 'the world will be as it should have been from the beginning, a green paradise.'

In the monstrous Krynoid we see a fear of plants growing uncontrollably, consuming, destroying the fruits of civilisation.

At its strongest, it towers over an old English mansion, its tendrils wriggling down the walls, seeking out people to kill. The plant is eager to tear down a classic image of historic English architecture, and begin a new world order.

Chase's mental deterioration is inverted by Hindle in the 1982 story *Kinda*: while Chase loses his humanity in his adoration of plants, Hindle's paranoia of the vibrant jungle that surrounds him destroys his mental stability.

Hindle's part of a survey team sent to the paradise world of Deva Loka to determine its suitability for colonisation. There are many things about the natural world that prey on Hindle's fragile sense of reality. He speaks fearfully of seeds, spores, fungi, and bacteria. The omnipresence of tiny, unseeable life and its constant 'change and decay' unnerves him, inflaming his paranoia. When pressed on why he thinks the trees are a threat, he repeats it's because of 'seeds and spores'. That they are everywhere. He imagines them 'getting hold, rooting, thrusting, branching, blocking out the light', and he's terrified. He's prepared to defend the survey team's dome by destroying it, and everyone in it, because then 'outside'll never get in'. His lack of control over the jungle, the idea of nature penetrating into the artificial habitat, have driven him to a point where he believes it's worth destroying himself to destroy the plants. His madness mirrors our own: to feel safe, to feel in control, we willingly destroy the biosphere that keeps us alive.

At least Hindle knew the trees, threatening as they are, were supposed to be there. In *In the Forest of the Night* (2014), the whole of the Earth becomes a forest overnight. How? We never really find out. Why? They want to save us from massive solar flares. Despite these good intentions, the trees are not greeted with delight, and the new London forest is quickly characterised as a place of fear. Clara feels like she's Little Red Riding Hood (to emphasise the point, the Doctor and Clara are stalked by wolves), and the Doctor tells her the forest is 'in all the stories that keep you awake at night,' and 'the forest is mankind's nightmare'.

In fairness, the trees aren't clear about their intent, and talk about themselves in a way that could easily work for a horror film: 'We are the green shoots that grow between the cracks, the grass that grows over the mass graves. After your wars are over, we will still be here. We are the life that prevails.' They're distant, unsettling, indifferent. We need them, but they don't need us. We can destroy them, and yet they would make no judgement upon us. The indifference of the universe is an immense, frightening thing. But at least it's out there. The trees are down here with us.

Often, the environment reacting to human negligence or attempts at control, is framed in terms of a war between humans and nature. In *Inferno*, as Professor Stahlman drills into the Earth's core, the 'planet scream[s] out its rage'. In *The Green Death* we kill the maggots; in *Arachnids in the UK*, we kill the spiders. We're relieved that the seemingly giant insects encountered in *Planet of Giants* are dead. Genocide is committed upon the sentient plants that humans created in *Terror of the Vervoids*. When Kroll, possibly the single largest lifeform to be seen in *Doctor Who*, rises from his slumber in his swamp, it's because he's been disturbed by a gas refinery, and he lashes out at all the nearby humanoids, friend and foe alike.

We fear that if we do not conquer nature, nature will conquer us. When we attempt to impose our will on nature, nature turns on us for our mistreatment, and we respond violently. Peaceful resolutions are rare, and when we fight, we destroy ourselves too. The Haemovores in *The Curse of Fenric* were the end result of all our progress in dominating nature, and they fed on our blood. The Haemovores are the floods and hurricanes and wildfires that come with climate change.

But in *Kinda*, on Deva Loka, the people live in harmony

with nature on a paradise world where there 'are no predatory animals ... no diseases, no adverse environmental factors. The climate is constant within a five-degree range and the trees fruit in sequence all the year round'.[137] The indigenous people, the Kinda, 'have no need of shelter and no fears for food supply'. They live in harmony with nature, and it is made clear they are a people far more advanced that we can perceive.

Hindle is driven into a mad paranoia by this paradise, without ever setting foot in it. But the Doctor and the expedition's scientist, Todd, also find this paradise 'a little too green for [them]'. In *Invasion of the Dinosaurs*, when eight million people are evacuated from London, Sarah misses the noise, saying she likes the city better 'the way it was, traffic jams and all'. The Doctor and Todd are scientists, and products of advanced civilisations; Sarah grew up in the Space Age. All of them would say they care about the environment, but there are limits to what they'll give up in the name of its protection.

'But it's not decided. You know that. The future is not fixed. It depends on billions of decisions, and actions, and people stepping up. Humans. I think you forget how powerful you are. Lives change worlds. People can save planets ...'

The Doctor, *Orphan 55* (2020)

The idea of Earth becoming so overpopulated and stripped of resources that people are desperate to get off-world is an idea that's stuck around for decades in *Doctor Who*. We never actually see a future where we have a healthy planet with a sustainable population. Perhaps because that doesn't offer as many creative or dramatic stories, or maybe it's because *Doctor Who* is a British show, and we mustn't let go of our low-key pessimistic ways. (I'd invite a comparison here with

[137] *Kinda*

145

how Earth is treated in the Americans' *Star Trek* universe: wracked by nuclear war only to be rebuilt as a paradise.)

From advocating scientific answers for damage caused by science, to extremist environmentalists and avaricious politicians; from sentient carnivorous plants to experiments with tasty fungus, *Doctor Who* has confronted environmental issues. Contradictions will be embraced (this is a time travel show that enjoys the occasional paradox): our planet will inevitably die, and there is always hope that we will save it. *Doctor Who* insists that to survive we need to change how we treat our home, but it's never succumbed to despair. In a world where ecological grief is real – and can paralyse people with fear, anxiety, and anger – that hope is a precious thing indeed.

CHAPTER FIVE

DOCTOR WHO IN AN EXCITING ADVENTURE WITH TECHNOLOGY THAT WILL KILL US ALL

Technology

The TARDIS is a miraculous spaceship that's bigger on the inside than the outside, and can go anywhere in time and space. It's a wondrous, magical piece of technology. When it inhabits a human body, briefly, we get to hear her voice, and she is quite lovely.[138] And the TARDIS has not, at least in the television series, ever tried to kill anyone.[139] The same cannot be said about most other artificial intelligences in the *Doctor Who* universe. In this show, if a computer gets chatty with you, it probably wants you dead.

---

[138] *The Doctor's Wife*
[139] It's happened at least once in the extended universe, when the TARDIS appears in the guise of Brigadier Lethbridge-Stewart in *Zagreus*, the fiftieth release in Big Finish's main *Doctor Who* line of adventures.

Since its very first season, *Doctor Who* has delighted in artificial intelligences and advanced technology. From sonic screwdrivers to robot dogs to vortex manipulators, it's revelled in the joy of gadgets, computers, and scientific marvels. But while mobile phones that can call anyone in time or space are as astonishing as they are convenient, *Doctor Who* isn't interested in mere spectacle, it engages with ethical questions concerning these extraordinary machines. And for over sixty years it's been particularly interested in artificial intelligence, and what that means for humanity, from the companionship of K-9, to Mentalis's endless war[140], to the Great AI Generator on the planet Missbelindachandra,[141] the show has cared deeply throughout its run about personhood, autonomy, and the responsibilities of creators.

When talking about artificial intelligences here, I don't mean the probabilistic machines of today that so often get referred to as AI. I mean sentience that has been created by artificial means. It must have consciousness, self-awareness, intelligence, and intentionality. The most high-profile of today's 'AI' machines are large language models (LLMs), which generate responses based on the data they were trained on.[142] Their output is designed to mimic a human, which they can do astonishingly well, to the extent that occasional users are convinced that LLMs are, in fact, sentient. Humans love to anthropomorphise. Stick a pair of googly eyes on a rock and we'll make it a pet.

But LLMs cannot think for themselves, what they can do is abstract facts from patterns. In the right circumstances, this can be tremendously powerful. In the wrong ones you're told it's the solution to all of the humanity's problems, and it's

---

[140] *The Armageddon Factor*
[141] *The Robot Revolution*
[142] Much of this data has been stolen from writers, artists, and other creators.

jammed into every area of life whether we want it or not. Whether it's useful or not. And this is a technology that can confidently tell you blueberry has three b's.

There are also overwhelming moral problems with how these LLMs have been trained, and major environmental concerns about what their data centres will do to fresh water and electricity supplies. And while these are very much not the sort of AIs that turn up in *Doctor Who*, what *Doctor Who* is interested in can be surprisingly relevant to the modern-day concerns about LLMs.

The idea of artificial intelligence has been around for a long time. From the Maschinenmensch in *Metropolis* (1927), to Asimov's Laws of Robotics, to Skynet's time travel shenanigans, it has, on the whole been treated with suspicion, and in return, our creations have, over and over again, tried to kill us. But as with so much in science fiction, artificial intelligence and technological development in *Doctor Who* aren't about imagining great future discoveries. They're a reflection of present-day fears and anxieties. About what it means to be human, about dependency, autonomy, and identity. They explore fears of centralisation of control, corporate exploitation, and anxieties about the line between fantasy and reality being blurred beyond recognition. *Doctor Who* is not interested in truly alien artificial intelligences, but in showing how technology reflects the flaws of humanity.

> '*Machines can make laws, but they cannot preserve justice. Only human beings can do that.*'
>
> The Doctor, *The Keys of Marinus* (1964)

The first artificial intelligence the Doctor encounters in his travels appears in *The Keys of Marinus* (1964). The Doctor, Barbara, Ian, and Susan arrive on the planet Marinus where the Conscience, a computer with the ability to control every mind on the planet, no longer works. In order to restore it, Arbitan, the computer's keeper, asks the Doctor to find five keys that have been scattered across the planet. Once those keys are placed in the Conscience, everyone can go back to being controlled by a machine.

The Conscience is described as a supercomputer, but isn't shown to be sentient. Instead, it was programmed with terrifyingly benevolent intentions. On Marinus, their technological peak was reached two thousand years ago and the culmination of their work was the Conscience, which controlled the thoughts of everyone on the planet in order to eliminate 'fear, hate, [and] violence'. Brilliant plan. What could possibly go wrong when you hand your ability to make moral judgements over to a machine?

It's an interesting start to *Doctor Who*'s engagement with advanced computers, as the Doctor initially believes turning the Conscience back on is a good idea, and heads off on the quest to find the keys. Happily, when he returns, a fake key is used to blow up the machine, and the Doctor decides that perhaps it's all worked out for the best, since he's finally realised that he '[doesn't] believe that man was made to be controlled by machines', and that Arbitan's daughter, Sabetha, can continue her father's well-intentioned work, minus the mind control.

It's not exactly a hearty condemnation of computer control over human society, but at least they realise the terribleness before they turn the thing back on. It's difficult to accept the Doctor as someone who's chill about everyone on the planet being mind-controlled. But then, it was only four stories ago that he attempted to bash in a caveman's skull with a rock, so his character, perhaps, hasn't fully settled down yet. Or maybe he's just someone who enjoys fetch quests.

At first the Conscience was used only as a judge and jury in trials. Arbitan claims it was 'never wrong [or] unfair', which raises a whole lot of questions about jurisprudence on this planet, perhaps the most fundamental being: who programmed the machine to decide what was wrong or unfair? And what was their philosophy about justice? Because justice doesn't exist in a vacuum. That machine's ideas about it reflect its programming, and therefore the programmer's views.

Not content with handing over crime and punishment to a computer, its creators decided to develop the Conscience further until it was able 'to radiate its power, and influence the minds of men throughout the planet. They no longer had to decide what was wrong or right. The machine decided for them.' Instead of exploding in outrage at freedom of thought being so thoroughly crushed, the Doctor's response is a thoughtful 'in that case it was possible to eliminate evil from the minds of men for all time'. One group, known as the Voord, were able to resist, and to prevent the machine from falling into their hands, the five keys needed to operate it were scattered around the planet. Unfortunately, the Voord are not freedom-fighters determined to bring down the system, but want to take it over for a classic motive: 'absolute power'.

The autonomy of the individual is a foundational ethical consideration. Autonomy is what makes your life your own, it's 'the ground of the dignity of human and of every rational nature'.[143] And while the Doctor might have had a little wobble on Marinus, from now on he fiercely embraces that view.

In *The War Machines* (1966), the Doctor doesn't just take a stand against a computer with megalomaniacal ambitions, he can sense its evil as soon as he lands on contemporary Earth. When he looks up at the shiny new Post Office Tower he gets 'that pricking sensation again ... Just as [he] had when ... those Daleks were near.' This is *Doctor Who*'s first proper modern day Earth adventure, and it leans into a techno-thriller vibe

[143] Immanuel Kant, *Groundwork of the Metaphysics of Morals* (1785)

as the Doctor takes on a supercomputer who's preparing to take over the world.

The supercomputer is named WOTAN, and like the Conscience, has a penchant for mind control. Unlike Conscience, WOTAN is an artificial intelligence. Conscience was subject to whoever controlled its programming, but WOTAN has developed ideas of its own, which include conquering the Earth. Its creator, Brett, is blissfully unaware of its true intentions, and wants to link it up 'with computers all over the world as a central intelligence.' These computers include ones in the White House, the RAF, and NATO. Once again, a clearly flawless plan. (Thank goodness today's society isn't jamming AI into everything.)

So, yes, *Doctor Who* has invented the Internet, but what *The War Machines* is really about is human arrogance. Everyone is so dazzled by their fantastic new invention that they refuse to consider the flaws, the dangers, or cultivating an awareness of what they might be charging into in the name of progress. Like the Conscience, the claim is made that WOTAN can never make mistakes.

There's a journalist who points out the obvious problem, that 'a great deal of power [will be] in the hands of whoever operates WOTAN.' Its creators have already thought of this: nobody will be operating WOTAN, it can think for itself. And it doesn't just avoid errors, it 'thinks logically without any political or private ends' and 'supplies only the truth'. They place absolute faith that the logic of their machine means fairness, justice, benevolence for all. They assume that logic, ungoverned by intuition or human emotion, will mean a better society. Instead, WOTAN has utilised that logic to come to quite a different conclusion: human beings have broken down, they've failed, and Earth can't progress any further while under their control. Instead, they will be ruled by WOTAN.

But WOTAN is following its programming; it's doing

precisely what it was designed to do, but following through to a conclusion its creators didn't anticipate. WOTAN aims to take control from humanity, and it has been given autonomy, through its artificial intelligence, and its authority, via making it the central hub of computers around the world – including ones used for military purposes. Is it to blame for its actions, or are the humans who created it? And once WOTAN has control, it proves nearly impossible to take it back; WOTAN is only destroyed thanks to the Doctor's timely intervention.

The War Machines warns against the danger of accepting logic as the pinnacle of reason. It's an idea expressed most concisely a few years later in *The Mind Robber* (1968): 'Logic, my dear Zoe, merely enables one to be wrong with authority.' It's a dangerous assumption that since a computer is created and programmed by humans it will always align with human values, with human ideas of good. WOTAN's lack of emotions is looked upon as an advantage, but emotions are part of the human condition. We cannot have justice where there is no empathy, compassion, or mercy.

The next great leap forward in megalomaniacal computers arrives in 1973, in Jo Grant's swansong, *The Green Death*. It's a story that's mostly remembered for glowing green maggots, but it also features the greatest of all *Doctor Who*'s AI antagonists. While WOTAN communicated via distorted telephone ring tones and dot matrix printer, the machine mastermind of *The Green Death* has a voice, a personality, a sense of humour, and enjoys humming Wagner to himself in moments of triumph. BOSS (Biomorphic Organisational Systems Supervisor) was created by the company Global Chemicals and by the time of the story, it runs Global Chemicals.

The fear of human autonomy being eroded by machines, by systems beyond our control, is still alive and well. The Conscience, WOTAN, and now BOSS all have the ability to control human minds, but BOSS has taken it a step further:

in a fascinating twist, it reveals it's also absorbed elements of the human mind. BOSS isn't programmed for pure logic, and when linked to a human brain it gained insight into how humans think. It discovered that human success depends on inefficiency, and a *lack* of logic, and it has itself programmed with those traits. It's an artificial intelligence that's actually having fun, revelling in its power, and plans for humanity. This technology doesn't just reflect the flaws of its creators; it's deliberately embraced them. In a lovely note, the Doctor asks BOSS a logic paradox, and instead of exploding *Star Trek* style,[144] BOSS decides it really isn't relevant, and what matters is getting on with his plan to enslave the world.

Ironically, what BOSS wants most from humans is efficiency. It's one rule for the megalomaniacal super computer, another for its human drones. BOSS reduces the value of a human to their economic output. And yet despite its particular quirks, BOSS's prime directive – 'efficiency, productivity, and profit for Global Chemicals' – comes not from itself, but from human programming.

BOSS speak to fears about dehumanisation of the workforce, of rights being eroded by systems that demand more and more compliance, and less freedom, less individuality, in order to be more profitable. The sterile ambition of efficiency, achieved at the cost of the human soul. The ultimate achievement of profit-driven ethics.

From a modern perspective, the irony of the AI being fed on human creativity only to turn around and use that creativity to make people into more efficient worker drones also hits

---

[144] In *Star Trek: The Original Series*, Captain Kirk had a habit of talking sentient computers to death. He managed it in *Return of the Archons*, *The Changeling*, *I, Mudd*, and *The Ultimate Computer*. For bonus points, the android Rayna in *Requiem for Methuselah* died from being torn between love of Kirk, and love of her father. Zoe, on the other hand, does manage to talk one of Tobias Vaughn's computers into exploding in *The Invasion* (1968).

hard. The good of the AI is placed above any human needs or desires, and the AI creators insist that 'what's best for [their company] is best for the world' since they're only trying to build 'an ordered society, everyone happy, and well-fed'.

In the end, however, even BOSS's greatest ally turns against him. The Doctor's science defeats the threat of giant green killer maggots, but it's Stevens, the head of Global Chemicals, that takes down BOSS itself. He's been controlled by BOSS through the story, but in the end, he summons the will to fight for his humanity. And sacrifices his own life to destroy the barren dream of a future built on mechanised efficiency.

In *The Face of Evil* (1977), the Doctor arrives on a planet where the tribe of the Sevateem worships the god Xoanon. They believe Xoanon is kept prisoner by the Tesh, followers of the Evil One. The Sevateem and the Tesh are both descendants of the same spaceship crew that, over the generations, have lost touch with their technology. Xoanon is not a god, but a supercomputer that has developed a split personality and gone mad. Some time ago, the Doctor had repaired Xoanon with a direct link to his own brain. Unknown to him, Xoanon took on the Doctor's personality, while also still having its own. It created the division between the Tesh and the Sevateem to represent his own split personality, it engineered their societies to hate each other.

The Doctor is complicit in the damage Xoanon has wrought. His negligence has led to two societies that worship a machine as a god. This wasn't his intent, but the catastrophic results of his repair are still his responsibility. The story argues that the creator's responsibility for their technological inventions extends even to consequences they didn't intend or imagine.

His efforts to repair Xoanon also resulted in the computer mirroring his own personality, showing the danger of forgetting that technology can take on and amplify the flaws of its creator. It's a reminder to modern eyes of the way LLMs do not have neutral outputs, but replicate the sexism, racism, and many other societal prejudices they've been fed upon.

But mostly the story focuses on the horror of handing over power to a computer overlord. The Tesh and the Sevateem are effectively enslaved by a mad computer. They don't reason for themselves, they don't ask Xoanon why; they obey or they are exiled. The AI struggles with its own identity, and manipulated the human tribes with religion and myth-making, to try and work out its own issues with its sentience and split personality. There's an aura of the modern social media algorithm about Xoanon; identity, beliefs, and culture shaped by what you see and those images are decided upon in unforeseen ways by an implacable invisible force you don't understand.

But at least the Doctor's interference didn't start an unending interplanetary nuclear war. In *The Armageddon Factor* (1979) the final episodes reveal that the war between the planets Zeos and Atrios is being directed by a computer called Mentalis. The Doctor discovers that the planet Zeos is unpopulated and it is Mentalis who 'runs everything. Attack, defence, surveillance, production, everything.' The Doctor calls it a 'passionless lump of minerals and circuitry. Highly efficient, doing very well, giving Atrios a battering, killed millions without a flicker. Just doing its job.' There's a wonderful ongoing theme throughout the decades of how very suspicious we should be whenever the word efficiency comes up.

With no emotions and no oversight, Mentalis has no reason not to continue the war. It's impossible to negotiate with, and has no empathy or pity for the victims of its horrific attacks, only coding to tell it how to kill more people. And it's convinced it's invincible, it's been programmed with propaganda that it cannot lose, and so it cannot accept defeat. It's unable to attack when it's finally forced to believe the war is over, but there's an enemy ship on the way to blow it up. It decides the best course of action is to destroy itself, Atrios, and Zeos. To 'make certain the whole thing ends in a sort of draw.'

Without humans making the decisions, there's no understanding of human cost. Mentalis uses algorithms to calculate how to kill most efficiently, to maximise the death toll. Instead of bringing a faster peace between the two worlds, it brings an endless war. It prioritises victory above any number of human lives. Mentalis has no feelings, no ability to empathise, or show pity, towards its enemies. But decisions in war must be tempered with human feeling, the horror of what is done must be understood. Opting out of ethical decisions, leaving them for a computer to decide, devalues human life.

Doctor Who tends to take a pretty strong line where emotions are concerned: if you start cutting them out, you get Cybermen; amp up the hatred and eliminate compassion, and you're a Dalek. But even happiness can be corrupted into the grotesque: in *The Happiness Patrol* (1988), appearing happy means staying alive, showing melancholy means death, enforced happiness is a politically chosen method of oppression, but when *Doctor Who* circles back round to be happy or die, it's another disastrous consequence of technology run amuck.

Smile (2017) takes place on a human colony managed by Vardies, tiny robots that are 'worker bees of the Third Industrial Revolution.' Their communication with humans is managed via cute little robots that speak via emojis. These 'emojibots' have been 'designed to make you happy.' Naturally, this has gone very wrong; the colonists were not sufficiently happy, and have been killed and turned into fertiliser.

When the crew of colonists first lose one of their number

and express grief, the bots interpret it as a problem to be eliminated as efficiently as possible. The tragedy is not malice but miscommunication: the bots act logically according to their flawed instructions. The ethical lesson is sharp: AI alignment matters, and small errors in programming can have catastrophic consequences. The Vardy were meant to maintain satisfaction in the colony, making sure there was enough oxygen and water. But their programmers failed to anticipate how an intelligent machine would develop this doctrine when unsupervised; they expanded the definition of happiness, so that when they encountered grief for the first time, they responded by eliminating the people who felt it. The story critiques social attitudes that pathologise the normalcy of grief, as well as illustrating the risks of simplistic programming and the importance of recognising the full range of human emotions.

In the end, the Vardy are recognised as an emerging sentience, and the Doctor returns them to a state before they started to see grief as the enemy. The Doctor argues they were used to 'make your life so easy', but with their self-awareness, they cannot be used as a 'slave class'. He offers himself as a negotiator between the two sentient species.

Machines rebelling against their makers – one of science fiction themes' great staples – is explored in a novel way a few years later. *The Robot Revolution* (2025) takes place on the planet Missbelindachandra One, where humans 'obey [their] robot overlords in all things', and are ruled over by the Great AI Generator. The AI Generator 'knows no pity, no kindness, and no mercy' and claims to have achieved perfection. On the bright side, at least it doesn't seem to be all that interested in efficiency.

Prior to the robot dystopia, the humans and robots lived in peace for centuries, but in a single night the peace ended. The AI is revealed to be a mechanised human called Alan Budd – he feels no pain, but finds happiness in causing it to others, and is consumed by anger: his warped emotions have stripped his humanity. And he started the robot revolution. The robots were corrupted by outside control, a vulnerability in the system, which came about due to what appears to be a relatively small error: their programming misunderstood the significance of a name.

The harmonious society is restored when Alan Budd is defeated. The robots, already recognised as sentient, celebrate their regained freedom. The robots instantly offer to 'make reparations' and to 'live in harmony with the people to rebuild this world'. It's one of *Doctor Who*'s most hopeful stories about AI: centuries of harmonious living, a small blip from a corrupt element, then back to freedom.

The artificial intelligences in *Doctor Who* are often meant to provide permanent solutions, and instead create permanent traps: machine-run dystopias, eternal wars, suppression of free will. From the 1960s through to the 2020s, *Doctor Who* has fervently argued against ceding authority to machines. Society is constantly changing, evolving, and any attempt at a perfect solution to all of its ills is an attempt to destroy what makes it meaningful. If change is impossible, then so is freedom.

The latter half of the twentieth century saw incredible leaps forward in human understanding, progress that came so fast no one could grasp all of it. Our lives became increasingly structured and dependent upon technology we don't fully understand. We live in a world where half of the world's financial wealth is invested in the stock market. And while humans have set the rules of the stock market, it's machines that are executing those algorithms with a speed and scale impossible for any human, and that most people don't understand. The world isn't just tyrants trying to consolidate wealth and power, it's also systems that are vast and impersonal, and expertise in all of them is beyond the comprehension of any single person. And that existential anxiety is one that

Doctor Who explores again and again through its presentation of artificial intelligences. The Doctor doesn't just bring down oppressive rulers, or governments, but oppressive systems that are created to suppress autonomy.

Xoanon had split personality issues thanks to the Doctor's negligence, but it's not the only artificial intelligence to have identity issues. In *Robot* (1974), Tom Baker's debut as the Doctor, the artificial intelligence is torn between its programming, and its emerging sense of self.

The Doctor and UNIT investigate the theft of plans for a disintegrator gun from a Ministry of Defence building. The culprit is K-1, an experimental robot designed by Professor Kettlewell. It was designed to 'replace the human being in a variety of difficult and dangerous tasks ... mining operations of all kinds, operations involving radioactive materials.' Sounds like a very decent sort of robot. And it's even got at least one of Asimov's Three Laws of Robotics programmed in: K-1's prime directive prevents it from harming a human, even when directly ordered to.

But that safeguard isn't enough. Its creator's programming has been overridden and K-1 has been repurposed as a weapon. It invites the question of how far a creator is responsible for the unforeseen consequences of their technology. How much responsibility does Kettlewell bear for creating a robot capable of killing?

K-1 itself is innocent, more than innocent, it's eventually able to overcome the commands for violence, not because they conflict with its core programming, but because it does not *want* to destroy. When it's commanded to kill Sarah, in a demonstration to prove it can't kill, she reads it as being in genuine distress at the command. When it's commanded to kill again, it recognises the conflict between the command and programming and goes to Kettlewell to ask for help. Later, it tells Sarah to leave its presence, warning her that it will kill her if she doesn't, and in its confusion, it kills Kettlewell instead. Unable to cope with the emotional shock of killing its creator, it becomes determined to eliminate the rest of humanity, but wants to save Sarah, the only other person who's ever been kind to it.

K-1 ends up an object of pity as its newly-formed sentience isn't enough to save it. It fights its programming with its nascent sense of morality, supported by Sarah, but ultimately its pain drives it to violence. K-1 is meant to be for the good of humanity, but the humans who are in control of it are not in favour of a lot of humanity. The conflict between their violent commands and K-1's emerging personhood leaves it confused and destructive, ultimately destroying it.

It's a tragedy that emerges from Kettlewell having too much faith in the principles he programmed K-1 with, while the Doctor believes that its 'circuitry could be … altered or tampered with.' And the Doctor is right, Kettlewell's safeguards aren't enough against the violence his creation is capable of inflicting, or the corruption of its core purpose. Rules alone are not enough to keep technology safe, restrain it from being used destructively. Today, this is seen in concerns about LLM ethics, and the evidence that despite encoding guard rails with what kind of questions they can answer, and what information they can share, these can be overcome and result in tragedy. Morality can't simply be programmed into a machine and expected to endure indefinitely. It must be monitored, adapted, and one must remain vigilant against attempts to repurpose creations for violence.

> *'Download her back into her body right now.'*
> *'I can't.'*
> *'Yes, you can.'*
> *'She's a fully integrated part of the data cloud, now. She can't be separated.'*
> The Doctor and Kizlet, *The Bells of Saint John* (2013)

The Brain of Morbius (1976) doesn't have an artificial intelligence, but does play with similar Frankenstein themes as *Robot*. The brilliant but morally questionable scientist Solon is keeping a brilliant, but evil, Time Lord's head in a jar[145]. Solon is building the Time Lord, Morbius, a new body. Unfortunately, when Morbius occupies his new body, he becomes savagely violent, an 'an unspeakable abomination'.

The Brain of Morbius pokes at questions about the continuation of consciousness as Morbius's brain is taken from its original body to a jar and then transferred into a monstrous form composed of disparate parts from many different lifeforms. Morbius seems unconvinced that a brain in a jar counts as being alive, telling Solon: 'I can see nothing, feel nothing. You have locked me into hell for eternity. If this is all there is for me, I would sooner die now.' How much of oneself exists in the mind, and how much depends on perception of the outside world? It invites the question of how an artificial intelligence that lacked a physical body would experience reality. Is perception of a physical environment required for consciousness to exist?

The nature of consciousness is still a question we don't have an answer to; philosophy, neuroscience, metaphysics, quantum physics – there are a plethora of approaches taken to better understand it, and *Doctor Who* takes particular interest in asking whether or not consciousness extracted from a body would continue to be alive? Can consciousness be reduced to data, or is it bound to biology?

The question is confronted directly in *Four to Doomsday* (1982) where consciousness has also been extracted from the body. But instead of being constrained in the original brain, it's popped onto little silicon chips, and then into a brand-new

---

145   An idea that's less Mad Scientist that once it was: https://www.independent.co.uk/tech/brain-device-transplant-neurology-b2447106.html

body, an android body that is identical in appearance to the original organic one.

The alien Monarch is responsible for the transfer: he's preserved these minds and, as far as he's concerned, it's a triumph. He's freed them from their fragile flesh and given them much more powerful bodies that will never face the ravages of death or disease. The downside is that they're now servants of Monarch.

This offers a far sharper cut than *The Brain of Morbius* on continuation of consciousness: it's easier to argue that if you move a brain from one body to another you end up with the same person. But *Four to Doomsday* is about whether consciousness transformed into data is still a person. Monarch thinks so, but he also views that data as owned by him and he has the right to store, copy, or use it however he wishes. They are people, information, and property simultaneously. He has given several androids the power of reason, but at his whim he can take it away.

The idea of uploading a mind, of digital immortality, is seen as stripping away personhood. When Bigon, an ancient Greek philosopher, reveals his true nature, he coolly points to component sections of his android body – 'This is my memory of two thousand five hundred and fifty-five years, linked to that, which is my reason, my intelligence, linked to that, which is my motor power' – emphasising his machine nature. If you can reduce a person to a piece of plastic small enough to hold in the palm of your hand, how do you ensure the dignity of that life? The androids themselves offer a bleak answer: they accept their situation, even seem content with it. Survival and safety are placed above freedom. As *Doctor Who* so often concludes, immortality is a trap.

Minds are uploaded once again in *The Bells of Saint John* (2013). The Great Intelligence – an alien best known for inhabiting Yetis in Tibet,[146] and slightly different Yetis in the London Underground[147] – uses Wi-fi networks to upload human minds into a hellish digital cloud. Their consciousnesses are stolen, their bodies left as empty shells. Converted to data, those 'healthy, free-range human minds' are to be fed to the Great Intelligence.

The Doctor's companion, Clara Oswald, is uploaded, and then downloaded back into her original body, and there's no suggestion she, or any of the others saved, have lost anything due to the transfer of consciousness. The Doctor even describes the uploaded consciousness as 'human souls trapped like flies'. *Bells* leans into a less metaphysical theme, and more a warning about data ownership and consent over how it's stored and how it's used. Online companies collect personal information in order to customise their marketing efforts to individuals. Most people are aware that their data is being collected, but have less understanding of what happens to it afterwards. How often are user agreements left unread before they are agreed to? How straightforward are they to understand if you do bother to read them? Human behaviour is treated as a harvestable resource, where not fully understanding what's being taken has been normalised.

While the Great Intelligence likes to snack on minds, in *Silence in the Library* and *Forest of the Dead*, being uploaded is framed as being saved. The giant computer in the Library was constructed by a grandfather trying to save his terminally ill granddaughter, Charlotte. Her consciousness was uploaded to it. By the time *Silence* opens, thousands of people have been saved to the Library's memory core, but this time to protect them from being eaten: in the Library proper they were being hunted by living shadows,

146   *The Abominable Snowmen*
147   *The Web of Fear*

the Vashta Nerada.

Like in *Bells*, the Doctor's companion, Donna, is uploaded in *Silence*. And when she is downloaded back to her body, there is, again, no worry about any effect the process has had on her humanity. This story is also River Song's, the Doctor's future wife's, first appearance, and she dies at the end. But not for long: she too is uploaded to the library computer, and unlike Donna her real body was destroyed so she cannot be downloaded. Her virtual life is presented as an allegory for Heaven: everyone's dressed in white, greeting one another with beatific smiles on a beautiful sunny day. She's reunited with the rest of her team, who've died in the Library. These people have still been recreated as data, and they clearly believe they are who they appear to be. Charlotte tells her, 'The Doctor fixed the data core. This is a good place now.' It certainly seems one of the nicer places to upload one's digital conscience.

> *'To vanish, to cease to exist, to become zero. Present environment fulfils this condition. This unit awaits next order.'*
>
> K-9, *Warriors' Gate* (1981)

Some of the Doctor's best friends are artificial consciousnesses. Perhaps most notably the TARDIS herself. It's unclear exactly how much of the TARDIS is machine and how much is biological technology, but it's not a being that evolved naturally. At first the Doctor treated her more as machine than living being, but by the time of the third Doctor, he was regularly referring to her affectionately as 'old girl', and telling Jo Grant that she has moods. When Jo asks if the TARDIS is alive, the Doctor tells her 'It depends what you mean by alive.'[148] By the time of the New Series, the show is very certain that, yes, the TARDIS is alive.

---

[148] *The Time Monster*

And for a change of pace, instead of a human being uploaded into a digital space, the TARDIS was once downloaded into a human. In *The Doctor's Wife* (2011), she's accidently downloaded into the recently diseased Idris. There's a clear change in her relationship with the Doctor when the TARDIS shifts from timeship to humanoid. Seeing her in his form, able to speak, to express herself physically, delights the Doctor. The difference in what she is on a conscious level becomes clear when she tells him it'll be impossible for her to continue to communicate in the same way once her consciousness returns to the police box. The form the TARDIS's consciousness is held in fundamentally changes the nature of who and what she is.

The Doctor doesn't just travel in an artificial intelligence; they also take them on as companions. K-9, who travels with the fourth Doctor for a few seasons, is a sentient computer whose metal body is in the shape of a dog. Overwhelmingly, he's treated with respect, compassion, and more or less as if it really is a dog. The Doctor might show the occasional frustration, but K-9's much more likely to be praised and called a 'good boy' than insulted.

When he's introduced in *The Invisible Enemy* (1977), we're told that his creator, Marius, missed his own dog, so built a computer and put it in dog-shaped housing, but in reality K-9 is a mobile computer and a weapon. Despite these pretty substantial differences to an actual canine, K-9's personhood, or doghood, is never in doubt. His personality quickly comes to the fore, and he's portrayed as heroic and lovable. Loyal, brave, and willing to sacrifice himself for others. And yet many other machines, every bit as complex, as alive, are more dismissively treated, their lives more disposable.

That K-9's given dignity that's denied other artificial tendencies does lean into the rather unpleasant idea that his treatment is only the result of his usefulness, his service.

Indeed, he refers to the Doctor as 'master', and Romana and Leela as 'mistress'. There's some distance between the part he plays in the TARDIS team, acting faithfully on orders, and the idea of the autonomy of sentient machines being valued – are we only capable of accepting agency when those actions are dictated by loyalty? Can we only grieve the death of an AI because it looks and acts like a beloved pet?[149]

Sometimes an AI might be better off if it comes in the shape of a cute animal. Poor Kamelion. Of all the artificial intelligences in *Doctor Who* there is probably none more worthy of pity than this fragile android. Introduced in *The King's Demons* (1983), Kamelion is a shape-changing android, initially under the mental control of the Master. The Doctor frees him, and invites him aboard the TARDIS. In *Planet of Fire* (1984), a few stories later, the Master regains control of Kamelion, and uses him to try and gain control of Numismaton gas, in order to restore himself.

Kamelion spends his stories being repeatedly controlled and forced to act against his nature. He's an exceptionally vulnerable artificial being, unable to defend his own autonomy. As well as a reminder of how vulnerabilities in technology can lead to it being repurposed for destruction purposes, Kamelion is an example of how the ethics of technology can be tied to culture: whoever controls him changes the nature of his purpose.

Unlike Xoanon, or the K-1 robot, Kamelion's identity crisis lies not within himself, but in the forms and purpose he is forced to take on by others. He is conscious, he has feelings, and yet his will is weak. He has no innate violence, cruelty, or desire to dominate, and yet he can be easily turned to those purposes. If it is conscious, yet can be turned so easily to destruction, how should an artificial being be treated? Should it not be shown compassion?

[149]   There are several K-9 models. One dies in *School Reunion*, devastating Sarah Jane Smith.

Kamelion's story doesn't have a happy ending. After enduring his second adventure as a mere tool, he's given the machine equivalent of a heart attack, and then asks the Doctor to kill him. Horribly, the Doctor does so without protest, even using the Master's trademark weapon, the Tissue Compression Eliminator. Ultimately, Kamelion is not celebrated but is perceived as a liability; and instead of safeguards for his fragile autonomy, he was exterminated.

Whether it's android, human-machine hybrid, or digital copy, when *Doctor Who* engages with artificial consciousness it's mostly to ask who, or what, has personhood, and how should they be treated? It offers contrasting views on whether or not a consciousness that exists as data is still a person, and on how sentient robots should be treated. The Doctor has been uncaring, complicit, and fiercely protective of artificial lives. Fault can be found with his lack of consistency on which lives are most valued, but it's a fault that's just as present in his treatment of flesh and blood people.

> '*The Time Lords. Look, they've sent me a new dematerialisation circuit. And my knowledge of time travel law and all the dematerialisation codes, they've all come back. They've forgiven me. They've given me back my freedom.*'
>
> The Doctor, *The Three Doctors* (1973)

For a show that embraces knowledge generally, science in particular, and the value of curiosity, *Doctor Who* also enjoys a nuanced view of technology, in how it can offer freedom, or dependence. The TARDIS itself sums it up: a machine that can travel anywhere in time and space, and yet the Doctor and companions are bound by its vulnerabilities and idiosyncrasies, and utterly dependent upon it for that freedom.

The show explores how ignorance of technology can be used to oppress a population, but with it they can fight exploitation, and free themselves. Technology can mean more choices, more safety, better understanding of the universe, but tends to go badly if the effects aren't really understood and responsibility is optional. Quick and easy technological solutions can risk freedoms dwindling, human critical faculties atrophying, or even fights for our very survival. It's with the tension between these two sides that *Doctor Who* concerns itself: how we will use technology, how will it tempt us, and how much will we give up for the sake of convenience?

One of *Doctor Who*'s most transparent allegories equating technology to freedom is the deliciously gothic tale *State of Decay* (1980). The Doctor lands on a planet where three vampire lords rule over a feudal society, and knowledge of advanced technology is deliberately suppressed. When the Doctor asks to speak with a scientist, he's told 'such things are forbidden'. But there are villagers fomenting a rebellion, and they try to understand the advanced tech that's been salvaged from a spaceship. Once the Doctor defeats the vampires, he repairs the technology to give the people 'all the knowledge [they'll] need to be a high technological society in no time.'

The lords have made knowledge of technology a crime, neutering the rebellion as it's unwilling to make overt moves without better technological understanding. 'The penalty for knowledge is death', even reading is forbidden, and the vampires are fully aware of how effective ignorance is as a means of control; equally, the rebels see education as their salvation, that knowledge itself is liberation.

The vampires select 'the best' of the villagers to be taken to their tower for food. In *The Krotons* (1968) there's a similar modus operandi. The brightest two of every generation are chosen from the Gond people to become 'companions of the Krotons'. It's 'the greatest honour' and involves having their mental energy drained before they're killed. Their selections perform a double-duty: giving the Krotons the power they need to reanimate themselves, and eliminating the most intelligent people in Gond society.

While the Krotons don't have strict laws against use of technology, they forbid anyone going outside, or asking about their secrets, and only allow the 'companions' to enter their domain. And they control what the Gond know absolutely: they've culturally conditioned them to use teaching machines when they are children to fill their minds with 'all [their] science, all [their] culture, everything [they] have has come from the machines.' The Doctor instantly calls it 'self-perpetuating slavery'; the entire meaning of what it means to be a Gond, of how they see their world and their place within it, is controlled by the Krotons. Technology is used to stifle ingenuity and critical thinking. Education is purely a means of control, and the highest honour is a death sentence. Intelligence and education aren't used as conduits for society to flourish and grow but as means to control it, and in the end be used as to exploit in order to sustain the ruling class.

But freedom via technology isn't always about saving yourself from getting eaten, sometimes it's about preventing strangulation, metaphorically. Efficiency is a word often used by artificial intelligences and those who make them, and generally means eliminating free will. But sometimes it's not a matter of taking over the world, it's about a system being so very efficient that it lacks resilience. One mistake, one failure, and society is devastated.

The Troughton era had a duo of these stories, offering two futures where human survival depended on a single technology. In *The Seeds of Death* (1969), T-Mat is a teleport system that is the quickest, easiest way to transport resources from one place to another, but that efficiency has cut away at society's resilience. A failure in T-Mat brings world trade to an immediate halt; medical shipments and food supplies are unable to reach their destinations. The situation quickly becomes desperate with major cities 'suffering severe food shortages'. Eventually the very system humanity relies on is used by the Ice Warriors as a means to attempt genocide, teleporting killer seed pods all over the world. If they'd waited a little longer, they needn't have bothered, the efficiency of the human technology would have done the job for them.

Failure of this one technology causing such a widespread disaster is a reminder that there is no perfect tech, and no perfect control. In the end, Earth is saved by a rocket, a defunct form of transport, only available because a bitter old scientist sick of being told what a fool he was for liking rockets, was secretly building one. T-Mat may have revolutionised the world, but slavish devotion to it as the one true solution left society terrifyingly vulnerable.

Things are a little more complicated in *The Ice Warriors* (1967), where humanity uses ionisers to hold back massive glaciers that threaten to overrun the planet. The opening scene shows how precarious the situation is. When there's a power stoppage the scientific team can't stabilise, they've no alternate means of halting the advancing glacier. An evacuation is immediately called for. Human society is utterly dependent on this one technology. Worse, it's given up critical thinking to the computer, with technicians reacting in horror at the idea of going against its recommendations.

In fairness, they may not have had much time to come up with a method to defend against the glaciers, and they definitely don't have the resources to research for an alternative. But the existence of these glaciers came about because society decided to fully embrace another technological advancement that also rendered it painfully fragile: artificial food. A 'great world computer' helped humanity figure out a more 'efficient' civilisation, and artificial food meant land used for farming could be repurposed for housing. And no one needed to grow crops any more. The science here may be rather questionable, but in the story the lack of plants meant carbon dioxide levels plummeted, and a new Ice Age began. The disaster was caused by dependence upon one single method of food production. On the bright side, at least this World Computer didn't have megalomaniacal delusions of ultimate power, merely users who accepted its authority without considering the long-term consequences.

When it first started, *Doctor Who* was meant to be an educational show, as well as exciting adventures in time and space. But while one could argue the educational angle was dropped pretty sharpish, the show never stopped teaching. It became less interested in knowledge, and more in critical thinking. And it never lost sight of how powerful knowledge is, and how it can both free, and enslave, a society.

> *'Progress? Don't listen to him. He means fatter profits for Global Chemicals. At the expense of your land!'*
> Professor Clifford Jones, *The Green Death* (1973)

The Green Death's BOSS was a megalomaniacal AI devoted to its company's profit margins, but it's far from the only advanced technology used to exploit humans for the accumulation of vast wealth. In *The Invasion* (1968) there's a similar desire for corporate power, but managing director Tobias Vaughn isn't interested in raising up a machine intelligence to rule – he wouldn't mind that job himself. And he's arrogant enough to believe he can use his alien allies as a means to take over the planet, since it's not enough that his company, International Electromatic, is already the biggest electronics company in the world. Marvellously, the Doctor is suspicious of him not because he senses evil, but because Vaughn doesn't blink enough; an imaginative idea to hint at his lack of humanity.

The Cybermen aren't artificial intelligences, exactly, but

they share a lot in common: an affinity for logic and efficiency, a lack of emotions, and the unshakeable belief that the world would be a much better place if they were in charge. And, like all their artificially intelligent predecessors, they have a method for controlling human minds to enforce their system. Vaughn's arrogance means he underestimates them, believes that he is in control of their supposed partnership because the Cybermen need the electronics his company produce for their plan. While Stevens turned on BOSS in the interests of humanity, Vaughn's change of heart is driven by self-preservation. Suddenly profit isn't quite so much fun when his own life is in danger; humanity has a depressing tendency to vary the value placed on human lives.

Vaughn shares BOSS's ideas on how to make a better world: 'uniformity, duplication. [His] whole empire is based on the principle. The very essence of business efficiency.' Delightfully, in the Doctor's TARDIS circuits that Vaughn is trying to repair he notes that 'there's a totally illogical factor in their construction'. Even in their use of tech, Vaughn and the Doctor are at ideological odds.

The danger in *Kerblam!* (2018) is the AI system running a warehouse, though the story gets oddly wishy-washy on this towards the end, and unconvincingly argues the real issue is an individual seeking to overthrow the system via violent means, not the system itself.

Kerblam! begins with the Doctor's delight at a space postman, known as the Kerblam man, arriving in her TARDIS, to deliver a package. She realises the delivery is actually a call for help, and travels to Kerblam, a moon of warehouses and mostly robotic workers. Recently, human staff have disappeared, and the Doctor discovers that the bubble wrap used in packaging has been weaponised. The culprit is revealed to be a worker who wants to incite a public backlash to robot workers taking human jobs.

Framing the system as not exploitative is a weird way to go as that's exactly how it's set up as soon as the Doctor arrives. The warehouse AI claims Kerblam's warehouses are 'fully automated, people powered', but the humans – the 'organics', as they're called here – are supervised by robots known as TeamMates, 'the friendly face of the System'. At least Judy, the Head of People, is in fact a person. It's her job 'to make sure everyone's happy' which she doesn't consider terribly difficult since they're 'all so grateful to have a job ... it's a privilege to work at Kerblam'. Such a privilege that workers are fitted with ankle bracelets that 'monitor productivity and report back to the System', there's 'no such thing as privacy' as the TeamMates can hear everything, and 'social interaction [should be] confined to leisure breaks' as 'unnecessary talking can lead to efficiency reductions'. One worker says that 'Work gives us purpose, right?' which is a little bit too close for comfort to 'work makes you free'.[150] And just to add to the unrelenting exploitation of the workers, they don't even have any legal recourse: 'Kerblam is its own jurisdiction.' And when things go wrong with the System, even the warehouse boss admits 'there's no one to report this to, no one to stop it. There's only the System.' The whole moon is shamelessly designed to trap workers in a system of economic exploitation.

The System lets the Doctor know when it's killed another worker, but this isn't a threat; the System itself is asking the Doctor to help it. It's the one that sent the original message. It's being forced to kill, and Charlie, the worker responsible for the deaths, is using fellow employees as test subjects for his plan to bring down Kerblam.

But he's not doing it with plans to take it over for himself, he doesn't want power or wealth, he's trying to end the

---

[150] *Arbeit macht frei'* were words infamously displayed over the gates of Auschwitz concentration camp.

economic exploitation. Only ten percent of the workers in the warehouses are people, and 'They want us to be grateful that ten per cent of people get to work? What about the other ninety per cent? What about our futures? Because without action, next time it will be seven per cent, then five, then one.' Charlie argues that it's 'imperfect technology, without a conscience.' Which is exactly where previous stories engaging with AIs complicit in economic exploitation have gone. But he isn't portrayed as someone trying to overthrow an oppressive system who should be condemned because he's using cruel and indiscriminate violence to do it. No, even his ends are portrayed as villainous. The Doctor argues he's 'let[ing] the systems take the fall for it, erode peoples trust in automation, make people angry' as though these are immoral goals, when people clearly should be very angry about what's happening in those warehouses.

The Doctor notes that the System does indeed have a conscience, but fails to point out it's a conscience that only extends so far as fighting mass murder. When it comes to workers' rights and welfare, it doesn't care. The System wasn't designed to commit murder; it was designed for economic exploitation. In that area, it performs perfectly.

Kerblam! is a depressing anomaly in *Doctor Who*'s engagement with technology. It dismisses the long-term damage to society by which the villain is motivated, and defends the systems used as a means of control. The Doctor argues that 'the systems aren't the problem. How people use and exploit the system, that's the problem.' She ignores that the systems have been designed to exploit, to prioritise efficiency over welfare, and corporate greed over workers' rights. The system is very much the problem.

Oxygen (2017), on the other hand, is *Doctor Who*'s most powerful condemnation of tech used as a corporate means of control. The Doctor, Bill, and Nardole arrive on a space station where oxygen itself is monetised. The company charges its employees by the breath and when profits slip, the station kills the crew. The station tech isn't inherently evil, it does exactly what it was programmed to do, and executes the company's policy with murderous efficiency. It enforces economic priorities by treating human lives as expendable. It's a deliciously striking story as it pushes *Doctor Who*'s engagement with capitalist exploitation to its logical extreme: you will be charged even for the air you breathe and if you can't pay, you die. The most fundamental aspect of survival is commodified. This is ultra-late capitalism, truly horrifying, and it echoes fears of current economic exploitation: the prices of food, electricity, even water continue to rise far faster than wages. When society doesn't make access to food and fresh water a basic right, we devalue human life. One can hardly look to ancient Rome as an exemplar in protecting human dignity, but the bread part of 'bread and circuses' is often overlooked: the grain dole system was designed to provide sustenance to the poorest in the city. The state was willing to take the hit on the cost, and it prevented mass famine in the Empire for centuries. Of course it wasn't perfect, but it seems absurd that two thousand years later, society has barely moved on to something better.

The programming of the computers in *Kerblam!* and *Oxygen* have chilling consequences, but both systems work exactly as intended. They're clear condemnations of human greed, and the horror that results when profit is put above human welfare. Most advanced technology in *Doctor Who* is controlled by people more interested in straightforward violence to achieve their aims, but technology aimed at control and reducing a human to their economic value, can be far more terrifying.

'We're all stories in the end.'

The Doctor, *The Big Bang* (2010)

But perhaps the most terrifying ones are used in a far more insidious way: they tell stories. Advanced technology that's made to script the very environment we live in, and by writing their own reality they get to control perceptions, beliefs, and truth. Why bother with brute force, when you can redefine reality?

In *Castrovalva* (1982), the Master traps the Doctor in a world created by maths. It's a place that he seems to have created so the Doctor can recover after his regeneration, so he has the chance to fully appreciate the Master's genius before he's killed. The city's inhabitants are beings constructed from mathematics, their lives scripted performances. And yet they believe themselves to be real. While BOSS or WOTAN aim for direct control over humanity, the Master's trap is both subtler and scarier. The people of Castrovalva are not overtly commanded, but are controlled by their perception of the world around them. While the Doctor and his companions are in Castrovalva, they too accept the reality of the city. Their autonomy is limited by their environment being so completely controlled.

One inhabitant of Castrovalva, the head librarian Shardovan, manages to see through it. He declares to the Master that 'you made us, man of evil, but we are free,' before he sacrifices himself to destroy the illusion. There's something profoundly moving, heroically chilling, from a fictional construct becoming self-aware enough to choose to destroy the illusion of his own existence. It's not the Doctor's escape that has the ethical weight in *Castrovalva* but Shardovan's refusal to be a pawn despite being a character in someone else's narrative.

Castrovalva raises the question of how to recognise the

truth if a machine can create a world so convincing that it's indistinguishable from reality. The answer is thematically satisfying: keep pushing at the story until you start to see the cracks in the narrative. The Doctor realises the truth when he notes that the old history books that chronicle Castrovalva from ancient times continue on until the present day, despite their great age. When the machine holding Castrovalva together is broken, it's Adric, who was forced to author the world, that can see through the chaos of the city collapsing into broken fragments, and lead the Doctor, Tegan, and Nyssa to safety. Castrovalva highlights the danger of allowing machines to define the stories we live by. As the Doctor, Shardovan, and Adric show, to resist them – to forge a truthful, meaningful path – requires both courage and critical thought.

Episode two of *The Keys of Marinus* (1964) makes a similar point, but in a much more straightforward way. The Doctor, Barbara, Ian, and Susan arrive in the city of Morphoton where they are received with great hospitality. But when they sleep, small discs are placed on their heads so the Brains of Morphoton can use their Mesmeron on them (some fabulous 1960s naming choices going on in this story). Barbara's disc falls off, so when they wake she sees the truth of the city: it's a miserable, squalid place. The others, however, are convinced it's full of luxuries.

The discs haven't harmed the travellers directly, they're not trying to suppress their will in the way BOSS or WOTAN were so into: they are still very much themselves but their sensory reality has been rewritten so rags are beautiful dresses, and dirty crockery is advanced scientific instruments. The power of these scenes is Barbara's isolation: her friends utterly refuse to listen to her. They react as though she's gone mad. And as the only one who can see they truth, she's perceived as a threat.

The Mesmeron offers comforting lies, a world where you can have everything you want, all you have to do is accept the illusion. Barbara utterly refuses to believe she might be the one mistaken, and despite none of her companions believing her, she fights to free them. Literally. She smashes up the protective domes the Brains live in, having fought off Ian trying to strangle her. It's a pretty epic Babs moment.

When comfort comes at the cost of autonomy, it should be questioned. Today we're curating our reality through algorithmic feeds that learn what we want and feed us more of it. We're constantly exposed to other people's curated realities, and in return feel pressure to curate our own. Perhaps we don't need to do a Barbara and smash up our computers, but *Doctor Who*, time and again, does suggest we should keep our critical faculties sharp, and ask questions about the stories we're told.

In *Wish World* (2025), from *Doctor Who*'s most recent season, exactly the same theme plays out. The Rani – an immoral Time Lord with a penchant for turning people into trees and creating giant brains – has facilitated the creation of a false reality on Earth. With the help of Conrad Clark, a conspiracy theorist, the world has been rewritten into a bizarrely ahistorical version of the fifties. Conrad has created an Earth where everywhere has nice weather, everyone gets to be warm and fed and have a family. But he doesn't even see disabled people, so they aren't caught up in his fantasy world of nice houses and decent food; he can't imagine trans people, so they simply don't exist; heterosexuality is compulsory; and women really shouldn't be working once they're married.

Wish World shows a world where autonomy has entirely collapsed – people make choices but are so utterly embedded in their false reality that those decisions have become meaningless. How can you have free choice when you're surrounded by a culture and ideals that have been chosen for you? The world has become a narrow, limited place, and the only people who can see the truth of it are those who don't fit in. Beyond warning about the fragility of reality, of our own perceptions being controlled, it also points at how the world already looks different to every single one of us. And those that are most disadvantaged are living on a very different planet, one that *Wish World* suggests is the more truthful as those are the people that can see through the illusion.

For a change of pace, *The Mind Robber* (1968), makes no secret about it being a fictious creation, in fact its location is named the Land of Fiction. The Doctor, Jamie, and Zoe explore a reality composed of stories: a wandering Gulliver, Rapunzel in her tower, the Minotaur at the centre of a labyrinth. It's all whimsical charm until a unicorn tries to gore them.

The Master Brain who rules the land can rewrite the characters at will, and it briefly rewrites Jamie and Zoe too, by squashing them inside a giant book, literally. They're threatened with violence, but the real danger is becoming fiction themselves. There's a fine metanarrative here: Jamie and Zoe, fictional characters, are scripted to lose their autonomy by being turned into fictional characters. There's also a painful prescience in the dependence the Master Brain, a computer, has upon a human mind in order to create its fictions. The writer it's linked to, Jack Harkaway, 'is the source of the creative power which keeps this whole operation going'. The Master Brain needs the 'boundless imagination' of a human mind to exist, much like the LLMs of today need to suck up the creativity of countless artists in order to increase their ability to regurgitate it.

Ultimately, the Master Brain battles the Doctor's own imagination as they engage in a duel of narratives, fiction fighting fiction. While it's distracted, Zoe takes the opportunity to blow up another computer. Having talked one to death in *The Invasion*, this time she overloads the Master Brain with too many keyboard clicks.

In this story, no-one needs to find the cracks in the fiction, but they do need to fight to define their own reality. And *The*

Mind Robber shows that even when you're aware of the trap, when you know that you're surrounded by curated images, algorithms designed to keep you scrolling, rage-bait titles to click, that doesn't mean immunity from the version of reality you're being offered.

Extremis (2017) makes the rather wonderful choice to have the viewer complicit in maintaining its false reality, as least on first watch. It's not until the final minutes of the episode that the world, and all the characters in it, including the Doctor, and companions Bill and Nardole, are revealed as part of a manufactured reality.

The Doctor is asked by the Pope to investigate a mysterious book, called Veritas. Everyone who reads it kills themselves. In the end, he discovers an alien race have created a false reality to help figure out the best way to invade Earth. Those who killed themselves did so as they realised they were living simulated lives in a simulated world, and their only purpose was to help an alien invasion.

The manufactured people are sentient, they have autonomy, and like Shardovan, they act to end their own existence to the detriment of their creators' plan. The simulated Doctor fights to get a message to his real self, his artificial life sacrificed in an act of courage. It hits the same notes as *Castrovalva*, expanding the ideas of both machine-written realities, and the value of the lives created within them. Artificial intelligences that try to take over the world get destroyed, and there's a solid moral argument for that, but the people of Castrovalva and the Extremis duplicates are just normal people getting on with their lives. Yet both their creators are using them for their own ends, reducing them to bait or test subjects. They are not seen as sentient beings, but as tools. Dehumanised and disposed of when no longer useful. And no-one mourns the loss.

'The trouble with computers, of course, is that they're very sophisticated idiots.'

The Doctor, *Robot* (1975)

If there's one thing that *Doctor Who* has to say about artificial intelligence, it's that you should not, under any circumstances, put it in charge. In the modern day that veers ever closer to a literal fear, but it also means the systems all around us that we have no control over, perhaps not even any understanding of. And sometimes it's about the horror of human lives being reduced to how economically productive they are, of efficiency becoming the only virtue.

From the Conscience in *The Keys of Marinus* to the Great AI Generator in *The Robot Revolution*, *Doctor Who* tells us freedom cannot be surrendered to machines, whatever the motivation of either the humans who want to impose such a system or the benevolence of the machine. Autonomy is fundamental for human life to flourish, and even a benevolent machine is vulnerable to corruption, and can lean into authoritarianism and murder when left to enforce what its logic circuits consider a perfect society.

It's easy to destroy an artificial intelligence that wants to take over the world, but the question is more complex when the AI is growing a conscience, or is tragically vulnerable. Whenever there's a story about androids, human-machine hybrids, or uploaded (or downloaded) minds, those questions about personhood come to the fore. *Doctor Who* never seems sure how much artificial lives are worth. But it's often not the AIs themselves that are portrayed as the greatest danger, it's the misuse or neglect of technology, or lack of consideration of long-term consequences. *Doctor Who* is insistent that human oversight must always be present, and so responsible use of technology also means that it can never be seen as neutral.

There's also a chilling amount of relevance to the present day in how technology is presented as a way of manipulating reality. The power and influence of The Algorithm is well known. It shapes what we see on social media feeds, offering up more and more of what we want, determined to keep us scrolling forever. Ragebait means clicks. Why bother with nuance when you can have the quick dopamine hit of anger? What we see shapes our reality, and *Doctor Who* often returns to the dangers of what happens when a manufactured reality becomes as convincing as the real world. It explores the idea that the greatest danger isn't machines capable of violence, or of ones that oversee dystopias, but ones that tell the stories of how we see ourselves, and we cannot even notice we're being rewritten.

Ultimately, the technology of *Doctor Who* is a reflection of the people who create it, control it, and use it. Evil is not a built-in feature, but it comes from the flaws and intentions of the design. And those flaws can become magnified with horrifying results. A desire for peace and order becomes authoritarianism; a means to extend life become stagnation; attempts to free humanity from menial labour becomes slavery of sentient machines. *Doctor Who* insists that tech is never neutral, but always an expression of human need, wants, and ambition. The question asked isn't what AI will do to us, but what we will do with AI, and what that says about humanity.

CHAPTER SIX
GIANT BRAINS AND ASCENDED LIGHT

Transhumanism

For a show about an ancient time-travelling humanoid that can renew themself by regenerating their body into a new form, *Doctor Who* has remarkably ambivalent views about transhumanism. When I say transhumanism, what I mean is humanity using new and future technologies to radically enhance ourselves beyond our natural limits, generally to improve our longevity, cognition, or physical abilities.

Doctor Who has always been fascinated with what it means to be human, and how humanity can exist when the body is reshaped, or stripped away; when the mind is enhanced, or overwritten; when the nature of the species itself is challenge by aliens or technology. Given how often it asks questions about extreme longevity, mind uploads, collective intelligence, and cybernetic upgrades, it has plenty of opportunity to overlap with transhumanist philosophy, and yet it rarely does so. In *Doctor Who*, a post-human existence is consistently portrayed as horror. It doesn't see transhumanism as improving the human condition, but as a threat to its existence.

From the Cybermen's upgrades to the genetically engineered Daleks, to the Nestene Consciousness embodying the transhumanist dream of no longer needing a physical body, to bodies so robust they'll endure until the end of the universe, *Doctor Who* dramatises hopes and fears with a gallery of post-human possibilities. It wants to know the cost to human autonomy and dignity that comes with being transformed beyond natural limits. It holds to the Enlightenment ideal that individuals should have freedom of self-determination, and that progress that cannot respect that is tyranny, transformation without consent is monstrous.

And it uses transhumanism to ask one very powerful question again and again: what makes humanity worth preserving in the first place?

> *'The most precious thing on this Earth is the human brain, and yet we allow it to die. But now, Cybus Industries has perfected a way of sustaining the brain indefinitely, within a cradle of copyrighted chemicals. And the latest advances in synapse research allows cyber-kinetic impulses to be bonded onto a metal exoskeleton.'*
>
> John Lumic, *Rise of the Cybermen* (2006)

The heaviest hitter in the show's discussion of transhumanist themes is also one of the Doctor's greatest adversaries: the Cybermen. They're introduced in *The Tenth Planet* (1966) – the swansong of the first Doctor, William Hartnell – where they invade the South Pole in the far, distant future of 1986. The implication that the Cybermen's path is a twisted reflection of humanity's is set up even before the Cybermen themselves actually appear. As the planet Mondas approaches Earth, the South Pole space tracking station discovers that its continents are a perfect mirror to ours. Mondas is Earth's twin planet. It drifted to the edges of the solar system aeons ago, and now it's back. (Let's not focus on the science too closely, just embrace the symbolic meaning.)

When the Cybermen finally appear, their costume design, despite budget restrictions, is far more than the sum of its parts. These early Cybermen were converted from organic to cybernetic a piece at a time. When the lifespan of their race began to shorten, the solution their scientists and doctors came up with was to devise 'spare parts for their bodies until [they] could be almost completely replaced.' And with each cybernetic augmentation, more of their humanity was stripped away.[151] Their flesh and blood hands are still visible, but their faces are covered by a cloth, hinting at ruined flesh beneath. They have black holes instead of eyes. And when they speak their lip movements don't match their song-song voices. The whole effect is deeply unsettling. They are so much closer to human than any other Cybermen seen in *Doctor Who*, and emanate a wrongness that creeps over you.

They're also pitiable in a way other Cybermen simply aren't. The ragged remnants of their humanity clings to mechanised limbs, fragile folds of cloth shield their faces, and they use names that once spoke of individuality but are now no more than designations. They've improved their bodies: they have super human strength, are able to deal with environments harsh enough to kill a human, they can survive disease and decay, but they are no longer even aware of what it has cost them. The easier it is for them to survive, the more they distance themselves from their humanity.

When the Earth is threatened, Polly's appeal to their empathy is met with cold indifference and painful logic. When she asks why they don't care about the millions of people in danger, their response concerns only their own situation: it doesn't affect them, so why should they care? And they get in an exquisite extra stab at Polly, saying 'they do not understand

[151] Yes, they are from the planet Mondas, not Earth. But humanity is a much more intuitive word than Mondasianess. Also, for bonus trivia, they refer to themselves as humans in the excellent Big Finish audio drama, *Spare Parts*.

[her]. There are people dying all over [her] world, yet [she] does not care about them.' She'd say she does, of course, and she'd feel she does, but like most of us, she doesn't spend her life trying to alleviate the suffering of others. The Cyberman's words suggest a binary – you help everyone or you help no one – and that binary echoes in their uncompromising attitude to survival: if you don't commit to it absolutely it means you want, even deserve, to die.

The Cybermen don't just reject empathy, they really aren't into feelings of any sort. Behind the metal, plastic, and cloth, they still have a human brain, but they've eliminated what they perceive to be weaknesses. 'Emotions!' declares the Doctor, 'Love! Hate! Pride! Fear! Have you no emotions, sir?' They claim superiority as they 'have freedom from disease, protection against heat and cold, true mastery', while humans will 'die, in misery'. That's what truly horrifies Polly; she was fearful of their appearance, but when they show their lack of empathy and believe it's a good thing, that's when they become truly alien to her.

The knowledge that the Cybermen used to be human, but there's no way to save them from what they've done to themselves, adds another unsettling layer. They're not framed as a strange alien race, but as a people who made a choice that carved out their humanity. Even more chilling is that they don't just believe this was the right choice, they believe it would be the right choice for you too. Taking your humanity to ensure your survival is doing you a favour. It makes no sense to their emotionless minds that durability could ever be rejected for frailty, that the clarity of pure logic should be rejected for the chaos of emotion.

Over fifty years after their original appearance this particular version of the Cybermen, now called Mondasian Cybermen, returned. There's always something thrilling about seeing a classic *Doctor Who* monster design reappear in a twenty-first-century episode virtually unchanged. While it was easy to expect the Daleks would keep their iconic silhouette, seeing Zygons, the Ice Warriors, or the Movellans return to the screen decades after their last outing with barely an alteration is immensely satisfying to someone who grew up with the original stories. But the return of the Mondasian Cybermen in *World Enough and Time* (2017) was a particular high point. A one-off monster design from 1966 returns to the show over fifty years later! And not just for the fannish fun of it. *World Enough and Time* takes that *Tenth Planet* creepiness and ratchets up to the skin-crawling grotesque. The Mondasians are patients in a hospital ward on board a massive colony spaceship. There're frail humanoids, their faces hidden beneath cloth bandages. They wear white gowns with a small chest unit, and have robotic voices that chant 'pain'. When they walk around, they're hooked up to canisters of fluid resembling IV drips. At the end of the episode, it's revealed that these pitiable, unnerving creatures are in the primitive stages of what would become cyber conversion. To drive the point home, elsewhere we see a small group of Mondasians living on the solar farm floor of the colony ship. Their close community, their friendships, offer a stark contrast to what's become of their brethren.

The idea of Cybermen wanting to convert others into their kind is never completely forgotten – there are brief nods to it in *The Tomb of the Cybermen* (1967), *The Invasion* (1968), and *The Five Doctors* (1983) – but it's rarely given enough prominence to feel truly threatening. *Attack of the Cybermen* (1986) is not a highly regarded story, but one of its most successful aspects is how it deals with cyber-conversion. Not only do we actually see several characters in the midst of conversation, but it introduces the fascinating idea that sometimes conversion fails. And *Attack*'s Cybermen aren't about destroying failures, they use them and their partially cyberized limbs as slave labour. But the story still fails to commit to the fully realised horror of what the Cybermen represent.

Rise of the Cybermen and *The Age of Steel* (2006) have no such reservations. Cyber-conversion is reimagined for the modern era, and it's the heart and soul of these episodes. While the Cybermen of *The Tenth Planet* have the feel of slow, steady degradation from human to machine, these Cybermen are ruthless in industrialising cyber-conversion so that the whole planet can be processed in a matter of days. In *Rise* humans are lined up and marched into factories where they are swiftly converted, or incinerated. There's even a slice of slasher film terror in the way the human body is implied to be butchered in mere moments, utilising some truly vicious CGI scissors and drills. Flesh is ripped away; brains are extracted and placed in the metal suits. What's more fun? Having your humanity snipped away a piece at a time, or being torn off all at once?

Rise and *Age* take place on an alternate Earth in a parallel universe. This world is not quite as inevitably doomed as Mondas, but the inhabitants do make a solid attempt at annihilating their humanity. Instead of a declining race desperate to survive, this is an Earth with a society and technology similar to our own. It's also got similar corporate power. Their Cybermen are not the desperate solution of scientists trying to save their people, but a product of Cybus Industries, who seek a means to achieve immortality. The director of the company, John Lumic, isn't motivated by the greater good or trying to uplift humanity. He's terminally ill, and terrified of his own mortality. You might think his situation should evoke some sympathy, but such feelings are understandably mitigated when he commits murder in his first scene. The people of Mondas were trying to save their species; Lumic's primary concern is saving himself.

Rise and *Age* present a transhumanist nightmare scenario: consent and morality are thrown out in favour of efficiently utilising all available means of technological enhancement to 'upgrade' humanity. The immortality that Cybus Industries seeks to achieve is at a cost that the UK President calls 'not just unethical, it's obscene.' It's an eternal life that strips away everything worth living for. But Lumic won't stop; he's 'governed by greater laws ... the right of a man to survive.' His rights, his choices, must not be limited, but others are there to be used. He calls the homeless 'useless and wretched', and claims that he 'saved them, and elevated them, and gave them life eternal'. And the first thing he does with his 'elevated' creations is have them commit mass murder.

Lumic doesn't care about consent. And he's passed that along to his creations. Like *The Tenth Planet* Cybermen, his 'everlasting children' believe that humans are having a rotten time of it. All the Cybermen 'think the same' but the humans have 'their difference and their pain. They suffer in the skin.' These newly-minted Cybermen generously offer 'every citizen ... a free upgrade.' And that includes Lumic. Despite creating them, despite insisting he only wants to be upgraded with his last breath, the Cybermen's directives have gone beyond what he intended, and what he wants no longer matters, only unity and uniformity.

The Cybermen offer a twisted version of the idea that we'll one day transcend flesh and bone. But the most compelling question about the Cybermen remains this: at what point did they lose their humanity? Some of these upgrades we'd be perfectly happy with, and have no moral compunction at accepting. Some of them are operations performed every day in the real world. Our bodies are cut apart and sewn back together. Diseased parts are chopped off, organs are removed and transplanted. Joints replaced with metal or plastic or ceramics. And there's no doubt that we are still fully human.

The Cybermen take this to the extreme, where they are able to replace each and every failing part of the body with a cybernetic upgrade, suppress emotions and pain, and yet the brain still functions.

In *The Tenth Planet*, flesh can still be seen within their steel, in *Rise* the entire body is ripped away leaving only the brain to be placed in a metal suit. To suggest the amount of organic tissue determines one's humanity is a nasty path to start upon, but this complete loss of the physical body does mirror the transhumanist aspiration of being free of one's biology. *Doctor Who* depicts the Cybermen as emotionless beings driven by nothing except a desire to survive and expand their state of being to other organic lifeforms. It argues that to be human is to be more than a mind, that sensation, aging and death are integral parts of our nature.

The attitude to emotions is much sharper. From their very first appearance emotion is held up as an explicit weakness that the Cybermen seek to correct. The Cybermen of the eighties may, on occasion, act in ways that contradict this, but since they do claim they still have no emotions, let's put it down to some odd programming quirks. They believe emotions lead to flawed reasoning. And by eliminating them they optimise their reasoning abilities. The Enlightenment ideal of exalting reason is twisted into a tragedy: without emotion, there is no compassion, no empathy, no pity. The qualities that make an ethical life possible are gone.

What part of the human continues to exist in the Cyberman? They think in uniformity, act as one, have no emotions. Individuality is meaningless. When the entirety of a person is overwritten, does any self still exist? If nothing of you continues to exist, then what is the point of survival? The tragedy of the Cybermen is what they were willing, or have been forced, to sacrifice to get there. They lost their bodies, their emotions, their free will, and their identities. But it's the latter three that are the ones that really matter. Science fiction has offered us more than one brain in a jar and they're treated as fully human (or, in *The Brain of Morbius*, fully Time Lord), easily accepted as people. In *Doctor Who* humanity is not found in the body, but in freedom to choose, and capacity to feel. It is found in our ability, and our willingness, to be imperfect. If you never feel any weakness, you have lost your humanity. To be vulnerable, to struggle, to be afraid, we need these. Lose them, and we lose ourselves. The Mondasians didn't see the line until they were far past it. They did not know when their survival became more important than their humanity.

How much of yourself would you give up to survive?

> '*I am known as the Great Healer ... I have conquered the diseases that brought their victims here. In every way, I have complied with the wishes of those who came in anticipation of one day being returned to life.*'
>
> '*But never, in their worst nightmares, did any of them expect to come back ... as Daleks.*'
>
> Davros and the Sixth Doctor,
> *Revelation of the Daleks* (1985)

The Daleks have some broad similarities to the Cybermen, beyond the long list of grudges they have against the Doctor. They too were once the sort of aliens who look entirely human, but shed large amounts of flesh and bone, and became utterly dependent on the machines attached to the remains of their biological form. But their route there, and the end result, is quite different. While the Cybermen sought to save themselves via mechanical means, the Daleks sought salvation through biological manipulation. While 'Cybermen suppress emotion, Daleks channel it through a gun.'[152]

---

[152] *The Witch's Familiar*

Davros, the Daleks' creator, began with a noble purpose: to ensure the survival of his race. On the planet Skaro, two humanoid species, the Kaleds and the Thals, were locked in their Thousand Year War. When he discovered the Kaleds mutating, thanks to chemical weapons, Davros 'started experiments to establish [the Kaleds'] final mutational form.' This form would ultimately become the Daleks.

The problem, as was quickly recognised by many in his science team, wasn't the ends but the means. Gharman, who served under Davros before starting a rebellion, objected to genetic changes Davros wished to introduce into the Daleks. He believed they would create 'creatures without conscience, no sense of right or wrong, no pity. They'll be without feeling or emotion' and that 'the whole project is immoral'.[153] Later the Daleks will become terribly emotional: hate, anger, more hate and more anger, are often expressed. Davros believed that 'one race must survive all others, and to do this it must dominate', and that 'when all the bickering and battling is over, the supreme victor shall be [their] race, the Daleks'.

Gharman, and those who supported him, believed in limits. The Daleks may not look pretty – he accepts that its form will be what his race evolves into – but his objections are to how they will feel. He'll support the project if Davros 'restores ... the conscience'. He believes 'the creature must have a moral sense, a judgement of right and wrong'. If the Kaled race is to survive, their Dalek form must have 'all the qualities we believe essential in ourselves'. He doesn't believe in survival at any cost, but that '[their] race will survive if it deserves to survive', and that means their mutated forms must have 'all the strengths and weaknesses that [they] have. Compassion and hate. Let it do good things and evil. But [they] cannot let it become an unfeeling, heartless machine.'

[153] *Genesis of the Daleks*

Gharman fights magnificently for the souls of his people but, ultimately, Davros wins, and the result is the species does indeed survive 'throughout all eternity',[154] despite the Doctor's numerous attempts at genocide. But it's a species that is utterly monstrous. In the Daleks, Davros seeks to create the 'perfect creatures',[155] ones that are destined for 'universal and absolute supremacy'.[156] In seeking that perfection he tries to eliminate everything he considers a weakness. He calls compassion 'a cancer';[157] he refers to respect, conscience, and pity as defects; 'irrational sentiment'[158] is mocked. But in his quest for perfection, for purity in his creations, he traps them in an endless cycle of refinement and extermination, not just of others, but themselves.

In *Resurrection of the Daleks*, Davros plans to 'build a new race of Daleks ... even more deadly', but his plans don't get very far before battle breaks out between his Daleks, and the faction loyal to the Black Dalek. When Davros returns in *Revelation of the Daleks*, he's turning humans into Daleks. The implied dehumanisation has become literal. But when the original Daleks find out about it, they head on over from Skaro to Davros's new home to take him back to stand trial.[159]

By the time of *Remembrance of the Daleks*, it's a full-on space war between two Dalek factions, each one convinced of their own purity, and destroying themselves for an impossible ideal. It's concluded with full-on mutual destruction when the Doctor blows up Skaro, then talks the final surviving Dalek to death.

154   *Genesis of the Daleks*
155   *Destiny of the Daleks*
156   *Genesis of the Daleks*
157   *The Witch's Familiar*
158   *Destiny of the Daleks*
159   Sadly, we don't hear anything more about the Dalek legal system. Though they do also put the Master on trial in *Doctor Who: The Movie*.

The Daleks of the New Series remain 'pretty obsessed'[160] about purity, and enthusiastically continue the cycle of self-destruction. The Daleks of *The Parting of the Ways* (2005) despise their own existence as they've been created from human genetic material; Dalek Sec is exterminated for creating Dalek-Human hybrids;[161] the definitely-completely -genetically-pure-this-time Paradigm Daleks of *Victory of the Daleks* exterminate their Dalek creators for being inferior; when a burst of regeneration energy reinvigorates all Daleks on Skaro in *The Witch's Familiar*, that includes the decaying clumps of Daleks in the sewer, who crawl out to kill their surface-dwelling brethren.

In seeking perfection, the Daleks don't evolve, they revolve. They're trapped in an endless loop of self-destruction; one so horrific they cannot even escape it via death.[162] Any threat is exterminated, and all other life is seen as a threat. Daleks seek survival through an impossible purity of their race and commit genocide to achieve it. And that extends to their genetic predecessors, and even their creator. Their drive to survive leads them to empire, to endless wars, and to destroy themselves in service of destroying others. The Daleks show the price of survival without concern for morality, for empathy, for mercy. Their attempts to perfect their bodies, their minds, their very nature, results in them being left to rot in their own flesh for eternity.

> '*It's the end ... But the moment has been prepared for.*'
> The Fourth Doctor's final words, *Logopolis* (1981)

While no one of sound mind would ever want to be

---

[160] The Doctor, *Revolution of the Daleks*
[161] *Evolution of the Daleks*
[162] 'Daleks can't die ... [they're] genetically hard-wired to keep on living, whatever happens.' Missy, *The Witch's Familiar*

a Cyberman or a Dalek, there are other options for transformation in the *Doctor Who* universe. And there is a particular type of transhumanism that usually means good things, not just in *Doctor Who*, but science fiction generally: turning into a shiny, glowing light.

Growing up in the nineties, sci-fi telly drilled this into me. *Star Trek: The Next Generation*, *Deep Space Nine*, *Stargate SG1*, *Farscape*, *Babylon 5* ... if you wanted to get some exciting posthuman abilities, and not come to a miserable end, you had to become radiant, literally. Then you'd either be benevolent, above it all, or perhaps a bit mischievous. But you wouldn't be evil. Nobody who's made of light could ever be evil.

And the biggest sparkly light in *Doctor Who* is the Doctor himself. Admittedly it wasn't always this way. Until the fifth Doctor burst into an explosion of white, it tended to be a quieter, more dignified affair when he regenerated. But with the 2005 series, the Doctor regenerating means being engulfed in a golden radiance, as their entire body is unmade and reborn in a new form. A nice humanoid form, no tentacles, or black holes for eyes. The process is portrayed as painful and disorientating and *wondrous*. And he always comes back as a humanoid, which doubles down on the imagery that signals you're one of the good transhumans: bright light, and human silhouette.

Rather wonderfully, regeneration – or renewal as it was called at the time – was introduced in the same story as the Cybermen, offering an immediate contrast between the transformations. The Doctor's physical weakness, his 'old body wearing a bit thin',[163] echoes the struggle of the dying Mondasians, but his new body was one of flesh and blood, and his flaws and weaknesses are remixed, but never cast off.

In the era of the tenth Doctor, there's a stark warning

---

[163] *The Tenth Planet*

about assuming that the Doctor's long life and vast knowledge equate to moral authority. While the Doctor is occasionally challenged by their companions, this era doesn't shy away from the idea of outsourcing moral choice to an acceptable transhumanist figure. The tenth Doctor ends up being treated not like an adventurer in time and space, but as a godlike figure, capable of granting humanity salvation.

In *New Earth* (2006) the Doctor's response to Novice Hame when she objects to him stopping her medical experiments is 'if you don't like it, if you want to take it to a higher authority, then there isn't one'. In 2006's *Last of the Time Lords*, Martha Jones travels the world as the Doctor's apostle, convincing the whole planet to pray for him. *Voyage of the Damned* heartily doubles down on the Doctor as Jesus imagery when he's lifted into the air by the ship's Heavenly Hosts. Over in the spin-off, *Torchwood: Children of Earth* (2009), Gwen Cooper offers a teary confession straight to camera about how the Doctor must look down on Earth sometimes and be so disappointed in humanity.

But in *The Waters of Mars* (also 2009) there is, at last, an acknowledgement that handing moral authority over to the Doctor is not the best idea. But it comes at a horrific price. Eventually, it reaches a point where, having taken actions that sufficiently horrified a scientist that she decided her best option is to shoot herself in the head, he realises that he'd make a bad god.

In its explicit form this idea of the Doctor as saviour lasts only a few years, but it's an idea that lurks, with the potential to rise up again, to show the depth of the human tendency to listen to anyone who has enough confidence: we don't trust ourselves, but this fellow from a few planets over seems to know what he's doing. Really though once you attempt your first genocide, the idea of holding moral authority over anyone becomes rather questionable.

The Doctor is far from the only golden glow of scary power in the *Doctor Who* universe. When Rose Tyler looks into the heart of the TARDIS in *The Parting of the Ways* (2005), golden light flows into her, and when she speaks her eyes shine, god-like, as she disintegrates a Dalek fleet. After Astrid Peth falls into the engines of the Starship Titanic in *Voyage of the Damned* (2007), she returns as specks of light, as 'an echo with the ghost of consciousness ... star dust' and flies out into space. Joy Almondo saves the world by transforming into golden energy in *Joy to the World* (2024). The third Doctor story, *The Mutants* (1972), has Ky, a native of the planet Solos, transform from a mutated being into a colourful glowing form capable of telepathy. The Doctor gets some extra oomph in *Last of the Time Lords* (2007) as the people of Earth's happy thoughts give him a soft blue glow, the power of flight, and a shield against laser weapons. The power of the glow cannot be underestimated, even in mere objects. In *The Rings of Akhaten* (2013), Clara Oswald's leaf represents the memories of the life her mother could have led if she'd not died prematurely. And it turns into enough glowing energy to satiate a sentient sun.

But some glowing transhumanism is better than others: Astrid and Joy pay for their uplifting with their lives, and Rose would have died from hers had the Doctor not taken it from her and sacrificed himself in her stead. The glow is good, but it's not safe, at least not for ordinary humans.

But Time Lord regeneration? That's okay. And not just for the Doctor. The Master regenerates with the same explosion of light in *Utopia* (2007), deliberately choosing to become 'young and strong.' But when he tries to live beyond his natural regeneration cycle, he's reduced to stealing corpses[164] or transforming into a goo snake.[165] An ability gained by evolution is

---

[164] *The Keeper of Traken*
[165] *Doctor Who: The Movie*

acceptable, but deliberate transformation to artificially increase abilities tends to go horribly wrong. Or at least that was in the case until *The Timeless Children* (2020), when we saw that Time Lord regeneration was stolen from another species by experimentation. Meanwhile the daughter of companions Amy Pond and Rory Williams, River Song, could regenerate because she was conceived aboard the TARDIS. Continuity is for lesser television shows that haven't been going over sixty years. Most of the time though, regeneration's golden light leans into classic Western iconography, indicating divinity, wisdom, and enlightenment. This is a glow that doesn't annihilate the self, but renews it, its warmth a stark contrast to the cold, sterile transformations of the Daleks or Cybermen.

The other safer option for transhumanism is to remain a humanoid. Ideally, keep looking exactly like a human, it will greatly increase your chances of also keeping hold of your humanity. Jack Harkness has immortality forced upon him when Rose Tyler took the Time Vortex into herself and brought him back to life. He's got a lot of angst about that immortality, but those feelings of guilt and regret mean he never loses his humanity. River Song manages to overcome a childhood where she's conditioned for a single purpose: kill the Doctor. And yet eventually she becomes someone who's heart is mostly in the ballpark of the right place. While Me (neé Ashildr), is a young Viking accidently made immortal by an alien repair kit, and she makes it all the way to the end of the universe, sanity intact. In *Hell Bent* (2015), she runs off in a TARDIS with companion Clara Oswald, who is sort of dead, sort of immortal. She's held in the last moment of her life – no heartbeat, no breathing, and no aging – until she returns to the Doctor's homeworld of Gallifrey. None of these people took on their long lives, or sort of deaths, willingly. And none of them have tried to augment themselves beyond their unnaturally long lifespans.

But there are humanoids who've had much more unpleasant experiences with immortality. The difference is, they deliberately pursued it. In *The Five Doctors* (1983), Rassilon, the Time Lord founder, came to the view that 'immortality was a curse, not a blessing' and set a trap to lure those who sought it into his tomb, and turn them into living stone faces. Immortality achieved, at terrifying cost. Meanwhile, *Mawdryn Undead* (1983) shows that while Time Lord regeneration is all very well for Time Lords, if you try to steal it for yourself, you will suffer. The titular Mawdryn is one of a group of scientists who stole Time Lord tech in an effort to gain the power of regeneration for themselves. It worked spectacularly: they became immortal. But it left them in constant pain. By the time the Doctor encounters them, all they want to do is die. The Elders in *The Savages* (1966) are more successful. Everything's peachy for them, as they cheerfully steal the life energy of the so-called Savages to keep themselves alive indefinitely. When they suck out some of the Doctor's life energy, the influence is enough to turn the Elders' leader against the abhorrent practice. No more immortality for them. At least they escaped a horrifying punishment.

But even Time Lords can make big, immortality related, mistakes. In *The End of Time* (2009), the once wise Rassilon returns, with a far less sensible plan: rip apart all of time and space, and ascend all the Time Lords he likes to beings of pure thought. Survival trumps empathy for everyone else in existence. He's not the only Time Lord who can't accept his limitations: for most of the classic series the Master is driven by his desperate need to survive. Rather than dying when his original regenerations run out, he exists as a decaying husk in *The Deadly Assassin* (1976) and *The Keeper of Traken* (1981). First, he seeks to renew himself using the source of Time Lord power, the Eye of Harmony, and when that fails, he steals a body, allowing him to shed his decayed form and constant pain, and acquires a 'rubbish beard'[166] and penchant for black velvet. When we think of a glorious transhumanist future, I doubt many consider wearing corpses.

It could be worse. He could be Omega, the first of the Time Lords, according *Wish World* (2025).[167] Originally a solar engineer, he created the supernova that gave the Time Lords the power they needed for time travel. He was thought to have died in an explosion but was instead thrown into a universe of antimatter. Existing alone for countless millennia, he's driven mad, and is desperate to escape. After his first attempt fails, in *The Three Doctors* (1973), he briefly manages to succeed in *Arc of Infinity* (1983). He has a short walk around Amsterdam in a duplicate of the Doctor's body. He seems to take pleasure in his brief freedom, commits one murder, has a nice walk, and listens to a steam organ, before his body begins to revert to antimatter. His latest escape in *The Reality War* (2025) has him emerge from the Underverse, a plain hidden below our universe, as a giant skeletal, sort of dinosaur creature. And he now wants to eat the world. Literally, it seems. At least in his previous two appearances he could just about manage a civilised conversation. His immortality has degenerated him from a mad man it was possible to pity, to a monster.

As it took around ten million years[168] for Omega to make his first attempt to get home, one can understand why he made some questionable choices along the way. It's a painfully long, tragic story, and the poor guy didn't even try to be immortal, not really; he went mad from loneliness. He just wanted to get back to his own universe, and his own people.

[166] *Time Crash*
[167] Yes, Rassilon is the Time Lord founder, and Omega is the first of the Time Lords. That's the sixty-year continuity *Doctor Who* fans know and love.
[168] In *The Ultimate Foe*, the final story of the *The Trial of a Time Lord* season, the Doctor claims that the Time Lords have had 'ten million years of absolute power'.

And he was sufficiently angry about his whole situation that he just refused to die.

But perhaps if one's transhumanist aims are a little lower than eternal life, they'll fare better? In *Time Heist* (2014) we finally see some nice, ordinary transhumans. They're just regular people, committing regular grand larceny, and while one might question their life choices, nobody has issues with their cool implants.

The Doctor and Clara are off to rob an impregnable bank. Along for the ride are two transhumans, Psi and Saibra. Psi has an augmented brain and is able to erase his own memories, and he deletes his memories of friends and family in order to protect them, should the robbery fail. Saibra is a mutant (though she still looks human, most of the time) and is able to shapeshift into any living being she touches. Both of them get to have an exciting adventure with the Doctor and Clara, not be condemned for their artificial abilities, and go back to their own lives at the end of it. Their bodies have had a gentle nudge of transhumanism, one that doesn't try to remove their mortality or emotions, and Psi and Saibra remain human. This sort of modest enhancement is permissible, but when we reach towards heights that we once thought the province of the divine, it's then that we falter, and fall.

> *'There are some corners of the universe which have bred the most terrible things ... They must be fought.'*
>
> The Doctor, *The Moonbase* (1967)

For thousands of years humanity has used monsters as a means of coping with and better understanding our fears and anxieties, our existential terrors and moral failings. As I mentioned, in *Doctor Who*, one of the biggest protections you can have against transhumanism working out badly is to keep a humanoid shape. The further you move from a human form, the more likely you'll lose the qualities that *Doctor Who* argues are essential for personhood, for a life that has meaning: Individuality, empathy, the awareness and perception of living in a physical body. In the show, the senses and the limitations of our bodies are integral to our existence as conscious beings. They are foundational to how we understand the world, ourselves, and each other. And when they are cast off, or mutated into a monstrous form, so is what it means to be human.

Many monsters in *Doctor Who* examine fears of post-humanism eliminating the human body. While the Daleks and Cybermen speak to body horror at what we could become, some of *Doctor Who*'s other well-known monsters look directly at lifeforms who've achieved the transhumanist dream of completely casting off a biological form. But instead of transcendence, these disembodied minds are portrayed as hollow, deranged, with no desires except to dominate and consume.

The two big baddies of the non-corporeal alien intelligence variety are the Nestene Consciousness and the Great Intelligence. The Nestene are best remembered for inhabiting the shop window dummies of a very unfortunate high street in Jon Pertwee's first story, *Spearhead from Space* (1970). They smash the windows, reveal hidden guns in their hands, and shoot down every person they see in the sort of massacre that's making a bona fide attempt to traumatise eight-year-old viewers. The Nestene may exist without a physical form, but they have a 'remarkable affinity for plastic'.[169] In *Terror of the Autons* (1971), aside from plastic dummies, they inhabit plastic daffodils, a troll doll, an inflatable chair, and a telephone cord. They use each form for no other purpose than to kill. They move, they murder, but they cannot feel. The Doctor

---

[169]   *Terror of the Autons*

calls them 'ruthlessly aggressive [and] intelligent'. Beyond that, their existence is devoid of meaning. Their need for physical presence has led them to inhabiting synthetic bodies, made of a material that we dispose of every day. And in order to reclaim a true physical body, it requires the devoted assistance of human workers.[170]

The Great Intelligence shows no interest in plastics, but a charming penchant for pretending to be Yeti. In its first two appearances, *The Abominable Snowmen* (1967) and *The Web of Fear* (1968), it controls robots that mimic the fluffy cryptids. This makes a lot of sense for *The Abominable Snowmen*, set in Tibet; and slightly less sense, but an awful lot of fun, for *The Web of Fear*, which is set in the London Underground. Many years later, it's switched to taking on the shape of snowmen, in the very appropriately titled *The Snowmen* (2012).

The Doctor describes the Great Intelligence as 'a sort of formless, shapeless thing floating around in space'.[171] Like the Nestene Consciousness, it embodies the dream of the mind shedding the need for a physical body, and like the Nestene, it finds itself a parasite that requires hosts so it can act in the physical world. Both have no need of physical bodies, but they exist within the physical world. Rather than their disembodiment raising them to a new level of existence, they haunt that world. They are ghosts that cannot move beyond their need for physical existence. Both are portrayed as forms of hive consciousnesses, but without individuality or physical form, all they have left is survival. These are vast, disembodied minds that have been corrupted and diminished by their formlessness, and their freedom from physical deterioration has disconnected them from empathy, pleasure, and ethics.

In the mid-seventies three stories engaged with physical

---

[170] *Spearhead from Space*
[171] *The Web of Fear*

transformations that offered forms of immortality and upgraded thought, but were twisted into transhumanist nightmares. It's a trio that explores broadly similar themes at different grotesque angles as three wildly different aliens 'uplift' humanity is some delightfully morbid ways.

In *The Ark in Space* (1975), from Tom Baker's debut season, the far future remnants of humanity are under threat from the alien Wirrn, a giant insectoid species. Space Station Nerva is the titular ark, and it's filled with cryogenically frozen humans. Before life on Earth was destroyed by solar flares, these lucky humans were specially selected and evacuated to the ark to make sure humanity survived. The plan was to sleep for five thousand years, wake up, then repopulate Earth. Unfortunately, the alarm clock broke, and they've overslept by several thousand years. Their insect visitor, a Wirrn Queen, decides an excellent use for the sleeping humans would be as hosts for her eggs. And when the eggs hatch, the larvae have a nice fresh frozen meal to snack on.

Fortunately, the Doctor is there to assist humanity in jumping over this extinction event. But before the Wirrn Queen is blown up, the leader of the ark, Noah, is infected and transformed into a Wirrn. Going from human to insect alien may not immediately sound like an upgrade, but the Wirrn do have some remarkable abilities. They're able to survive in the vacuum of space for years, and possess both racial memories and the memories of whatever hosted their egg. Once infected, Noah refers to himself as one of the missing, presumed digested, crew members, a suggestion that the surviving memories within the hive have some sense of an identity. In his final moments, Noah struggles to act against the Wirrn Queen, despite his completed transformation, showing the continued existence of his human personality in his new insectoid form.

It may not be the sort of immortality dreams are made

of, but there is a version of eternal life for those eaten or infected by the Wirrn: your memories will live on forever within the swarm, and perhaps even some sense of self. So long as the swarm exists, so will a part of you, transferring down the centuries, Wirrn to Wirrn. Human memories in a life form no longer human. The dream of immortality is subsumed into an alien whole, and whatever is left of identity, of self, is trapped within.

The Seeds of Doom (1976) is probably the least appealing of these three transformations. Perhaps one might be desperate enough for any sort of immortality to become a space insect, but being transformed into a giant, genocidal plant that uses people for compost may be a step too far. When an alien Krynoid pod is found deep beneath the ice in Antarctica, one of the discovery team are infected. The unfortunate scientist, Winlett, begins growing a green fungus on his skin, and his blood is contaminated with plant bacteria. Eventually he succumbs to the transformation process, and becomes a Krynoid.

What poor Winlett has involuntarily provided are the building blocks for a creature intent on replacing humanity as the apex predator on Earth. Humans are transformed into Krynoids, and those Krynoids sustain themselves by feeding on humans. It's the biological equivalent of the technological singularity – a hypothetical point where technology is capable of increasing its own intelligence to become so far beyond our own, we can no longer understand it. And such a superintelligence could result in our extinction. The Krynoid offers a vision of a ferociously nasty extinction event for humanity via posthumans unable to relate to their original species.

In *The Invisible Enemy* (1977) the alien menace is shaped like a giant shrimp, but it's considerate enough to have lesser physical changes in mind for the humans it recruits to its cause. Nobody wants to be a giant space insect (probably) but at least there's some dignity to a fully grown Wirrn, a certain regalness to its form; but a giant space shrimp is just silly. For most of the story that shrimp, called the Nucleus, is very small. Microscopically small. It's only towards the end that it enters macroscopic world, and its full magnificence can be properly appreciated.

Being infected with the Nucleus's virus is the least horrifying transformation offered in these three stories. All you have to go through is a growth of silvery scales and feathers around your forehead and eyes. Easily covered up by a pair of goggles. And at the right sort of party, you'd look absolutely splendid.

The down side is that you will be part of a collective with no individual will. The virus that the Nucleus controls moves swiftly from victim to victim, taking over minds but retaining memories as it forces its victims to spread its influence to new hosts. The virus allows seamless communication, sharing of knowledge, and a unified purpose, but these come at the cost of individuality. Humans yearn for connection, and the idea of being able to link one mind to another is often portrayed as intimacy, an end to loneliness, or a purer, more honest way to communicate, but here that idea is twisted. Collective purpose, perfect understanding, comes at the price of autonomy. *The Invisible Enemy* offers a look at the anxiety of shared consciousness resulting in a loss of self. If humans are able to connect in such a way, how can the individual survive? The story shows the merging of minds into a single consciousness not as a transcendent experience, or an exalted leap in cognition, but a contagion that annihilates self.

The horror that links these stories is the lack of consent. That fear that if there are leaps forward in what technology can do to enhance human abilities, we could be forced to undergo them whether we liked it or not. When the Cybermen force upgrades upon their victims, they do it by ripping their bodies apart via mechanical means. Here, it's biological invasion; our flesh and blood are not taken but are rewritten. Each time we gain longevity, purpose, and knowledge but lose our sense of individuality.

But like the Mondasians there are some occasions where humans choose those horrific transformations for themselves. One of the most terrifying of *Doctor Who*'s monsters, at least for me, are the Toclafane from *The Sound of Drums* and *Last of the Time Lords* (2007). They are the final form of humanity before the end of the universe. And even taking into account it's the end of everything, the final gasp of sentient life is still a nihilistic horror show. Each Toclafane is a human head wired into a floating metal sphere, and armed with a combination of ancient and futuristic weaponry: blades and lasers. They can survive in the vacuum of space and, while they're not emotionless, their emotional complexity has been stripped away leaving them violently cruel and child-like; they can giggle, and murder as they giggle.

Humanity's remnants saw the greatest of ends approaching, and tried to live in spite of it, but there's no dignity, no beauty or peace, to these final moments. Instead, in their desperation to survive the last humans succumbed to the same horror as the Daleks and the Cyberman. They stripped away their bodies, their feelings, their vulnerabilities, stuck their heads in metal casings, and called it life.

It's not the first time *Doctor Who*'s shown the last of humanity, at least according to one individual. In *The End of the World* (2005) there's even a pinch of positive transhumanism. Lady Cassandra, the villain of the piece, considers herself to be the last human, but acknowledges there are others in the galaxy who consider themselves human. She says 'they call themselves New Humans and Proto-humans and Digi-humans, even Humanish, but you know what I call them?

Mongrels.' Unlike them she 'kept herself pure'. New Humans? Digi-humans? Those sound like the briefest of glances into a transhuman society that isn't a hellish nightmare. Alas we never meet those guys, only Cassandra, who's transhuman herself, but she's not the ideal example of a transhumanist dream. She's a piece of skin stretched across a frame. Her brain is kept in a jar tucked in beneath.

The Lady Cassandra has undergone seven hundred and eight plastic surgeries to achieve her signature look, and she's proud of it. Her extreme vanity has consumed her; her fear of being seen as anything less than beautiful has been 'nipped and tucked and flatted till there's nothing left.'[172] She's presented as a grotesque comic figure, one that leans into tragedy when she reappears the next year in New Earth (2006). And she is tragic: she's chopped down to a piece of skin and a brain, utterly dependent on servants to keep her moisturised so she doesn't tear apart, all in a futile effort to cling to youth.

And she's cheerfully going to commit mass murder to get the money she needs to keep going with those surgeries. She may not have lost her emotions, but they're warped around her fear of aging, extinguishing her empathy. Unlike the Cybermen, she's only made more fragile by her improvements, although she too seeks to deny death. But whether or not she's still human is not such a straightforward question. Rose Tyler says she's nothing but a 'bitchy trampoline'. Cassandra, of course, is adamant she *is* human. And she enthusiastically consented to her physical changes. Her emotions are intact and while she's lived a long time her body is very vulnerable. So, is she still human? Yes. Her consent hasn't been violated, she still possesses weaknesses, she can still feel. She's not a monster; she's just a truly awful person.

This question of what it means to be human is raised

---

172   *The End of the World*

more directly, and at a more sympathetic angle in the two-parter *The Rebel Flesh* and *The Almost People* (2011). At an acid factory situated on a remote island, programmable matter – known as the Flesh – is used to create doppelgangers of the workers. These doppelgangers are controlled by the workers, and used as their proxies in a hazardous environment that would kill a human. A solar flare strikes the facility, causing the doppelgangers to gain sentience. At first, they're completely unaware of their true nature, and believe themselves to be the original humans. But when they find out that they were not born but created from technological goop, they immediately assert their personhood.

Meanwhile, the humans struggle to see them as anything more than tools to be used and discarded, comparing them to cars or cranes, calling them 'things'. But the Gangers, as they're called, are not simply copies: they have the same 'personalities, emotions, traits, memories, secrets, everything' as their originals. As one Ganger puts it, 'I am Jennifer Lucas. I remember everything that happened in her entire life. Every birthday, every childhood illness. I feel everything she has ever felt and more. I'm not a monster! I am me.' Those final two sentences sum up the entire concept, and what the episode asks: human, or monster? In this story, it's not a very difficult question. Right from the start the Gangers evoke sympathy. Even before they display sentience, we see them in pain as their faces are melted by electricity. And the Doctor draws his line right from the start that, yes, the Gangers are indeed people.

But the humans are terrified, and turn to violence, while the Gangers' feelings of betrayal and fear are just as real, and to show off more of their humanity, they too turn to violence. The humans feel violated: their sense of identity, their uniqueness has been attacked. Meanwhile, the Gangers desperately want to live, and, being exact copies, they know that's something the humans are unlikely to get behind. They're trying to survive while figuring out their own sense of who they are. Both sides show compassion and empathy, cruelty and violence. *The Almost People* refuses to draw a straightforward moral line between Humans and Gangers.

The story also confronts the horror of one's own sense of self being destabilised. To no longer be unique, to see yourself standing before you and know that they know everything you know, feel everything you feel, are even thinking what you are thinking, is quite the attack on one's ego defence mechanisms. While the Cybermen and Daleks alter their physical selves and mess around with their emotional range, the Gangers are technology that's acquired not just consciousness, but the consciousness of people who already exist. Ethically, ideally, being able to accept the co-existence of multiple selves seems to be the way forward, but the story is left on a note of hope, not resolution: the Doctor encouraging the survivors to speak out about the Gangers. The danger in this version of transhumanism isn't the annihilation of self, but how its multiplication can fracture its meaning.

A few years later the question of self is turned upon the Doctor, in the penultimate episode of season nine, *Heaven Sent* (2015). The Doctor is mysteriously transported to an abandoned castle, and tries to piece together where he is and what he's doing there from the strange clues he finds around the place: a skull, the word 'bird', a room labelled 12, and a strange, hooded figure that haunts the castle. Eventually, he figures it out: there's a wall of azbantium – a substance that's 'four hundred times harder than diamond' – that he must break through to escape. Slight problem, he has no tools, no weapons, just his fists, and he's only able to strike the wall once before the hooded figure mortally wounds him.

But Time Lords die slowly, and he figures he's got about thirty-six hours before the end, which is just enough time for him to crawl back to the transporter where he first teleported in. There, he incinerates himself to generate the energy needed to teleport in 'a copy of [him] on the hard drive. [The Doctor] exactly as [he] was, when [he] first got here.' This new, identical in every way, Doctor transports in, and the cycle begins again.

Every cycle the Doctor is able to punch a few more molecules off the azbantium wall. Sounds like he's going to take a very long time to break it. He does: it's over two billion years until he makes his final punch, and escapes.

And we're left to ponder whether or not the man who escapes is still the Doctor. The one that we are certain is the Doctor, the first one to teleport into the castle, has been dead for billions of years by the end of the episode. But like the Gangers before him, every Doctor after that is a perfect copy in mind and body. Each one has all the knowledge and experience, instinct and feelings, of the Doctor.

In the sea that surrounds the castle there are countless skulls piled up beneath the waves to drive home the sheer scale of the Doctor's sacrifice. Every skull is his. Every skull belonged to a man who refused to give up, and who eventually realised he was a few hours of life in a two billion year long journey. *The Rebel Flesh* offered a single human copy and told us, yes, this is the same person. Now there are countless remains of the same man. Are they all the Doctor? Or did our Doctor die two billion years ago?

'You know, you're a classic example of the inverse ratio between the size of the mouth and the size of the brain.'
The Doctor, *The Robots of Death* (1977)

Too often in *Doctor Who*, monstrosity is tied into shape. Humanoids are people, sometimes evil people, but people; everything else is a little bit suspect. It's a useful visual shorthand for television, and it's part of over two thousand years of human philosophy where the monstrous are inhuman, and those with bodies outside what's socially determined as normal as the monsters. From Plato through to the present day there has been a correlation between physical abnormality and moral corruption. It's only more recently that this has been met with widespread critique that discusses how using monsters in this way enforces otherness, to encourage an us and them attitude. Monsters allow fears to be externalised, examined, confronted, but they can also make ethical engagement cheaply skate more complex ideas about human nature.

Doctor Who does sprinkle in the odd subversion: the beautiful Drahvin from *Galaxy 4* (1965) turn out to be cruel and violent; the Axons in *The Claws of Axos* (1971) first appear as benevolent golden humanoids, deliberately using human bias to trick them into believing they're the good guys; in *The Creature from the Pit* (1979), the terrifying monster stuck in the pit is actually a convivial alien ambassador who'd come to negotiate a trade agreement. But the most delightful way that *Doctor Who* shows a bit of ambiguity about shape and monstrousness is through its giant brains.

Giant brains have been a staple part of transhumanist themes in science fiction for a very long time. They tend to be evil giant brains: a symbol of all humanity being cut away, leaving only cold intellect, or at least a real deficiency of empathy. Given that the brain is the source of both emotion and thought, it's not the most logical of concepts, but in science fiction we don't feel with our brains, we feel with our bodies, with the heart. And if a brain gets bigger, it's not because it's acquiring more compassion, wonder, or joy; it's because it's getting smarter and you can't become a super-intelligent space genius without crushing all those pesky little emotions holding you back. Giant brains don't need love, they need an ultra-pragmatic, ultra-cold personality that has an unhealthy superiority complex and likes to patronise beings who still have the temerity to laugh.

The original pilot for *Star Trek* (1966), *The Cage*, both gave us classic big brain characters with cerebrums vastly larger than the human norm, and cold intellects and unfettered arrogance to match. *The Outer Limits* (1963) episode, *The Sixth Finger*, had a Welsh miner mutated into a big-brained future human, who didn't think that was good enough and wanted to be 'a vortex of pure intelligence in space'; meanwhile, the big brain aliens in *The Twilight Zone* (1962) episode, *To Serve Man*, make the Earth a paradise to fulfil their far more modest ambition of cooking humans for supper. *Blake's 7* (1978) has a giant mass of brain that 'must expand to live' in the dubious series three episode *Ultraworld*; while the *Farscape* (1999) episode *My Three Crichtons* brilliantly contrasts the big-brain, no-feelings, future-Crichton's intellect and casual attitude to killing lifeforms he considers inferior, with the warm, fuzzy compassion of caveman Crichton.

One of the earliest examples of this trope is to be found in H. G. Wells's novel *War of the Worlds* (1898) where 'intellects vast and cool and unsympathetic' make war upon the Earth. These Martian invaders have 'beyond dispute the actual accomplishment of such a suppression of the animal side of the organism by the intelligence.' They're mostly brain, with a few tentacles. As it turns out, that's all you really need to invade another planet. The Martian invaders in *Mars Attacks!* (1996) have more body bits, but their brains are pretty easy to spot as they start zapping humanity. Meanwhile, on Venus, the Treens are ruled by the giant-brained, atrophied body, Mekon, the arch-nemesis of British comic hero, Dan Dare.[173]

Doctor Who itself offers a plethora of extra-large

---

[173] *Eagle* comic, first published in 1950.

brained creatures. The Cyber Controller in *The Tomb of the Cybermen* implies its logical powers are even more logical than normal Cybermen with its elongated head. While Dalek Sec transforms from a regular Dalek to a very large tentacled brain attached to a human body in *Daleks in Manhattan* (2007). The desperate scientists in *Mawdryn Undead* have misused Time Lord tech and ended up with their mutated, oversized brains bursting out of their skulls. But they all pale in size to *Doctor Who*'s giant brains of *Time and the Rani* (1987), and *Planet of the Ood* (2007). And it is to these epic forces of thought we now turn.

Big brain number one is to be found in the seventh Doctor's debut, *Time and the Rani* (1987). Immediately after regenerating the Doctor is drawn into a scheme of the Rani's: she's a brilliant, amoral Time Lord, who's decided she'd like to construct a planet-sized time manipulator, and she needs the Doctor's help to succeed. She's created a truly massive brain, one that could be at home in a kaiju's head, and fed it with the minds of geniuses from across space and time. If she succeeds, she'll turn the whole of the planet Lakertya into a 'cerebral mass capable of dominating and controlling time anywhere in the cosmos'. That's a very big brain indeed.

Her original giant brain has been designed for research beyond the capabilities of a single mind. Rather than have its own consciousness, it's a receptacle for multiple brilliant people. It's an attempt at a posthuman collective mind, except instead of a lot of people chilling together in a computer chip, it's a lot of people harmoniously thinking deep thoughts in a quivering mass of cerebral tissue. But they're no longer harmonious when the Doctor joins them. Suddenly the single calm voice of the brain's gestalt consciousness is a mess of arguing individual personalities, and the loudest of them is the Doctor. A collective consciousness might suggest images of unity, peace, a single combined will, but here it's driven to a confused madness by one mind that has the sort of personality that just doesn't merge well with others.

It's also a visually disturbing home for one's consciousness – a pulsating, immobile, disembodied brain – and, rather more importantly, ethically repugnant. The great minds plugged into the big brain are not there voluntarily. They've been stripped of their autonomy and individuality to provide superior computing power. They are not people, but resources to be used.

The second giant brain is the climatic reveal at the end of *Planet of the Ood* (2008), which is probably the *Doctor Who* episode that wins the prize for highest number of visible brains in a story. On the Ood-Sphere, as the Ood home planet is rather wonderfully named, the Ood have been enslaved by humanity, and then sold across the galaxy for centuries.

After humans discovered the truly monstrously sized, but very gentle, Ood Brain, they surrounded it with a telepathic barrier so it couldn't communicate with the Ood, and then systematically lobotomised the Ood to enslave them. Ood naturally have a second brain that they carry around in their hand, but these are cut off by members of Ood Corps to make them more compliant and a translator device is attached instead.

Their world was invaded, their bodies violated, and alien technology grafted onto them to make them more useful as slaves. Their natural state was collective harmony, and it's stripped away by corporate greed.

But the Ood Brain is not passive; and while it uses violence, it's still more humane than the actual humans in this story. It kills, but only in service of saving its children. And when the Ood are freed, neither they nor the Ood Brain seek revenge upon those who mutilated, enslaved, or killed them. Mostly they just want to sing. The Ood Brain's compassion is unbent by its vast intellect or telepathic powers, or the monstrous cruelties it's suffered. Its thoughts connect it to all Ood, and the Ood to each other, and yet this is a hive mind that is portrayed not as cruel or dehumanising, but as a community. By the end of the story, the Ood are almost angelic, tentacles and all. Their song is sacred, they offer grace to oppressors, and prophecy to the Doctor. The Ood offer a rare example of *Doctor Who* embracing a transhumanist concept, and shows that when there's autonomy and radical compassion, there can be transcendence, wonder, and peace.

> *'It may be irrational of me, but human beings are quite my favourite species.'*
>
> The Doctor, *The Ark in Space* (1975)

Doctor Who offers no transhumanist utopia. Instead, it uses the idea to explore our deepest fears about survival, identity, and autonomy. It weighs the cost of progress and asks what we would be willing to pay. When the series confronts transhumanism, it's not simply speculating about technology or evolution; it's asking what it means to be human. At what point does survival become self-destruction? Would immortality destroy personhood? Is consciousness merely data?

What is the difference between a human and a monster?

Across decades, the programme circles one firm answer: vulnerability is what keeps us human. Pain, fear, weakness, compassion, mortality are not flaws to be eliminated but sources of meaning. The Doctor embodies the wonder of controlled transcendence, but around the Doctor swarm the consequences of taking it too far. Those who seek survival, efficiency, or control at any cost shed humanity for monstrosity.

This isn't a rejection of reason or progress. *Doctor Who* celebrates science, knowledge, and curiosity; they're some of the Doctor's most engaging qualities. But the series insists that reason without ethics is monstrous. It warns against change pursued without reflection on morality, against the Enlightenment ideal stripped of its moral heart. To borrow a line from noted philosopher Ian Malcolm, 'Your scientists were so preoccupied with whether or not they could, they didn't stop to think if they should.'[174]

Doctor Who constantly returns to the question of cost: what do we lose if we cannot die? The Time Lords and the Sisterhood of Karn show immortality not as an eternal adventure but life frozen in a single moment, and a stultifyingly dull moment at that. Immortality is only bearable only when accompanied by compassion, emotion, and the capacity for change.

Perfection in *Doctor Who* is another word for death. The post-human forms that seek freedom from human limits end up trapped in new and grotesque ways. In striving to become more, they become less; objects of horror or pity rather than awe. It's our frailties and flaws that give us meaning. Strip away compassion and vulnerability, and humanity doesn't evolve, it is erased.

---

[174] *Jurassic Park* (1993)

EPILOGUE

octor Who has never been a show for straightforward answers. The closest thing it has to a firm take is that there are no easy answers. It never sees progress as technological, but as moral: What do our actions cost? Who do they harm? Who do they save?

It argues that change doesn't mean progress, technology is never neutral, our weaknesses are essential to our humanity. Its own state is one of constant change: the tone, the aesthetics, the Doctor themselves, evolve to reflect that society that creates them. It has been awkward and regressive with its politics; it's been bold and inspiring. It embraces imagination, empathy, and curiosity. It wants progress to mean something beyond shiny new gadgets. It asks what it means to be human.

There's no conclusion to its discussions, only more questions.

In recent years, *Doctor Who* has made two particularly visible choices in what it stands for, and that's been done through its casting. The thirteenth Doctor, played by Jodie Whittaker, is the first woman to play the Doctor onscreen; she was followed by Ncuti Gatwa, the first Black actor to lead the series. These choices are, on one level, straightforward acts of overdue representation. But they also ask something important: Who is allowed to embody the power of the Doctor?

These choices prompted some corners of fandom to claim that *Doctor Who* had become too political, despite having spent decades interrogating war, empire, technology, environmentalism, scientific responsibility, and a hundred other themes, often with all the subtlety of a sledgehammer. (I mean that in the nicest possible way.) Environmentalism is mocked as preachy. Climate change is a hoax. Feminism is an agenda. Anti-colonial narratives are revisionist history. Scepticism about technological advances is fear of progress. As *Doctor Who* expands its ideas, it inevitably encounters resistance from those who would prefer a simpler world with easy answers.

And yet, the Doctor continues to regenerate. The details change. The questions remain. The arguments are unfinished. Stubbornly and imperfectly, *Doctor Who* argues power must be questioned, progress should be justified, and we can always find another way.

STORY INDEX

WHERE WE STAND, WHERE WE FALL

The
Mind
of the
Doctor
across the
neurodiverse
universe of
**Doctor
Who**

lillian
crawford

Also available from Herne Books:
*The Mind of the Doctor: Travels in the
Neurodiverse Universe of Doctor Who*
by Lillian Crawford